AN EVIL SHADOW FALLS

W.T. DELANEY

Copyright © 2021 W.T Delaney

The moral right of the author has been asserted.

Apart from any fair dealing for the purposes of research or private study, or criticism or review, as permitted under the Copyright, Designs and Patents Act 1988, this publication may only be reproduced, stored or transmitted, in any form or by any means, with the prior permission in writing of the publishers, or in the case of reprographic reproduction in accordance with the terms of licences issued by the Copyright Licensing Agency. Enquiries concerning reproduction outside those terms should be sent to the publishers.

This is a work of fiction. Names, characters, businesses, places, events and incidents are either the products of the author's imagination or used in a fictitious manner. Any resemblance to actual persons, living or dead, or actual events is purely coincidental.

AN EVIL SHADOW FALLS

PART THREE OF THE SAM
HOLLOWAY TRILOGY

W.T. Delaney

"By wise guidance you can wage your war"

The Raven

The raven will be the last bird we hear
As disaster arrives and ploughs through Ash
Through Dante's vision of hell
With a brakeless, breakneck speed
And then the stars will appear reflected in shining skulls
And then the danger-dark will eventually bare its teeth
And no prayer or action will delay the beast
With one long, slow, hot breath, it will draw its prey in
And with sharpened claws, savage the earth
And extinguish the very last chance of love!

Barry Plunkett

Prologue

Abbottabad, Pakistan

He looked down at his most treasured possession and couldn't quite believe how something so small could be so deadly. The atomic cone of death was only four inches wide and eight long, but it enabled a Pakistani Army NASR Vengeance 4 battlefield tactical missile to deliver a nuclear strike of 0.5 to 5.0 kilotons. He took the device, cradled it in both hands and closed his eyes as he tried to envisage its awesome power. It made him feel reverential, as if he were handling something sacred. The denseness of the nuclear material made it unusually heavy, but that was truly outweighed by the awesome responsibility of being chosen by God to use it. The radiation did not worry him, as the explosion would kill him along with thousands of the infidels, and he was dying anyway. He smiled. *I am going to take the war to the Yankee unbelievers' doorstep.*

Chapter One

Canada, two months earlier

It was always the same dream. The man who had tried to kill her was staring into her eyes like a lover at climax, but it was the polar opposite of love. She held his gaze and felt pure hate reflected back at her, felt his evil slowly start to seep into her soul. It was like swallowing an ice cube that was slipping frostily towards her heart. The hate was hard, cold and unyielding. Her fear seemed to swirl, solidify and take form. It was as if she had become its ideal host; the shadow had found room and made itself comfortable inside her. And then the evil shadow became apparent, like a flickering ancient movie image projected onto the bedroom wall. Her fear fed it and gifted it an amorphous translucent shape made up of the faces of the dead – her own personal body count. The shape darkened and solidified as its claw-like tendrils reached out to claim her.

There was the white-bearded old man from Helmand dispatched with a double tap. There was the boy with the petrol blue eyes and the AK 47 whom she had tagged with a three-round burst, centre mass, and dropped into the choking dust of Helmand. And there was the Satan-eyed murderer with the combat knife. She had killed him with a head shot as he had attempted to decapitate Connor Cameron in Mosul.

An over-pressure of fear broke over her and she panicked, turned and fled, terrified and alone. She ran from the wraith-like vapour that chased her; her fear fed the shadow that grew and gained strength until she could feel it reach inside her.

"FUCK, FUCK, FUCK, NO!"

Sam screamed herself awake and instantly knew: *The ghosts of the past are back, and they have just kicked and clawed their way back into my soul.*

She was awake now, pulse racing, breathless, with wide eyes still seeing the faces of all the dead she had sent to Hell. Her past haunted her, especially that last mission.

It had been a year since the 'Weeping Willows' ambush, when the team had substituted a bullet-riddled and anonymous corpse for a living terrorist whom they had snatched for interrogation. The dead man was simply known in intelligence circles as a SNU FNU, or surname unknown, forename unknown, and he had died a year earlier than the Weeping Willows incident, in unrecorded circumstances that had a similar profile to the man that they were beginning to hunt. The CIA had supplied the body, of the same approximate age, weight, and ethnicity of the man it was meant to replace, a Tier One target known as Objective Cyclone. The team had finally managed to untangle the living terrorist mastermind from the bloody mixture of him, his weapons, and his comrades, and he had been snatched in a 'rendition operation', an Americanism for the arrest of an active terrorist for the purposes of interrogation.

It had been organised by MI6 and the CIA, using Sam and her team of 'Spartan Operatives' consisting of former British Special Forces soldiers. Nobody would mourn the loss of Objective Cyclone, or miss him, because this particular terrorist had twice been reported dead. First, in a US airstrike in a dusty little village in Syria, and more recently in what the British and international press had come to call the Spean Bridge Massacre, when the SAS had ambushed an Islamist terrorist ASU (Active Service Unit) near Sam's cottage in the highlands of Scotland. But the operation had forced Sam and her husband Nigel from their beloved croft cottage and into permanent exile. They were now under a death threat, or *fatwa*, and therefore had been incorporated into an intergovernmental resettlement package usually used for blown MI6 agents. The press had ensured that they couldn't safely stay in Britain. They had been 'outed' in several papers and news channels when directly linked to the killings in what the locals at Spean Bridge called 'The Weeping Willows'. The official inquest into the deaths had exonerated the SAS and concluded with a verdict of 'Lawful killing'.

DNA samples, harvested from a backstreet garage containing the target's car that had identified Objective Cyclone, had then been recycled for use by the Scottish coroner's office. The name of Jassim Emwazi had thus been officially recorded as one of those killed in the ambush, and EMNI (ISIS's security service) therefore thought that their future plans were safe, as Cyclone had taken their operational secrets to the grave with him. The small highland croft and the 'Weeping Willows' were now the scene of an annual all-night vigil, organised by London-based political activists and Islam4UK, to commemorate the four terrorists they called martyrs, accompanied by the inevitable counter-protests.

The operation's objectives had been brutal, and its violent conclusion still deeply disturbed her. It was the most unethical job that she and the team had ever been involved in; they had snatched a British-born terrorist from mainland Britain for interrogation by the CIA. It was a job Sam and the team had been given because they provided the ultimate firewall for the security services. It had been a deniable operation.

Canada had been kind to them; they lived in a beautiful rambling house, and the resettlement package had been generous. Nigel worked teaching surveillance techniques to a Canadian Special Forces unit known as JTF2 or the Joint Task Force Two, based in Ottawa. Everything had seemed blissful to begin with, but things had now started to unravel. The pressures of just living apart for a lot of the time had started to take their toll, and Samantha spent long periods with only her traumatic memories for company. The covert nature of their existence was also problematic. The small rural community in which they lived was curious about the newcomers, and that curiosity brought an element of resentment when it could not be satisfied.

Last year's global lockdown because of the Covid-19 pandemic had brought further problems. Her feeling of isolation was exacerbated by her husband's increasingly long trips away; she felt both isolated and homesick. They had also tried for a baby and failed; that was the one thing that they both desired and it was still just tantalisingly out of reach. Sam had been five weeks pregnant when she had lost the baby and it had broken her heart. But she hadn't told Taff; she felt that the burden was her own to bear, as she rationalised that this seemed to be the payback for all the lives she had taken on behalf of her country.

Maybe there was a God? Some all-powerful omnipresent being that thought that human life was too precious to be reproduced inside a killer.

Her moods had started to spiral into depression, with each day increasing her unhappiness. *But maybe she didn't deserve happiness; perhaps the terrorist with the hateful eyes had cursed her.*

The last operation had been a time-bomb on a very slow fuse. The truth about an Anglo-American operation of such complexity, with such a wide circle of knowledge, could not remain a secret for ever. The team had known this at the very beginning and had only agreed to get involved because they accepted that it was the only way that the future carnage planned by 'Objective Cyclone' could be stopped, while also knowing from bitter experience that former soldiers could very easily be sacrificed on the altar of political expediency in the future.

She closed her eyes, and for one fleeting moment wondered what was happening to the man they had snatched. She tried to recall his face, but all she could remember was the terrified look in his eyes.

CHAPTER TWO

A Black Site in Eastern Europe

That man, whom the British Army had called Objective Cyclone, didn't really know where he was. He was hooded and entombed by what smelled like damp concrete walls. The guards sometimes came in and hosed him with water, but they never communicated. He didn't know how long he had been there. The bar to which he was tethered meant that he only got respite from the pain of the shackles biting into his wrists when standing on his tiptoes. He had been kept naked, apart from a US-issued diaper, for so long now that he couldn't even remember the last time he'd been dressed. The only thing he smelt was the cold wet scent of the concrete and the sickly stink of his own excrement. He didn't know how long ago the blonde woman had sent him to Hell, but he knew he had arrived. His resolve had diminished in the never-ending, cold, smothering, and ear-splitting darkness, but his hate, and the suffering, served to nourish it and keep it alive! It reinforced his belief, and it filled his emptiness. He had been given a sacred task. He had set in train a series of events that would result in the final confrontation between the 'House of Peace' (Dar al-Salam) and the 'House of War' (Dar al-Harb) that the Prophet would bring to the world of the godless kuffar.

The cell was specifically designed for partial sensory deprivation, but his interrogator had also put his own homeboy spin on it. If the pain of the handcuffs wasn't enough to deprive him of sleep, then the constant pounding of country music at one hundred decibels compounded his suffering and vanquished rest completely. The driven, focused terrorist mastermind that had once been a Tier One target was blown out. He had lost track of time, and his thoughts did not race at all anymore; they had long since crash-landed in abject despair.

The doctor called himself Jacob, but that wasn't his real name; it changed with every interrogation he conducted. He didn't think of his methods as cruel, just necessary. He wasn't a torturer, as he got no personal enjoyment from human suffering. He was just a man that realised that, in this field of counterterrorism, you sometimes, for the greater good, needed to park your sensibilities – and even your humanity – at the front door of an interrogation cell. This man would be the latest in a long line of people that he had broken. He was very good at what he did. He had worked as a US civilian contractor since his time in Iraq and had hundreds of successful interrogations under his belt. He was the best that the CIA had.

He was a psychiatrist and primarily a physician, but thought of his special skill almost as a calling in the service of his country. He considered himself more a type of brain mechanic or psychiatric plumber. He knew how the brain worked under extreme pressure, what parts broke first and how best to repair them. He knew how to disassemble the thinking parts of the 'quivering orb' into its constituents and then rebuild it. The keys to all secrets were suspended in the trembling alabaster of the brain's limbic system, and he could strip it down to its basic parts as easily as the V8 engine of his beloved 1967 Chevrolet Camaro.

The limbic system was a set of brain structures located on both sides of the thalamus, under the medial temporal lobe of the cerebrum in the middle of the brain. This system controlled all behavioural and emotional responses. It consisted of equally proportioned areas of the hypothalamus, which managed sexual responses, hormone release and body temperature, and the hippocampus that helped to retrieve memories, *a vital part for an interrogator.* There was also the amygdala, which controlled fear and anger, and finally the limbic cortex that affected mood, motivation and judgment.

A successful interrogation had to rip all these elements apart and then reassemble them in a way designed to extract those dark, deep and hidden secrets within. At the moment, it was a waiting game - waiting for the subject's brain to scramble and disconnect under the techniques applied, until the time came to throw it all back together into a pattern that pleased him. He paused and observed the suffering in the darkened cell. Time was on Doctor Jacob's side. He knew it could take a week, a month or a year, but he also knew that the subject's isolation and hopelessness would eventually reveal his secrets, which would spew out in a torrent.

CHAPTER THREE

Her Majesty's Prison Wandsworth, London

In Her Majesty's Prison, Wandsworth, another prisoner considered his situation. The Victorian building had been the home of 237755T Richard 'Coco' Miller for over a year. Coco was an unusual inmate, even in such an unusual place. He was really just an internally displaced person, a refugee gangster sheltering from what the British press called the postcode wars, the ongoing battle on London's streets between rival drug gangs, and he was every bit as fearful for his life as the streams of migrants taking their chances in the English Channel in the hope of gaining illegal entry to the UK. He was a fleeing combatant and a fighting-age male who was also a top amateur boxer, known to MI5 as Codename CORKSCREW.

He was, as far as he knew, the only Security Service agent inside Wandsworth prison, in west London. It was one of the largest in Europe, maybe the oldest, and it currently housed him and 1,500 other pissed-off prisoners. From the air it looked like a giant sun-fried starfish washed up on a crowded Brighton beach. Its main body was a central hub from which protruded five long legs, each an ancient prison wing simmering with discontent. The design had been state of the art in 1851, intended as a panopticon system where all five legs could be under constant observation from the control point in the middle.

The prisoners just called it 'Wanno' or, maybe more descriptively, 'The Hate Factory' and the prisoners were as diverse as the metropolis they mirrored: white, black and brown, and drawn from across the city's cultural and social divide. Wandsworth was full of losers, choosers and chancers, the hopeful and the hopeless, the redeemable and the damned. A prison, after all, was only a reflection of all that is bad with society, and just a raw stinking slice of the entire shit that surrounds it.

It was everything bad outside squeezed up on the inside, including the previous year's Coronavirus epidemic. On the bright side, though, it was one of the few places in the country where the inhabitants were well used to wearing masks, so one of the few advantages of the controlled environment, combined with the enforced segregation of the penal system, was that the infection rates inside had been surprisingly low.

'A' Wing had been Coco's home since sentencing, and although it wasn't pleasant it was actually where he had chosen to be – but he still didn't like it very much. In fact, he detested the whole fucked-up monotony of it all. He hated the constant clanging noises with the rattle of keys, and the constant whining drone of fifteen hundred bitching convicts buzzing around the landings for a full fourteen hours a day. He loathed the food and the lack of privacy. The wing looked shabby in drab shades of magnolia and blue and echoed with the sound of long noisy metal corridors, clicking barred electronic doors, shouts, laughter and screams. As he looked up through the safety netting strung under the landing, the milky light of a summer's day struggled through the Victorian glass and bird-shit ceiling above. The lack of colour and light made it as grey as the prison issue tracksuits that everybody wore. The drug of choice on the inside was 'Spice', and that ex-legal high was smuggled into the wings in industrial quantities by people like him. The success of his venture resulted in the other shuffling tracksuits looking like the cast of a zombie movie, while the few prisoners who were not drugged seethed with discontent. Wandsworth was a societal pressure cooker primed to go off.

For the first couple of months of his sentence he had sat back and tried to understand the unique dynamics of the prison ecosystem. He didn't want to be perceived as too willing, too soon. He also needed to develop and enhance his own cover story and profile on the Wing first, and as a new boy on remand that meant standing your ground, as the predators inside prison walls always viewed a new inmate who failed to do so as an easy touch for the rest of his sentence. Coco knew that a prison was like any other social system, with both winners and losers, predators and prey, and in 'Wanno' they came in a variety of shapes and sizes. The old idea of a prison hierarchy, with full-time professional criminals, like bank robbers and Kray-type gangsters, and the notion of 'honour among thieves', really didn't apply any more. Coco thought that might be linked with the disappearance of that culture in London society outside; and the more fragmented it became outside, the more dangerous it became inside 'the Hate Factory'.

He thought of a quotation in one of the books now gathering dust on the shelf in his bedroom where he had lived in south London. An old French guy called Voltaire had said, *'Fear follows crime and is its punishment'.* Coco had hurt some people while doing business 'on the out'; it hadn't been personal as far as he was concerned, but others sometimes didn't take the same view, and thoughts of vengeance inspire potent and dangerous emotions. He had once scanned an article by some soldier-academic type, whose name he couldn't quite remember, about a thing called 'complexity theory'. It promulgated the view that all human social systems are basically organic and that they react as any living organism reacts, in an almost Darwinian way. It was natural that certain inputs into a biological system led to almost preordained outputs. It sounded about right, but when you have over 1,500 criminals banged up in the same space you have an almost unique ecosystem, with both unusual inputs and pretty violent outputs. The pre-Covid clampdown on gun and knife crime on the outside had taken the war from the streets to spike stabbings on the inside, and that made a new prisoner on remand a very vulnerable person.

Coco had already been involved in a couple of violent incidents relating to his former drug business, and some of the lads from other firms really believed they could fight. He thought it was a result of an overexposure to shit martial-arts movies and nonstop *Call of Duty* video games while coked out of their fairly underdeveloped brains, but generally they couldn't scrap and, unfortunately for them, he could.

He had always possessed a natural talent for violence that had been honed, developed, and sharpened by a decade of amateur boxing, and too many street fights to remember. He knew that, to be effective, properly applied violence had to be emotionless. He had been attacked on one occasion by some east London associates on remand and had managed to knock out all three in a flurry of punches before they could use the shank (knife) they had threatened him with. *Nobody tried that any more!*

And then there was the target organisation he had been tasked to infiltrate. They were known by various names on the inside – most cons just called them the 'Beardies' or sometimes the MooJ or the Mojos – but, whatever their nicknames, they were gaining strength inside all of Britain's prisons. The toxic atmosphere of self-imposed religious segregation allowed by the prison authorities almost made the road to radicalisation a common sense option for a new arrival. The Mooj were the only organisation that could provide the protection that a newbie prisoner needed. It was also common knowledge that once you converted to Islam you got more time on your own, with better food, and you got an easier time from the screws because they were shit-scared of being considered religiously intolerant or, even worse, racist. Once you were under the care of the 'Brothers', problems with the staff quickly evaporated; if they didn't, a quick chat to the nominated Race Equality Officer (REO), or the Government-employed mullah, and somebody on the staff had fucked his career.

At first, he had evaded and avoided them, and then slowly, and ever so gradually, he had let them think that he was listening. He had eventually led them to believe that he had been persuaded to convert, as in this particular prison the Islamist influence was everywhere, and it was the 'natural' thing to do. At times he actually missed his old dangerous life on the street and detested the person that he had needed to become. But it was all a game, and so far, he had played it well. It seemed to be the best approach; after all, the Mojos were a potent political force when compressed within a prison's walls, and inmates with extreme religious views were notoriously hard to handle. Violent criminals driven by faith also, by their very nature, provide an ideal breeding ground for further radicalisation.

Coco waited for the ideal situation, and his turning point came during a disturbance on A Wing, when he went to the assistance of a young Asian lad who had upset some members of a particularly nasty Turkish firm. He had been directed by his handler to try and get alongside a returned jihadist called Mohammad Ziaman, who was on remand on terrorism charges. He was a real nutcase at the lunatic end of radical Islamist ideology; he also had a large ego and a small brain. He had managed to annoy one of the Turks by preaching to him on the evils of smoking, accompanied by numerous unconnected quotes from the Koran. The guy had just snapped and was battering the fuck out of him when Coco intervened and stopped the attack.

The Turk was from the Arifs, a well-known south London family, and Coco dived in before the big man had really damaged Ziaman too much. The Turks knew Coco and, although they hated him, they didn't want any undue aggro. The incident had broken the ice, and the Mojos had finally offered him both their thanks and acceptance. Things had happened pretty quickly after that; the brotherhood had recognised his talents and, as he had made himself more useful, he actually made himself safer on the inside.

After that, in a few short months he became the main man controlling the smuggled mobiles and organising the import of drugs via the nightly drone flights. It made being an MI5 source inside the organisation a demanding task. He spoke to his handler at least once a week, and sometimes daily when a new Islamist prisoner was on remand. It was Coco's job to make sure that the new man had everything he needed, including access to a smuggled mobile that had been supplied via MI5's technical department. He had sometimes, during the course of these events, considered how strange life was, where one particular decision made at a particular time had changed how things had panned out.

Sometimes what you regarded as a small isolated incident sets up a chain reaction that results in a reality that you could never have foreseen.

He realised it now: that he had been identified, befriended and recruited by MI5 during a very skilfully run operation, and that all through that process, whenever he had thought he was making his own choices, he had actually been complying with another milestone in his MI5 handler's master plan. He was where they had placed him, but he bore no resentment. He, after all, had also planned it that way: it was his escape route from his life outside, his way of taking some time out before it was his blood on the pavement, instead of that of one of the other drug dealers in south London.

It had been a cathartic experience for him, and he had begun to see that life on 'B' Wing, where the Beardies held sway, was particularly strange. At first, he felt that slavish adherence to a religion was counter to his personal feelings. He had disliked his mum's strict observance of her own Catholic faith and had decided that religion of any type wasn't his thing. He had begun to realise, though, that strange 'groupthink' had some beneficial side effects. After all, everybody arrived on the inside at his lowest ebb and alone, and religious adherence behind bars gave the weakest a lifeline and others a routine.

Coco, like most of the other guys banged up in the Hate Factory, felt dispossessed. He had always felt incomplete, almost like a discarded and unfinished jigsaw puzzle that had been put away because some pieces were missing. Almost finished but not quite, therefore always unfinished and always partly lost. But he had slowly begun to understand that this slavish devotion to the idea of something immensely more powerful than oneself supplied something that troubled people really needed. He had also realised that the interludes of quietness and reflection involved in prayer could be good for his general mental health.

After all, this place was in his own city of London; it was mainly outside the prison walls that the madness reigned. The Somali gangs terrorised their areas with knives, while the Turks carved up the rest of north London in the same manner. All the drug money was laundered through the Albanian car washes in Tottenham and Kilburn, while the Vietnamese gangs grew and distributed two-thirds of the strong skunk brand of cannabis found on the capital's streets.

And why was that? He had his own thoughts; he read a lot, and he read things that other gang guys didn't read. *Maybe we are seeing a lost generation.*

Canada

Samantha hadn't been out of bed for twenty-four hours. She woke again with a headache and tried to focus on her immediate surroundings. She turned her head to the right and blinked at the evidence of her previous bout of depression. An empty wine bottle propped up her mobile phone on the bedside cabinet, alongside an opened container of painkillers. As she reached across to check for messages another bottle span aimlessly and thudded onto the carpet.

How have I managed to get so low?

The smart speaker still played her previous choice on a loop. It was classical music for sleeping. *And it had certainly helped with that.*

As Sam struggled to release her head from the pillow, she felt the vomit beginning to surge upwards and launched herself in an involuntary crouched stagger towards the bathroom. Her head was thumping as the acidic remains of the wine ejected themselves over the tiled floor. She wiped her mouth and stared towards the bathroom mirror.

I'm not ready for a mirror moment.

That was what her Dad had called it. *It was for after you had fucked up! When you looked at your reflection and asked yourself some really serious questions.* The woman in the reflection looked nothing like the super-confident Captain Samantha Holloway MC, formerly of the Special Reconnaissance Regiment. Her hair was a tangled mess, and the remains of what had been expelled from her digestive system were smeared across her face. What she could see looking back at her was the internal emotional carnage of the depths of her despair.

As she continued to brace against the bathroom cabinet, she felt a strange sensation on the inside of her arm, glanced down and realised what she was looking at. A large gauge canula dangled from her arm, and she knew in that instant what she had tried to do. The sight recalled a conversation from years before with an SAS combat medic around a fire pit in Baghdad, and she could hear his words as if it were yesterday:

"Fuck that slashing your wrists shit! Far too messy. Just whack a big size canula in your radial artery, take some pills, put some decent sounds on and get to somewhere where the blood can drain away easily and where it isn't gonna cause a health hazard for the first responders, who, after all, get their heads fucked up far too much by gory scenes."

She could remember the big smiling face of the 'blade'.

"Just 'cos you've decided to bail out, don't headfuck other people's lives with what you leave behind."

The house medical kit was lying in the bathroom. The zipper on the large black holdall was still open, with various pieces of discarded items scattered around it. It was as if desperate hands had scrabbled inside it to find something in a hurry – and then her drunken memories returned, and she felt her emptiness. She looked again into the mirror and studied her face. Her normally bright blue eyes were bloodshot pits of sadness. He skin was pale, and she looked defeated. Samantha Holloway stretched upwards, took a deep breath and, eyes tightly shut, thought of everything that was precious to her. She thought of her husband as she removed the canula and deftly applied a bandage. The bathroom smelt of vomit; she opened the window and felt a slight breeze begin to cleanse the foul air.

Never again. She mouthed the words soundlessly as she once more studied the mirror.

She turned quickly to the bedroom. In a corner of the room her bright pink Salomon S-Lab Ultra trail-running shoes attracted her gaze; they had been a present from her husband. She picked them up, opened the wardrobe door and snatched some running kit from the neat pile of clothes. She dressed quickly, and two minutes later she was running in the fresh Canadian air as she felt the soil under her feet. As she started the run, she felt her cheeks moisten with involuntary tears. *How could have I been so selfish?* she thought, as she started to relax into her stride.

CHAPTER FOUR

The Binner: the Joint Task Force

Within five miles of Coco's cell two men were discussing the information he had provided. They were working in room C7. The Joint Task Force (JTF) handlers called the room The Binner, but nobody really knew why. It was one of those words that had been handler-speak during the Troubles in Ulster, and it had somehow been passed down to their present-day equivalents. It probably referred to the time when source reports had been handwritten, all too often rejected by the Det boss and consigned to the 'secure waste' bin placed in the middle of the source unit, so that all could snigger as a dejected handler had to ceremoniously cast his report into the bin and start his rewrite. This 'Binner' was on the fifth floor of Thames House, in central London, the beating heart of Britain's domestic security services. But this twenty-first-century Binner was mega high-tech compared to the Neolithic days of source handling. It was a cyber-insulated and totally firewalled room with steel-lined walls, where the JTF's source handlers could compile their reports in total cyber security. Although the room was a sealed chamber it appeared bright, modern and airy; its interior was all white wood and light magnolia, like a healthy dose of Swedish modernism on steroids.

Standing against one of the magnolia walls was an Afro-Caribbean guy, working at a whiteboard with a somewhat perplexed expression. He was an ex Royal Marine Commando called Lou, and Agent CORKSCREW's Task Force handler. He was tall, burly and black, and the polar opposite of the other guy sitting across from him, who was perched at a desktop. The other MI5 man was somewhat small and slim, with the pallid shade of the office worker at Thames House that the Asian intelligence officers called 'London white'. He looked more like a trainee librarian than an intelligence officer. His defining feature was his intensely bright eyes, magnified by his latest purchase from Specsavers, that glimmered with the sort of native intelligence that others just didn't have.

He was Lou's partner in this source management brainstorming session. The handlers at the source unit just called him Computer Chris, the go-to guy for anything web-based. He was an unlikely MI5 man and nothing like the secret agent stereotype of popular imagination. Chris looked as smart as Lou looked dangerous, and had been recruited directly from a computer engineering PhD. His head was jammed full of computer analytics and weird algorithms, which was why he was employed at Thames House as the Security Service's expert on computer analysis. He was working diligently as the information from CORKSCREW was transferred from the whiteboard, where it had been roughly sketched out, onto the standard MI5 presentation screen. The two officers had their monthly case conference scheduled for the next day. It would be an important one for Lou: everything that his agent had produced from inside Wandsworth Prison would be discussed.

The ex-Commando glanced across towards the computer geek. Lou was tapping a red marker against the whiteboard, waiting for either internal inspiration or some external technical input from Chris. Lou would scan the whiteboard intermittently, and then his eyes would light up as he wrote another name into the rough link analysis diagram. The marker would then quickly scribble the next revelation onto the already cluttered board.

"What do you think?" he said, out of the corner of his mouth, at the only other person in the room. "It looks like a fucking mess, mate, but explain that last link again," Chris said with a smile – and he was the man that would have to 'get it', as he was simultaneously compiling this huge mass of source and technical information onto the link analysis diagram displayed on the 60-inch plasma screen on the wall behind Lou's wild dreadlocks.

"Yeah, OK." Lou looked towards him. "This is Ali Khan, the main man in B Wing, and this line, the green one, links him directly to this blue financial link line and this technical intercept, and this guy is Ahmad Rahim, the money man."

Another line connected both names. "Ahmad Rahim is the main fundraiser for Islam4UK, and he is linked directly to this local politician, who is the fixer for all the Asian drug gangs. He sends all the money to Kabul via the Hawala system. He is also Ali Khan's first cousin on his mother's side."

"Explain Hawala again, mate." Chris looked up; his brow tensely crinkled in thought, giving him an almost simian look.

"Yeah, Hawala is the unofficial system of transferring money from one place to another by trust, used extensively in the Islamic world. It's used all the time in the illegal drug trade. A guy pays money in London for a promissory note that is redeemed through an agent in the 'sand pit'. It's set up throughout all Islamic countries and makes the money virtually untraceable."

"OK, got it now!" Chris said, while a simultaneous flurry of his fingers on the keyboard changed the details on the display. The monthly conferences played an essential part in any successful source handling agency, and an integral part in developing Lou's own agent CORKSREW, who had gained unprecedented access within the Islamic State's acolytes in the British prison system. They also helped a good agent handler to maintain his peripheral vision and to look at the bigger picture. Lou knew that it was a cardinal error to become too focused on your own particular agent; it made you too insular, and therefore too possessive and concerned with your own personal fiefdom. Sometimes the deep and personal relationship that developed between an agent and his handler could blunt that perception.

After all, HUMINT is only one aspect of the vast amount of information that daily feeds the intelligence cycle, the process that keeps the raw information spinning until it can produce a proper intelligence product. Lou and Chris knew that an item of information is only properly verified when constantly analysed and compared with other products over the whole spectrum of collection, whether from other agents, surveillance operations or technical means. The monthly meetings organised by the JTF were a way for all operators to assess the latest data and get a quick reality check.

They also allowed the younger handlers to tap into the knowledge of more senior colleagues in order to get their own source deeper into a terrorist or criminal organisation. Producing a link diagram was a proven method of providing an accurate visual representation of the intelligence input from a source such as Lou's agent, presently residing in Her Majesty's Prison Wandsworth. Lou stepped back from the board, made an assessment and smiled.

Fuck, he has produced a lot!

The names of every major ISIS terrorist or acolyte in the UK were linked by lines in different colours, with all the phone numbers interconnected on the peripheries like some mad piece of modern art. He was amazed at what his guy on the inside had achieved. Mapped out in front of him was every phone and covert link that the ISIS prisoners had to their host organisations on the outside. Another set of data superimposed on the outer peripheries of the board indicated the main funding inputs from what was commonly referred to as the crime/terror nexus. This was where Islamist fundamentalism in London met its money. The link diagram outlined the drug connections, the fake charities and religious organisations, along with the criminal gangs in London that provided the funding for its operations inside the UK.

Everything his agent had achieved was there. He had taken the whole organisation apart. He had identified all the finance flowing the other way as well: money that had been generated inside the Wings by the Brotherhood and then directed back into the drug gangs and into the financial scams considered the most profitable. Lou knew that the network had managed to rob the British tax system of over thirty million in the past couple of years, and it was still doing it in ever more inventive ways.

Lou was still smiling, although in a thoughtful way, when he addressed his colleague, who seemed to have a somewhat troubled expression.

"What do you think, Chris?" The smaller man fidgeted nervously with his computer mouse.

"I think CORKSCREW has had amazing results but…" His expression darkened. "You are not going to like what I'm going to say!"

"What's that?" said a concerned Lou.

"I can see that you have a huge security problem here, mate." Chris used the mouse to highlight one of the links on the presentation screen.

"Now that we have all this information in a diagrammatic form, I can see clearly that all of it has been compiled from one major asset."

"How can you see that?" said Lou.

"I've instantaneously loaded it, as we've confirmed it, into an analytical programme from an American company called Palantile Expressway."

"And what?" Lou was worried.

"Everything decent that has been extrapolated from this link diagram leads it back to the only possible source."

Lou spoke through a thin-lipped smile.

"And in layman's English, please, my extremely bright friend?"

Computer Chris didn't smile. As he fixed Lou's eyes with a worried expression he simply said, "The ISIS computer department could easily have the same software; it's commercially available." Chris used the mouse to sketch from one link to another on the presentation screen.

"And, if they do, your source is blown. You need to get him out, mate. Prison isn't a place to be when people are trying to kill you!"

Lou took a deep breath. "Let's tell Tim," he said in a quiet voice.

Chapter Five

The following day

To Tim, the walk across the bridge was quicker than getting a driver to drop him off, and it also gave him time for some much-needed headspace. The bridge had only just opened again after a year-long closure owing to a row with the Mayor and the Government over who was going to pay the bill to repair it. He was glad that row was eventually resolved, because he needed the walk. Me-time had been in short supply since a promotion that had gifted him both a blizzard of work and a storm of responsibility. He looked around as he made his way towards the bridge. Lou's call had just released him from an otherwise mandatory two-hour seminar on 'mental health in the workspace' organised by the all-powerful health and safety Gestapo at Vauxhall Cross. It was the latest of the new 'woke' seminars that all employees had to attend as a 'tick in the box'. He thought of it as he walked.

It was bizarre that the twin organisations charged with the safety of the realm thought that agent handlers had the time to attend to anything but work since the fall of the so-called Caliphate and its last stand at the little Syrian border town of Baghuz.

A lot had happened since the Downing Street attack, and his department was still working against the clock to detect the next atrocity, despite the current relative lack of interest in security matters generated by both Covid 19 and the BLM (Black Lives Matter) movement. He had sat in one of the small conference rooms with the rest of his team, all eyeing each other with the *'What the fuck is this all about?'* look. It was two hours of operational time they would never get back, so he was glad of the walk. He had previously managed to dodge the lectures, but they had finally tracked him down.

Just another occasion where he found himself at odds with some of his more woke colleagues within the modern and politically conscious security and intelligence agencies. The sunlight glittered off the surface of a restful Thames as he paused and looked over the edge of Vauxhall Bridge. He still went through all the usual anti-surveillance procedures as normal, more through instinct than need. It was a given that the entrances and exits to MI6 might be under observation by hostile eyes, but the sheer number of people who worked within the building usually gave a handler a certain amount of cover. Like in any large organisation based on quasi-military lines, at least four backroom workers were needed for an agent to operate in the field.

He looked again at the bridge: a lot of water had flowed under it since the last London terror attacks in 2017, 2019 and 2020, and anti-crash barriers now provided some protection for the hundreds of pedestrians that used it. He thought he maybe knew why rivers and bridges were so important to Islamist types.

He had initially worked with the 'Prevent' programme, established to try and de-radicalise terrorist suspects. It had been a good way to learn the problem up close and personal, because a good knowledge of the Koran was needed to counter the Salafist narrative. To him, religion was a deeply personal thing, an internalised control mechanism that made you think of others. The naked ideology that he had encountered during his time with Prevent was more like Islamic fascism, black flags and marching fanatics included. The bridge thing, he thought, might be grounded in Islamic tradition. A hadith said that 'As-Sirat' is the bridge that believers must cross to get to heaven, or 'Jannah'. He half remembered the associated hadith:

> *The companions of the prophet ask, "O Allah's Apostle! What is the bridge?"*
>
> *And the prophet tells them, "Some of the believers will cross the bridge as quickly as the wink of an eye, some others as quick as lightning, a strong wind, fast horses or she-camels. So, some will be safe without any harm; some will be safe after receiving some scratches, and some will fall down into Hell. The last person will cross by being dragged over the bridge."*

Bridges and water, he thought, have always had a spiritual connotation within various religions, including Islam; *maybe that's why Islamist terrorists want to murder and kill and die on them?*

The only answer that the politicians had come up with was the hugely expensive Prevent programme. It was a mishmash of some of the more bizarre academic theories related to counter-radicalisation and, like most things academic, it had very little practical use. It consisted of just a series of interviews that took a committed Islamist through a box-ticking exercise to gain early release, or to stop getting banged up in the first place. It was a poorly designed series of modules, where a committed terrorist could easily gameplay the system and end up with the right result. He knew from bitter experience that the guys actively engaged in Jihad were sometimes extremely evil but never simply stupid; there is no talking therapy programme for those people.

It was just a waste of money, because about four hundred British Jihadists had now arrived back after the fall of Baghuz and were still untraced. The main problem was the present lack of resources to find them, or even to examine their motives. The limited resources available were further diluted by the ascendant 'woke' wings of MI5 and 'Six', who wanted to concentrate instead on 'Right Wing terrorist organisations' for the sake of diversity and very easy results.

It was always a lot easier to nail some deranged teenager in Croydon, say, who had overdosed on Adolf Hitler, than raise any political hackles within the London bubble in which they all resided. He sometimes thought that his world had changed so much that he needed to take one of the very lucrative offers that regularly came his way from blue-chip companies desperate for some sort of insight into the madness that seemed to be engulfing London.

The Covid epidemic had delivered the security services a disastrous 'double tap'. Half the backroom staff at Thames House and Vauxhall Cross were still working from home, and the empty streets during lockdown had made physical old-school surveillance nearly impossible.

He checked his watch; he had a meeting with Lou at 1400 hours, so he could take his time and enjoy an unusual glimmer of sunshine. He had had no time for reflection recently, as everything was happening at breakneck speed. It had been a hectic spell for the Joint Task Force, the hybrid group that the government had set up to cover the overlap between MI5 and MI6, to bridge the gap between the organisations that had led to problems in the past.

Tim walked more quickly now, as the first spots of rain started to fall. He unfurled his umbrella just in time for a typical London deluge. The rain stopped equally suddenly just in front of Thames House.

He loved the look of the building; it was, he thought, typically British. The MI5 HQ at Millbank had been built around 1930 in what architects call the Imperial Neoclassical style, by the same man who designed the Cenotaph in Whitehall. Its six storeys of chalky Portland stone towered over the embankment, a handsome building with all the Art Nouveau touches that one would expect of that era. The refined and elegant exterior, though, concealed the beating heart of the United Kingdom's domestic security intelligence effort, the London-based home of Britain's Security Service since 1994.

He walked through the main entrance, scanned his pass and walked to the tubes. The security staff watched as he stepped into the tube. The large full-body scanner briefly whirred and buzzed, then opened and allowed him access to the lifts. He was going to the Binner on the fifth floor. The bell tinged and the stainless-steel lift door opened soundlessly. Tim looked up at the camera opposite. It clicked, and a small green light told him that his face had passed another visual scanning test. The office he needed was only two doors down; he scanned his pass and waited for the airtight door to wheeze like an elderly asthmatic as it opened.

Lou and Chris looked up as he entered, and both faces mirrored their concern. Tim immediately picked up the negative vibes.

"What's the problem?"

"We have an issue with CORKSCREW, Boss." Lou glanced across to Chris. "Chris can probably explain it best, but we have a problem that we need to solve pretty quickly."

"Is he compromised? And if so, is the compromise time critical?" Tim looked at the presentation monitor and the indecipherable whiteboard.

"It could be!" Chris said, as he removed his glasses and cleaned them with the bottom of his tee shirt. "Do you want the long version or the concise one?"

"Concise. Go for it!" Tim looked pensive.

"CORKSCREW is either compromised or about to get compromised. We have run an analysis on all the information he has provided, and enough of it runs back to him as to make his present position untenable."

"What's the bottom line?"

Chris picked up the laser pointer and indicated the newly-compiled link analysis chart.

"OK, everything in red on the chart is information from the source that could be traced back to CORKSCREW if he came under suspicion. As you can see, he has been particularly busy reporting on the crime-terror nexus concerning the drugs trade. Unfortunately, some of this product, with a particularly small circle of knowledge, has already been acted upon."

"How did that happen?"

"Not sure." Chris returned the pointer to the desk. "My guess is that the raw information has hit JTAC too early and been given to other agencies without the proper checks and balances. Probably some government minister trying to score brownie points. There's a lot about Pakistan, opium, and the financing of the Taliban that our guy came up with that has been actioned."

"How long have we got?" Tim's voice mirrored his concern.

"Depends on the opposition's ability to replicate our findings, but we know they have the capability. It would only be a guess, but I'd say, erring on the side of caution, maybe days instead of weeks?"

"OK, let's get him out." Tim's decision was immediate. "Talk to legal and come up with a plan for his release."

"Roger that, Boss," said Lou.

CHAPTER SIX

Baker Street, London

Danny McMaster was at his office, listening to BBC Radio Three and working on the contracts for the Qatar World Cup job, when Tim called. He looked at the phone, recognised the number and took a deep breath. A phone call from Tim on his secure line always led him to the polar opposite of the safer world of commercial security contracts. His company, 'Hedges and Fisher', had become the security services' preferred choice for intelligence outsourcing. Its central expertise lay in the people it employed, all with the requisite British Armed Forces skills developed over thirty years in the ever-changing intelligence shadow wars with Britain's enemies. The company had become a one-stop shop for unofficial intelligence-related tasks. Danny hesitated slightly; phone calls from Tim had, in the past, led to dangerous times and places for the people he employed.

But why did he hesitate? The caution was almost subliminal rather than conscious. Being a company that operated below the radar of the official government position had its downsides, and in a liberal democratic country it often had more downs than ups.

In the past couple of months, he had heard disturbing rumours of an internal movement within the security services, a sort of left-of-field cabal of the new Generation X, who had been promoting what they called 'an ethical approach' to intelligence collection, and the extra time that people had been given to work from home had sharpened the new breed's appetite for change.

Danny had heard that certain people had passed stories to media outlets about some of the operations that Hedges and Fisher had been part of, and it was slowly leading to the headlines that the mainstream British media craved: the big anti-government headlines that captured readers of a certain type. Newspaper stories just like the ones that had named his star operative Samantha Holloway, and her husband Nigel Thomas, for their part in what the press called 'the Spean Bridge massacre', and that had ensured their permanent exile to Canada. The latest potential iterations were still probably in the tabloid editors' offices, as they examined the legal implications. The story was bubbling under the surface, leaked by Russian and Arabic media, but he had been already told what the possible headlines might be:

MI5 run by Uncle Sam!

CIA pulls the strings!

Why did they have to die?

5,000 bullets fired in SAS ambush!

Where is Captain Samantha Holloway?

His insider contacts within the mainstream media had told him that the press would ask why the terrorists involved hadn't been given a chance to surrender. Danny looked at his reflection in the office window; it seemed that every worry, every operation, etched yet more years into his face. *Did he need this?* It had now been four years since the outline scribbled onto an airline napkin had become an unofficial arm of Britain's covert policy both at home and abroad. It had been successful, but it was always dangerous, and the commercial side was now more profitable. The company earned more from Close Protection than its intelligence-based product. *Maybe, just maybe, this was the time not to answer the phone and concentrate on the Qatar World Cup.* But Danny did pick up the phone.

"Tim, to what do I owe the pleasure?"

"Can you attend a meeting?"

"Where?"

"VX" Tim used the insider term for the MI6 building in Vauxhall.

"When, mate?" Danny picked up a pen.

"One hour?" Tim said quickly.

"Yeah, OK." He put the pen back down.

"See you there, mate, Conference Room 10."

"Roger that" said Danny. His face wrinkled into well-worn lines of frustrated resignation. He still could not ignore a request to serve his country.

'A' Wing, Wandsworth, London

He had waited as Mohammad had stretched and finally roused himself from his slumbers. The ex-Jihadist was smiling and beaming with confidence as he stood up. Coco pictured him as a punchbag and felt better.

"Had a good nap?" He was smiling on the outside.

"Yes brother, thank you. I dreamed I was back in the Caliphate and felt closer to God."

"Allah be praised," said Coco, as Mohammad started to run his left hand under the sputtering tap of the cell's washbasin. The A Wing Muslims called it *wudhu*; it cleansed and prepared the believers for prayer, which they called *salat*. It was a lengthy process with twelve steps, starting with the left hand washing the right one three times. The ultra-religious in the wings, post-Covid, had staggered prayer times so that only six could gather at one time, and Mo was preparing for his time frame.

Coco just wanted him to fuck off so that he could make his call to his handler. By the time Mo had got to the fourth step of inhaling water into his nose, snorting it and expelling it into the prison wash basin, he just wanted to smash his face into the porcelain and keep smashing it.

You're losing it!

By the time the cell door finally opened to allow the Jihadist to go to prayers, his pulse was racing like he was waiting for the bell for Round One. He quickly gathered the phone from its hiding place under his mattress and dialled the number from memory.

"Yeah," Lou answered.

"Hi, mate, I'm phoning from Uncle Mo's." Coco gave the brevity code that told his handler that he was on his own and not acting under duress.

"How's it going, bro?"

"As you say, fucking grimmers, mate!" Coco liked using some of his handler's 'bootneck' sayings in conversation with Lou, although he was never stupid enough to use them elsewhere.

"Then you're going to like what I'm going to ask you to do, buddy."

Coco then just listened, and as he listened, he started to smile.

CHAPTER SEVEN

Canada

She had got out of bed quickly, just before sunrise, in order to follow her training schedule. It had been hard at first, but Samantha knew that sometimes you had to bend your body to your will. She lifted her small backpack onto her back as the front door slammed behind her. Her mind was healing now, and each day since her suicide attempt had left her stronger. The first run afterwards had been the toughest but now everything was easier. Sam was running hard as she ducked her head under a low branch and then clambered over the trunk of a fallen tree. She was three miles into it now. Her mind and body felt alive as her body reacclimatised itself to endurance work. Samantha felt the straps of the small-size Karrimor X backpack jerk comfortably into her shoulders as she used one outstretched arm to vault over another fallen tree. The last time she had timed herself over this route had been in direct competition with her husband.

They had designed the course with care, a route that followed the small winding logging tracks through the forest, a demanding run of over six miles. It was muddy, and the mixture of cloying clay and water puddles tested her strength, endurance and agility. She came to the firebreak, stopped momentarily and checked the time. *I'm getting quicker.* Sam took a deep breath of the cool air, scented with Canadian pine, and for the first time in weeks she felt truly alive. As she loped along the track the shade of the trees suddenly gave way to a wider logging track, then a small valley, and her destination on the high ground opposite.

The track fell away sharply, down a wet, muddy slope. She slipped and slithered downwards and adjusted her backpack as she steadied herself for the jump across the stream. She hurdled it smoothly, landed in a controlled manner with both feet hitting the far bank together, and then powered herself up the climb to the top. She sprinted, both legs now firing like pistons and forcing her upwards, and then she was there.

The clearing at the top was where they had set up the outdoor range. Sam removed the pack and neatly stacked the contents, ready for use, on a fallen tree trunk. A black leather gun belt, a speed holster and two mag holders. A Glock 19 9mm pistol, three 9mm magazines, ten boxes of high-grade Luger ammo and a 'Competition Pocket Pro' range timer. She remembered her training at Hereford as she organised the equipment. She thought back to the thousands of rounds of ammunition used on her two-week pistol package, and the countless hours of dry drills. The house combat days, the vehicle drills. The training had had the desired result: when she observed her hands preparing the equipment, it was almost like they were working independently of thought.

She 'bombed up' (loaded) three magazines for the first range practice. Her hands moved nimbly, pressing the shiny 9mm bullets into the mags. The first mag with five, the second with five and the third with six. She moved the mag holders onto her left hip and picked up each loaded magazine, forefinger flush to the top and to the front of the mag and pointing downwards. This ensured that each magazine would be correctly aligned when it was snapped into the pistol on a fast mag change. She adjusted the gun belt around her waist and tested the draw on the pistol. She drew the weapon at speed, slapped the first mag into it and slid the pistol back into the holster, where it gave her a strange feeling of completeness. It felt right, it felt natural. It was what she was meant to do.

The bond between an inanimate object designed only for death and the living, thinking part of the equation was hard to describe, *but the weapon is part of a soldier, and then the soldier is the weapon.* She placed the other two mags into the leather holders on the left-hand side of the belt. There is a kind of balance to the relationship that people who have not carried arms would find hard to understand. Her Special Forces training had raised her competence level from the normal to the superb, from the safe and capable to the near-ninja. Her life before her suicide attempt was now firmly in the past. The Samantha of before had been different. As she had cradled a tiny life inside her she had been happy, but the happiness had made her more susceptible to emotional upset. It had released hormones that had changed her and made her much softer and therefore weaker, but because that precious life had now been clawed from her body her strength was back. She felt focused now; the old Special Forces Sam from the Special Reconnaissance Regiment (SRR) was back.

Samantha removed three paper targets from her pack, along with a stapler and a timing clock. She soon found the place on the edge of the clearing where she had practised with Taff. She quickly stapled the 'Hun's head' targets to the pine trees, where the remnants of the previous pieces of paper had lost their battle with the Canadian weather, then took the Glock from its holster, smiled and weighed it in her hand. She loved the feel of the weapon, twenty-five ounces of steel and polymer, a comforting weight, and she felt at one with it. She had been around weapons for so long that they now represented the closest thing she had to happiness. She racked the weapon slide back an inch, saw the reassuring gleam of brass that ensured that a bullet in the breech was good to go, and returned the pistol to the holster. This was the first practice of the day, designed to test her competence from the draw. Her instructors at Chicksands had, for unknown reasons, called it 'El Presidente'. Sam stood with her back to the three targets.

They were six feet apart and stapled onto the pines at head height, simulating three bad guys in a group. Sam pressed the range timer and then raised her hands. The routine had been engrained into her muscle memory. On the signal she would draw, turn and engage the first target with a double tap, then double tap the second, fire a single shot at the third and then perform a speed mag change before reversing the process until all her ammunition was expended. The timer beeped down to the draw.

Beep, beep, beep, the counter ran down and then, BEEP, and her hand was already moving with the fluidity that only Special Forces training can deliver. She drew the pistol as she was turning, then the Glock was fully extended in the two-armed Weaver stance and she had the sight picture.

BANG, BANG! A double tap with two sounds so close together that they almost blended into one report. Another target – BANG, BANG! another double tap and then BANG! the fifth round hit the target, the weapon's working parts held to the rear and she was into the first mag change. She depressed the mag release button, the empty mag dropped from the pistol and the next mag held in her left hand deftly replaced it as she released the slide, pushing a fresh round into the chamber. Another target: BANG, BANG! The procedure was repeated the other way round, and all done in the split seconds it took to double-tap the targets in the opposite direction.

BEEP. The timer ended the action. Sam holstered the warm pistol and studied the targets. The first double-tap group was within a couple of inches in the forehead of the target, the next tighter but a bit too far to the left, while the third double-tap was flawless, as were all the rest, all at the very centre of the Hun's head and square between the eyes. Sam walked back to the ammo point to re-bomb her mags and go again!

SAS: Surprise, Aggression, Speed. And muscle memory, she thought, and smiled.

CHAPTER EIGHT

Wandsworth

Coco was having a bad day. He sensed that things were beginning to change on the inside. He looked into the scratched steel mirror at a reflection that he didn't particularly like. He didn't like the beard that sprouted at varying lengths from his young face, and he didn't like the prayer hat perched like one of his mum's lace doilies that had protected the table from the teapot whenever Father Murphy visited. He also hated the heavy snoring sound coming from his odious cellmate Mohammad, as he took an afternoon pre-prayer nap. He had left his prison-issue Covid mask on, and that made the snoring louder.

Coco had been inside for over a year now, and although being an MI5 informer in Wandsworth Prison had been a financial success it had not been much fun. Things had started to go downhill after he had been approached by the 'Brotherhood' and requested to be moved to D Wing. His cell on A Wing had been a happy place compared to here, because it was a remand wing and therefore had a large number of 'normal' criminals that he understood. But D Wing was different, it was where the prison authorities placed the most militant of the Brothers in a sort of internal, joyless, Islamic ghetto. There were no little snatches of normal life here, music was banned, smoking was frowned upon and laughter was seldom heard, with each of the wankers trying to out-Islam the next. It gave a whole new meaning to the phrase 'holier than thou'. He was genuinely worried for his own sanity, for the first time since he had volunteered to be MI5's man on the inside.

He had begun to have dark thoughts: if he had to endure another lecture on the 'holy book' from the deranged mind of Mo Ziaman, he would just punch the fuck out of him until he killed him. He had been trapped by his own success, as he had deliberately engineered the cell-share, but the close proximity to Mo had slowly chipped away at his sanity.

He had learned some interesting insights to pass on to his handler, though. Mo was a gobby bastard who obviously had never had the benefit of a 'Need to Know' lecture. He liked the sound of his own voice, and because of that some little gems of intelligence were beginning to glimmer out of the opacity of his self-serving boasts and innuendo. He had started to talk about his time in Syria and of how the blessed day of the great reckoning was coming. He got enthusiastic when he talked about the final showdown with the USA, the final conflagration that would bring 'Dar al-Salam', or the 'House of Peace', when Allah would rule all mankind.

Coco knew he had pressed all the right buttons. People who like talking will often talk long into the night. Mohammad talked more than most, and all the information was collected and passed. Something very big and nasty was on its way. Coco had learned that a rumour is sometimes more than a rumour when lots of people start referring to it.

What's the old saying? 'No smoke without fire'.

Getting the information to his handler had become much more problematic since the cell-share situation. The Mojos had lots of smuggled phones, and other prisoners paid a premium to use them. Coco had one, but it had been supplied to him by them and was therefore probably monitored. He also had his own, a small

'Beat the Boss' that had been supplied by Lou via the drone flights. It had come with what Lou called a 'sked' (schedule), a specific window during the day when he could phone information straight into the office. It had been difficult to reconcile the two elements he needed to make space for a call, but a window of opportunity, albeit a risky one, had now presented itself. His cellmate was leading the evening prayers for six of the Brothers, the maximum still allowed since Covid, and would probably go to the prison prayer room to prepare himself early. If Coco could grab five minutes after he left, he could call Lou. He looked again at his reflection in the mirror while glancing towards the slumbering form of his cellmate. It wasn't a happy face, and he had that old familiar glint of violence in his eyes.

***

Thames House

Less than five miles away, Lou was in a room at Thames House talking to one of the Security Service's legal advisors. Sheena was a pretty girl with bobbed blonde hair, bright red lipstick and designer clothes that looked like she had just walked off the set of 'Made in Chelsea', and she also spoke the same way. As with anyone in MI5, though, appearances could be deceptive; Sheena was a council house kid from Kilburn who had clawed her way upward and into a law degree at Brasenose College, Oxford, where she had excelled.

"So how long have we got?" Sheena was sitting at one of the white wood tables, on a Swedish-looking hardback chair and taking notes with an MI5 issue Chinese-manufactured biro.

"Not sure," Lou replied. "Chris thinks that they have the same sort of assets we have on the computer analysis side, so certain threads, that we know that they know we know, are going to be traced back to him eventually."

"So, no definite time frame for compromise yet?"

"No," Lou said.

"Well, that increases our options." Sheena started scribbling a mind map.

"Fuck," said Sheena as her MI5 issue pen stopped working. She normally spoke with a Sloane Street accent but swore in north London Kilburn cockney.

"Why do they buy shit that self-destructs on use?" she blurted out in rapid Kilburnese.

"If I was smart enough to know that I wouldn't need your advice, girl," said Lou.

"Fair one," she said as she delved into her designer bag for a writing implement that worked. "I have a possible solution to get him out that will look natural, but it has its downside."

"Let's talk downside," said Lou.

"Your source will no longer be viable and will lose all access."

"Yeah, I can live with that," Lou said in a resigned murmur. "What's the plan?"

Sheena looked up. She liked Lou and her eyes sparkled slightly. "Well, it's what a lot of the guys in his position do, especially when they are halfway through their sentence and coming up for parole review." She paused. "This is a particularly good option for him, because he didn't go in on terrorism charges and so will be deemed by the parole people to have been radicalised on the inside."

"Is this what the Islamist nutters inside call Plan B?"

"Yeah, Plan B: he goes to the official prison imam and says that he wants to go into the Prevent programme, that he has turned his back on extremism and wants some counselling."

"There's no time for that."

"Yeah, I understand, but hear me out." Sheena flashed a 'shut the fuck up' look at the big handler.

"The dynamics of Wandsworth are peculiar to that prison, and the strict segregation imposed after last year's Covid measures has further divided the inmates, especially on CORKSCREW's wing. What the normal criminals call the 'Beardies' are on the extreme Wahhabi side of Islam. However, since the last prison review most of the prison's imams are from the Hanafi school of Islamic jurisprudence. It's a softer side of Islam and they will always try to help a prisoner disengage from violence."

"How does that make a difference?

"This is where the geopolitics of Islam gets confusing inside prison walls. Wahhabism is the most extreme form of Islam and is Saudi-based." Sheena took a long breath. "The milder form of Hanafi Islam is also competing for space inside Wandsworth."

"How can we use this to get him out?" Lou picked up CORKSCREW's file from the desk and started leafing through it.

"As you know, it's going to be slow. The current Muslim chaplain is a Hanafi and will want to help him to get away, but it will take time."

Sheena was reflective for a moment and then came up with a solution.

"But I have an idea."

"I'm listening," said Lou.

Chapter Nine

Canada

Samantha hit the heavy bag again, and the frame shuddered as she used the momentum generated by her right hip to smash her shin into the leather. She had been going through her technique drills now for an hour, and both she and the bag glistened with sweat. Sam felt on autopilot in that strange, almost Zen-like state of consciousness, just living in the moment. The drills were always the same, and their familiarity and patterns gave her mind rest.

It was thirty strikes with the left shin followed by thirty with the right. Thirty left crosses from her left fist followed by thirty from the right. As each blow struck the bag her body relaxed into the routine, and the power and speed increased. She concentrated on summoning up the strength from her hips and through her frame, until it became a seamless stream of applied power. After a week of hard training the old Sam was nearly back; as her shins and hands had hardened, so had her mind. As she stepped back from the bag, she caught an image of herself in the shadow-boxing mirror. It was the Samantha she recognised. She was wearing one of Taff's old Commando sweatshirts that she had bastardised as a crop top. She could see her muscles glistening deep in her midriff as she took a deep breath. Taff was due back from an exercise with the Canadian Special Forces later that day, and she had decided that she would never tell him about the night she had tried to end it all.

TING!

An incoming message disturbed her thoughts. She picked up the iPhone that she had been using as a round timer; the WhatsApp message was from Danny.

'See you at the next seminar.'

Samantha knew something was wrong. This was the team's brevity code for an emergency REVCON (emergency contact procedure). It meant that she should phone her old boss from the Intelligence Corps on his secure line. Retired Colonel Danny McMaster ran the London-based PMC (Private Military Company) that she had worked for over the past four years. She was both extremely fond of, and indebted to, the legend that was Danny Mac. He had looked after her in Iraq and Afghanistan and given her a job when others had refused.

She knew that he wouldn't be phoning with such security if it were just a social call. Sam scrolled through the phone as she climbed the stairs from the basement gymnasium. She looked through her phone list for the name that said 'St Andrew's' and she just changed the last two digits of the phone number. She now had Danny's encrypted number. She looked around her - although she was alone in the house, she was unsure whether there might not be some sort of undisclosed technical assets installed for their protection. Her skin was still glowing from the bag session as she quickly draped her parka around her and snatched the emergency burner phone from its hiding place in the kitchen cupboard.

Sam checked the time: it was 0800 hours in eastern Canada, which was 1300 in London. She checked that the phone was fully charged and replaced it in her pocket. As she broke the seal of the door the light and warmth of the early morning sun bathed her face. She smelt the freshness of recent rain and her trainers slipped slightly as she made her way to the outside wood store. She opened the door, took the burner phone from her pocket and tapped in the number she had memorised, Danny answered immediately.

"Fortnum and Mason," he said, his company's code for being able to speak freely. "How can I help you?"

"Complaints department, please." Sam repeated her brevity code.

"Hi Samantha," he answered with real warmth.

Sam smiled. "Hi Danny, what's up?"

"Sam, how lovely to hear your voice."

Sam knew immediately that something was wrong. Danny McMaster had been her friend and mentor for over a decade, and she knew him well. She also knew that he wouldn't break the basic protection given to resettled personnel by a direct REVCON unless it was absolutely necessary.

"Great to hear yours as well, Danny, but why the call?"

"Just want you keep you in the loop of what's happening over here, kid."

"I read the papers, Danny." Sam took a deep breath as she knew what was coming. "I suppose the normal ambulance chasers are now involved in the last job?"

There was a short pause and an intake of breath on the other side of the line.

"Yes, you've nailed it, Sam, we've huge problems over here trying to keep the lid on the op, for obvious reasons. They are trying to reopen the Weeping Willows inquiry and they are actively trying to find out where you and Taff are staying. But that's not why I've called." Danny paused as if in thought, and then fired the question.

"I have a job for the team. The outline is sketchy at the moment but it's with the Task Force, and I think it will a UK-based training task."

"Any details?" Sam replied quickly.

"As I say, Samantha, sketchy. I just need to stand by some people to babysit and train a blown agent." Danny paused. "And that's all I can let you know at the moment."

"He must be an important one." Sam had a sceptical edge to her voice.

"There are other things going on as well; you'll just have to trust my judgement on that one."

Sam was momentarily lost in thought. *Do I trust Danny's judgement? The last job had started in a straightforward way and the team had done all that was required of them, including some elements of a dubious moral nature. They had trusted the security services then, but by the end of the mission she had lost her home and her career and had been exiled from the country she loved. And although they had delivered an evil man into thoroughly deserved torment, the success of that operation had depended solely on what they could extract from him. Because unless he talked, the whole operation would have eventually failed.*

But Samantha knew that she didn't really have an option. She needed to get home.

"OK, Danny, I'll talk to Taff, if you'll make the arrangements."

"Right, Sam, things are already in place. You and Taff fly RAF from Rockcliffe Airport, near Ottawa, in two days."

"Roger that" said Sam.

D Wing, Wandsworth

Coco worked to a strict timetable; he had to appear to act naturally, as he planned to do something that he had a natural talent for. A few things needed to be in place before he acted. He had to prepare the ground by an official meeting with the prison imam, a kindly old boy who was just totally out of his depth on the Wings. He had seen how the authorities in the prison had been game-played by the Beardies on numerous occasions. The 'D' Wing Islamists called the imam, a white bearded sexagenarian, Gandalf, as he was the spitting image of the wizard from *The Lord of the Rings*, and they considered him just another part of the ever-evil 'kuffar' system. But he was always ready to go in to bat on behalf of the prison's Muslim population.

The meeting was arranged very quickly, and the prison warders also played their part, as a visit to the 'D' Wing chaplain was subject to certain protocols. The oldest prison warder on 'D' Wing was an ex-serviceman, particularly attuned to the unique situation on the Wings. It was he who opened Coco's cell. "Miller," he said, in quite a friendly manner. He sometimes used the prisoner's nicknames to try to communicate more effectively but couldn't use Coco's because the word could be considered racist.

"Yeah?" Coco was sitting on his bed, thinking how he would make sure the plan would work.

"The prison chaplain is ready to see you if you are available."

"Cool," said Coco, as he followed the screw towards the single room beyond the locked landing door that was designated the Wing's multi-denominational prayer room. He sauntered behind the prison officer, who had the reputation of being a fair enough guy.

"Mr Patrick," Coco whispered, as they made their way along the walkway.

The prison officer was experienced enough not to turn towards Coco's voice.

"Your right hand." The officer opened his hand as Coco pressed a small object into it but said nothing as he unlocked the wing entrance.

"I will wait for you here, Miller," he said with a smile. "Enjoy."

Coco returned the smile as the prison officer opened the prayer room door.

The imam was studying the Koran as Coco entered the room.

"What brings you here, my son?" the kindly man asked.

"I believe my life is under threat."

Gandalf's gentle features darkened in reaction.

"Tell me why you think that's the case, son?"

Coco assumed his most contrite face, the one usually reserved for only three occasions: when talking to his mum or his handler, or when in court.

"I know what I've become involved in is wrong, and I've voiced opinions to certain people that I shouldn't have." Coco gave an extra-sincere look to the old guy. "I now believe that these people intend me serious harm."

There was a moment of silence as Gandalf processed this.

"Please tell me the names of those that intend you harm."

"You know I can't do that. I just need to get off this particular wing."

"Do you feel your life is in danger?"

"No, I can look after myself, but I want it on record that I let you know."

"I will see the Governor as soon as possible," the old man said. He knew what people were saying about the prisoner sitting opposite him and he agreed with the young man's self-appraisal.

"Please try and keep out of trouble if you can, my son; you are due release soon."

"I won't trouble anybody as long as they don't trouble me!" Coco stood and tapped on the door.

"Thank you" he said, as the door clanked open.

Coco looked at the large Victorian clock at the end of the prison landing. It had always seemed a bit cruel to prominently display the minutes of a prisoner's life ticking away, but today it served a purpose. In one hour, he had a meeting arranged with Mohammad and two of the most prominent Brothers on 'D' Wing.

The officer had known exactly what it was as soon as he felt it in the palm of his hand: a prison comm. A comm was the way some prisoners from organised groups communicated with others and their people on the outside of the prison. Although smuggled mobile phones were very much part of prison life they couldn't always be relied on. Prison authorities found it easy to jam phone signals, and the organised crime element of the prison population always considered the wavelengths that were not jammed as compromised.

The comm was a communication system first used by Irish Republican prisoners in Wandsworth; now the Beardies used it, and it wasn't the first one he had seen. It was a simple message written in very fine script on a piece of Rizla cigarette paper, and folded in a certain way to identify the sender to its recipient. It was then wrapped in cling film so it could be carried covertly, and it was designed to be secreted in many devious places on the human body. The screw hoped that this one hadn't been inserted into any of them.

He looked across the office at the burly frame of Billy, the prison's designated Intelligence Assessment officer. He was the specialist who was needed to unwrap the message. All prison intelligence was fed into an integrated computer system called Mercury, and that in turn eventually fed into the JTAC (Joint Terrorism Analysis Centre) at Thames House. On his desk rested some of the tools of his trade. A large, illuminated, magnifying glass was suspended seemingly in mid-air over an area of sanitised glass, and several small tools, including a scalpel, were resting on a workbench.

"What've you got for me, Pat?" Billy was from the Shankill Road in Belfast, and sometimes hard to understand.

"A comm from a known face on 'D' Wing, mate."

"Who?"

"Miller."

"Hey, that could be interesting. You know the lad – what do youse think?"

"Strange one, mate. He's never approached us before, and why use a comm, unless he wants it into the system straight away? He would know that anything like a comm would come to the Intelligence Branch."

"Well, let's find out!" the int guy said, while pulling on some surgical gloves. "Always a good idea to put gloves on, not only for the integrity of forensic evidence but also because these things sometimes spend time up somebody's arse."

Undoing and reading a comm was a specialist task. You needed to open it correctly, as each had a signature that was particular to the person that had painstakingly inscribed it. Billy first examined the general shape; a lot of the guys in prison are used to the types of drug wraps that were distributed around every council estate in London, but the ones distributed by terrorist groups inside were more complicated. Each comm was crafted in a certain way, and Billy had the ability to put them back together like they had never been opened, *but maybe that wasn't needed this time?*

"What's the timescale on this?" he asked Pat.

"Not sure." Pat looked thoughtful. "I should think that I'm the end user for this, so I doubt that a reply is needed."

"OK," Billy looked through the magnifying glass and reached for the scalpel.

"Let's just open her up" he said, as he sliced through the clingfilm. It was a pretty standard comm, neatly folded in on itself. The number of folds usually indicated the sender, and this piece of Rizla paper was folded sixteen times, which was a standard Beardie feature.

"OK, what have we got here?" Billy said, as he placed the unfolded piece of thin paper under the magnifying glass. The simple message was written in fine script, and Billy read it out.

"I have been threatened and I am in fear of my life. I have renounced my allegiance to the Brotherhood, and they intend to kill me. Please help!"

"OK, he's got to move." There was a hint of concern in Pat's voice.

The intelligence specialist reached across for the red house phone. "OK, I'll phone the Governor." The phone, a secure line direct to the main man's office, started to ring as soon as Billy lifted the receiver. "You organise the heavy mob to move him."

The older man was already hurrying towards the staff rest area. He knew what had to be done. Any prisoner-move after such a tip off or warning needed a segregation order, and the operation had to look heavy handed, to protect the whistle-blower. There was always a designated 'Tornado Team' of at least four officers in their own office near the main staff canteen.

As Pat reached the room and knocked on the door the team, already alerted, were donning their equipment, and four black-robed figures were making final adjustments as he opened the door.

"Where?" one guy said, as he reached down to pick up his extendable ASP baton.

"'D' Wing, but it's a cell move, not a riot."

"OK," the officer said, as everything seemed to slow. "What's the SITREP (Situation Report)?"

"Vulnerable prisoner under threat, standard cell move." Pat noticed how the team's excitement had somewhat faded. The Tornado Teams were the Prison Service's specialists in countering violence, so by implication were pretty violent fuckers themselves.

"Any violence displayed against the inmate so far?" The team leader said.

"No, just a straightforward cell relocation, uncontested," Pat said, stressing the final word. He could sense the disappointment.

"So, nothing should be happening in that cell when we arrive, yeah?"

"Correct, uncontested. The prisoner has requested the move."

In his cell, less than three hundred yards from where the guys in black continued to prepare for their routine task, Coco was sitting on his prison bed and chatting to the three most prominent Jihadists in Wandsworth. He had arranged for them to be there at that time. Mohammad was doing most of the talking, still preaching and still pissing him off. The other two guys had talked already, and now nothing could be changed; the plan was already in motion. Suliman had been a doorman in his twenties, looked like he could handle himself and had the reputation of being an enforcer on the religious side of life. He was the guy that castigated the other Brothers if they missed prayers.

He will go as soon as I've chinned Mo! Coco had made his assessment.

The larger and fatter man was one of the most important players. His name was Ibrahim; he had all the contacts to the Muslim Brotherhood on the outside. Coco had prayed with them all as he lived his double life. He had grown close to Suliman and Ibrahim and had ostensibly bonded with them over his time on the Wing.

Now, that shit changes!

Mo was still mouthing off, but Coco had long since stopped listening. His voice was now just a background drone as Coco focused on his mouth opening and closing. He chose his spot, just below the left side of the lower mandible, the sweet spot for shattering the jaw. It had to happen now. There was a look of horror on the faces of the other two as Coco closed the space quickly. Mo was half leaning against the washbasin as the right hook smashed his head into the steel mirror. The other two looked on in amazement as the first flurry of punches showered around them. Suliman managed to connect with a half-hearted blow that cut Coco's lip before he was knocked out. Ibrahim still had a puzzled look on his face as Coco hit him with a left hook.

Then, there was silence in the cell as Coco looked at his handiwork. All three were out for the count. He quickly reached under his mattress and found the shank, a six-inch piece of hacksaw that had been honed razor sharp and attached to the shaft of a toothbrush with black masking tape. He carefully wiped off his prints with the prison issue sheet and placed the improvised knife into the hand of Mohammad, who was now propped up under the wash basin. He stood and glanced into the mirror smeared with Mo's blood. He had just had time to sit down and rub some of the fresh blood from his lip over his face when the cell door opened, and the men in black appeared in the doorway.

"What the fuck happened here?"

Coco looked up from where he was seated on the bed and tried to look shocked.

"They tried to kill me!"

The first Tornado Team guy looked around the cell. The three other prisoners were in various states of unconsciousness, but they all seemed to be breathing.

There was almost a hint of admiration in his voice as he said, "They didn't do that too well, did they?"

Chapter Ten

On the way from Brize Norton

Sam, dog-tired, was being driven at speed in the back of a V8 Transit van. A no-frills military flight across the Atlantic and a midnight pick up at Brize Norton had dulled the blueness of her eyes. She looked across at Taff. He was asleep and looking childlike as his head nodded gently with the progress of the van. Its lights were flashing as it made its way on the team's latest mission. The last two days had been a blur, but she was glad that she had survived her night of despair. She was stronger now. She had chosen her own Commando brand of therapy to claw her way back to what she considered normal within the confines of her strange existence. Taff had not asked any awkward questions, but she felt that he had a good idea that she had been struggling.

She had used the time before his return to both regain her fitness and reinforce her resolve - and thereby regain her sanity. She would never mention that night to her husband; she didn't need either his sympathy or any questions about her ability. The team had to think that she was the old Samantha Holloway, the team leader and not a team liability. The message from Danny had not only reunited them but had also created more questions than answers. But both operators were used to this; a clear-cut answer was rarely expected in the smoke and mirrors of covert operations.

Was this a government job? Probably.

Being picked up after the flight in a government vehicle that looked disturbingly like a prison van, and with none of the normal inconveniences like passport control, made that look likely. The bulky driver of the vehicle had greeted them with a polite smile, a handshake and a friendly "My name's Julian. Danny sent me" but had otherwise remained tight-lipped and was obviously a spook of some kind. "This bit of kit is yours as soon as I've dropped you off," he said, as if that were all the information he had been told to impart.

A sign flashed by, telling Sam that they were on the A40 and moving towards London. She looked again at her sleeping husband. Taff was a real Afghan veteran, able to sleep on a clothesline if needed; it was a skill that she sadly lacked. She was beginning to realise that she needed help. All the progress she had made, through the initial therapy that she had grudgingly submitted to, had instantly been wiped out by the guilt she felt after the last job and its bloody conclusion. The loss of her baby had made things a thousand times worse. She thought that the only thing that had kept her alive during those dark nights was the love she felt for the big lump opposite her. She was beginning to realise something that she had always subliminally known. They were both happier when they were pushing the limits in that emotional no-man's-land of operational combat.

It was a fucked-up way to live.

The main man in her life made an involuntary nod as the van lurched slightly, as if he were unconsciously agreeing with her.

They had been given an A4 envelope by Julian as they left the plane. Neatly inscribed across its plain brown exterior, in Danny's handwriting, was a stark and simple 'Open only when required'. That time had clearly now arrived, since the package began buzzing: a mobile phone vibrated inside it. Sam removed the iPhone, swiped it and answered.

"Welcome back, Samantha," said Danny. "This is your burner phone for the duration of the task - if you take it." Sam examined the phone, a used iPhone 8. Danny continued. "The phone has all the same technology as the one supplied on your previous mission, as this task might require you to work independently at times." There was a pensive pause. "Please let me explain what's happening."

Sam prodded Taff with her foot and he woke with a start. She mimed the words 'Danny Mac' and pointed to the phone. Taff raised his thumb in acknowledgement.

"Please do," Sam answered. "Going to put you on speaker, Danny. Taff's listening in."

"OK, hope you two have recovered somewhat from the flight? I'm going to outline the task and what we know so far, but I've got to warn you guys that it's quite an unusual job."

"Life has been pretty weird lately anyway, Danny." Sam looked across at Taff. "Yeah, got to agree with you on that one, kid."

Danny's tone changed slightly.

"Basically, we have an intelligence training job for you two. Interested?"

"What is it?"

"Good question." Danny was business-like.

"I will outline the job and then take questions at the end, OK?"

"Yeah, fire away."

After five minutes of Danny's unusual download, Samantha began to realise just how different the next mission was going to be!

"You've got to be joking, Danny."

"No, Sam. It's a bit unconventional, I know, but sometimes the conventional doesn't work!"

"Well, it's definitely different, and it sort of fits with the Kitson idea of the 'counter-gang' thing."

"Yes, it has historical precedent. After all, that's how our organisations began!"

Sam was quiet for a while as she considered Danny's offer.

"Danny, we need to chat this end; can I call you back?" She glanced at Taff, who was wearing his 'What the fuck was that all about?' look.

"Of course, Samantha. Take your time."

There was silence as Sam took a deep breath and momentarily considered the options. She knew what Danny was referring to. General Sir Frank Kitson, a warrior-scholar with post-colonial experience in both Malaya and Kenya, had been an early exponent of British 'Black Ops' in Northern Ireland. He had been the guiding light in the use of what he called 'counter-gangs' or 'pseudo gangs', designed to penetrate terrorist organisations and destroy their operational effectiveness. It was a policy designed to 'turn' terrorists inside the IRA and then exploit the information they produced. In many ways he had been a precursor of what the press later called the 'Unholy Trinity', the secret fusion of the 'Troop' (the SAS in Northern Ireland), the surveillance experts of 14th Intelligence Company and the agent-runners of a military formation called the Force Research Unit or FRU.

She knew from her university days that it was far from a new idea: Sun Tzu, around 500 BC, had said that *"to understand your enemy, you need to be your enemy"*. But this was the decision point.

"What d'you think? Your call!" Samantha whispered to Taff.

"Well, I suspect that we've come a long way for nothing. I think Danny is just trying to keep us out of trouble for the next couple of months. Why doesn't Five or Six run it themselves?"

"I think there's got to be that 'Use a contractor for plausible deniability' thing going on again. But that's the service we provide, I suppose!" she said in a resigned voice.

"You in?" asked Taff.

It was Yes or No. That special moment when you could jump into trouble or choose the safe option. Sam blinked and looked across at Taff, who nodded in consent.

"Then we both are. It shouldn't be that demanding; it's only a training task," said Taff, smiling broadly, but knowing that any task that Danny and his company, Hedges and Fisher, gave them was always more than it seemed and was always intrinsically dangerous.

Julian, started to indicate right just before a roundabout and shouted from the front of the van.

"OK, guys, within the next half hour we will be at the safe house that you'll be using for the duration of the task. Danny has requested that you call him before we go any further and accept the assignment."

Sam made the call and Danny answered.

"Hi Sam, can I just chat before I get your answer?"

"Of course. I have the call on speaker and Taff is listening."

"OK, that's good. Before you two tell me if it's a goer, there is something that we must discuss."

"Yeah?" Sam looked a bit confused.

"The first thing is a given: if you don't want this type of task at the moment, we can go in another direction. I have a couple of other jobs that will get you out of the country until the dust settles on the last mission. The company will look after you." Danny paused. "Is that understood?"

"Yes, and it's appreciated."

"Yeah," Taff added.

"And, secondly, there are other things that might unfold from this task that could be of a much more military nature." Danny seemed to take a breath.

"Are you still interested?"

Sam looked towards Taff and they both nodded.

"Yeah, we are both in," Sam said.

"OK, stand by for a download on the location you are going to, and a full outline of the task. And welcome back!"

"Thanks, Danny," both operators chimed, almost in unison.

TING.

The outline of the Op Order arrived on Telegram. Sam used the company cipher and decrypted the message.

"Where are we going?" said Taff.

"It's a place on an estate in Oxfordshire called Repton Manor," Sam replied.

"I think I've heard of that," said Taff.

"Yeah, so have I." Sam smiled.

Chapter Eleven

Wandsworth Prison, 'E' Wing

Coco was getting to know his new surroundings. He was 'in solitary', although it wasn't called solitary confinement anymore. They now called it segregation, and he supposed it was quite an understandable reaction from the prison authorities after he had beaten three of his fellow-prisoners senseless. Coco had read a lot and realised that he had joined quite an exclusive club: after all, the poet Oscar Wilde and Ronnie Biggs, the legendary train robber, could have shared this same cell. He also knew that his own government-sponsored escape plan was already in progress.

The segregation cells on E Wing had just undergone a refurbishment following sharp criticism in a 2018 prison report, and, if he was honest with himself, he would have to admit that the move had given him a significant upgrade from his previous accommodation. These cells had only just been redecorated and being on his own was just the way he liked it. And he needed to be on his own as he heard the resounding clunk of the cell door being unlocked.

The newly painted prison-grey door creaked open slightly as he heard the prison officer outside almost whisper, "Step away from the door, Coco." This was the first time he had ever heard his nickname used by any member of the staff. An official brown paper envelope was pushed inside the cell, then the door closed and clunked shut. He picked up the envelope tentatively; he was a careful person, but he thought it might be his next set of instructions. He unwrapped the package slowly: some bubble wrap and then an old iPhone 6, obviously a burner.

As soon as he switched it on it vibrated; he swiped the screen and answered.

"Coco," said Lou. "You OK?"

"Yeah, sweet, bruv," a smiling inmate replied.

"OK, listen very carefully, as you are going to get ghosted."

He knew exactly what his handler meant – it was prison slang for what sometimes happened to troublesome prisoners after a violent incident. A 'ghosting' usually happened in the middle of the night. It was a way of breaking up and disrupting the normal powerbrokers in the criminal fraternity, in order to stop their influence spreading, and it was used a lot against the Beardies. A prisoner would disappear and be taken on a tour of various prisons at various times just to disorient him, a 'magical mystery tour' to stop him settling anywhere and establishing control.

"Just how ghosted?" There was a hint of scepticism in his voice. He had heard stories of prisoners disappearing in the middle of the night and getting a real kicking before they entered any prison transport.

"OK, this is the thing: it will happen in two nights from now, so it gives us time to organise where you're going. The Tornado Team will not hurt you if you play the game – they think it's a routine transfer to get you away from the Beardies – and I will pick you up personally."

"Sounds good," said Coco.

"Right, mate. Just delete this call, wipe the phone, rewrap it, put it back in the envelope and then place it just by the door where you picked it up. It will be collected in ten minutes."

"OK," said prisoner Miller, as he complied with his handler's request.

***

Repton Manor

As Samantha finally felt that she could sleep, Taff nudged her awake.

"We're nearly there," he said.

Julian, who they knew was a bit more than a driver, started his commentary from the front seat.

"Hi, guys." He indicated left. "We arrive at the Manor in ten minutes. It's on a private estate and I will run you through the inventory and sign it over to you; I'm the present custodian." The van jolted as it went over a pothole on the minor road. "I'm going to sign over a sixteenth-century listed building that is owned by English Heritage but used by Thames House." A few minutes later, as the van's tyres crunched on the gravel, Julian continued his commentary.

"This is Repton Manor, and it's had an interesting history. It was once used by the SOE (Special Operations Executive) during the Second World War, and then as an MI6 training facility during the Cold War. It also has a resident ghost, the spirit of a young woman who killed herself when her husband didn't come back from the English Civil War, so you could say it's a spooky house in lots of different ways. She was called Lady Elizabeth, doomed to walk the place at night until she has atoned for the sin of suicide."

Sam felt suddenly felt chilled, as if her secret had been laid bare by that simple statement from history. It was as if this affable Six guy had just clawed at a deep wound in her subconscious. She had tried to kill herself; she looked across, caught Taff's eye and felt ashamed of the memory.

"You OK, kid?" Nigel's accent always became a bit more 'South Wales' when he showed concern.

"Yeah, I'm OK," Sam said. "I've just had that 'someone's stepped on my grave' feeling with this place. Did you know that the original guys from the FRU (Force Research Unit) trained here as well?"

"No, a bit before my time with the unit," he said.

"Before mine as well, husband of mine, but you really should know more about the unit's history, especially as we both nearly got stiffed working for it."

"Don't like history, Sam," he said, with a broad smile on his face.

"Why not?"

"Because it has a way of repeating itself when you least expect it."

"Yeah, point taken. But this place is really part of the DNA of our old unit. The original people from the MRF (Military Reaction Force) and the FRU were trained here."

The van trundled along the drive, offering the odd fleeting glimpse, between the tall ash trees, of their destination. Tyres crunched a final time on the gravel drive as the van stopped, and Julian left the engine running as he unlocked the outer chain-link gate. A large yellow plastic sign saying 'Monitored by Clarion Security' featured the black outline of a CCTV symbol alongside the signage '24-hour surveillance'.

Julian threw the large chain that had secured the gates into the footwell of the driver's seat.

"OK, guys, this place has the same cameras that are used at Thames House, and the feed is monitored there. There is an override button in the exercise Ops Room in case you need to use it. This house is listed as English Heritage undergoing renovation, and it has been for the last ten years. Before that it was an MoD asset used mainly by Army Special Duties types."

The last of the summer sun was just starting to outline the three-storey facility. It was a substantial house that looked like it had been assembled at different times and in different styles for different reasons, as indeed it had. Its architectural style ranged from classical Elizabethan through Georgian and into post-war Army utilitarian. The extended building and its barn had started life as an Elizabethan manor but had ended up as a spy school. "Now that does look like a house with a history," Sam said.

An ancient oak tree, darkened with age, was outlined against the Manor's red brick exterior. "Yeah, it's got character and history in spades," Julian replied. "They say they hanged witches on the oak when it was all the rage. The barn and range were used more recently to train FRU agent handlers for Northern Ireland, in the good old, bad old days when guns and violence were their best defence. We also have some new kit, punchbags and training mats, that have just been delivered." Julian fumbled with a large bunch of keys as he searched for the front door one.

"There are only six functional rooms used at the moment, mainly for when the driving course works from here. The rest of the house has been mothballed as an emergency training establishment and agent safe house. It was also used by R Branch in the old days for debriefing blown sources in the 'RA' (Provisional IRA) before they were resettled."

Julian drove the van through the gates and secured them with the chain. He turned to Sam and Taff, holding the key on a large brass fob.

"All yours, guys, once you sign for it," he said with a smile.

"Thanks, Julian. What every girl dreams about – her own family spy school."

"OK Sam, it looks like I have another happy customer! I'll show you guys around. You'll get a call when the rest of your team arrive on the plot, Danny assures me that all the staff for this mission should be good to go by midday tomorrow.'

The ancient door of heavy, dark oak creaked as Julian pushed against it. It reminded Samantha of the start of one of those old Gothic horror movies she had enjoyed as a girl, before real blood and terror entered her life.

As she stepped inside, she got that slightly musty odour that such buildings exude when not in use, a mix of mothballs and strong disinfectant on linoleum floors. It was not an unpleasant smell, just vaguely institutional. She had a weird feeling, though, maybe a flashback to her boarding school days, as she peered into the darkness and felt that Repton Manor had, in a way, enveloped them and welcomed them in, as if they belonged there. Julian hit the light switch and harsh fluorescent light laid the house bare. The main hallway was a confused mixture of shapes and differing styles. Ancient Tudor beams coexisted with the ubiquitous military magnolia-painted Artex of the 1980s.

"Right, I'll start the tour. Welcome to Repton Manor, and please follow me." Julian turned and grinned. "And watch out for the ghost of Lady Elizabeth, guys."

Taff smiled but Sam didn't.

Chapter Twelve

Wandsworth Prison

Prisoner 237755T Miller R now knew that getting ghosted was quite a painless experience. The mysterious package with the burner phone had been pushed into his isolation cell in much the same way as before. Once he had removed the phone it had again vibrated, and Coco had listened to his handler Lou's instructions; he now knew when they would arrive and what to expect. The Tornado Team had come soundlessly in the night, dressed in black riot gear and tooled up for trouble. The team leader had opened the cell door and said, in a low, calm voice, "Prisoner Miller, we are moving you for your own safety and you are strongly advised not to resist. DO YOU UNDERSTAND?"

"Yeah, no problems," said Coco, as he placed his hands on his head to signal compliance.

It was all very quick after that; the team did not handcuff him, just enveloped him and guided him out of the isolation cell towards the visitors' wing. They stopped outside a room just before the main visiting area; he recognised it as what the cons all called the 'Hobbit Shop', a place where more compliant prisoners spent their sentence doing interesting shit like putting washers onto bolts or constructing mop handles. The door opened as soon as the team neared it, and a hand gently pushed him inside and closed and locked the door.

"How's it going?"

"Lou!" Coco recognised the voice immediately. "Pretty well at the moment, mate," he said with a broad smile.

Lou was dressed in the same uniform as the Tornado Team outside. "Black suits you, Lou."

"Thanks, son, it has a certain slimming effect, although this rig is a wee bit tight, to be honest." Coco noticed how the overalls were somewhat stretched over the ex-Marine's arms.

"Right, listen in." Lou pointed towards the clothes and personal effects that Coco had been wearing when he had first arrived at the Hate Factory.

"Get yourself dressed in that and then you're on the out soonest, mate. You have five minutes and then we move you to a safe house. I will be with you all the time, bruv."

"Excellent." Coco beamed as he recognised the clothes he had arrived in.

He could never have described to someone the sheer delight he felt as he shed the baggy grey tracksuit of his prison days and replaced it with the clothes from his old life. It was a transformational experience in more ways than one. He knew that he had actually changed on the inside while being banged up and was now a different person from the street-smart gangster that had arrived at HMP Wandsworth two years ago. He had changed in many ways that his handler would never ever know. He had different loyalties now.

"I hope this stuff is still cutting-edge of south London fashion," Coco muttered, as he finished lacing his expensive 101s.

"Fucked if I know," growled the ex-Commando. "But can you run in those smart pumps, bruv?"

"Run?"

"Yeah, run and do extreme phys."

"Where are we going?" Coco smiled. "A gym?"

"No, son, it's the start of your training. I promised you options when you went inside this shithole and we keep our word, but it won't be easy. You are going to be assessed by an independent training team. You either pass or fail and the effort must come from you. You up for it?"

"Yeah, I need a new start," said the young gangster, in a more contrite voice.

"You've got one. Follow me; we are going to meet your training team. You will know one of them because you tried to mug her at St Pancras."

"Fuck!" said Coco.

Repton Manor

"So, you think it's down this turning?" said Pat Paterson. He doubted that they had taken the right junction off the motorway. Pat had been one of the original crew on the hostage rescue in Iraq. He looked exactly as you would expect a 'blade' (SAS man) to look. A hard-looking face fitted onto an even harder-looking body. Twenty-four years inside the military grinder, from a fifteen-year-old Barnardo's boy, through an apprenticeship in military violence in the Parachute Regiment, to a decade with B Squadron 22 SAS. It had shaped him in the British Special Forces mould, both physically and mentally.

The guy sitting next to him, who was determined to navigate the old-fashioned way, was his SBS mate, Richard Scott, or 'Scottie the Hands', so called because of his oversized fists in comparison with his mid-sized height. He was the same age as Pat but looked younger, shaped from the same mould but via a different route. He had joined the Marines at sixteen and had spent the last twelve of his twenty-four years in the Corps as a Special Boat Service operator. He, too, had been one of the original members of the hostage extraction team.

"Next right, mate." Scottie said with confidence.

Pat indicated right, turning the Mercedes onto a minor road that looked a bit too minor for his liking.

"You sure? I think we should have taken the next exit off the motorway, mate."

"Trust me. I'm a Royal Marine and a good-looking swimmer-canoeist."

"Yeah, really," said Pat, as he looked for road signs. "Well, that's two possible reasons why we're hopelessly lost, then." He laughed. "Fuck! I sometimes think you fookers actually believe your own propaganda." Pat's Yorkshire accent had been somewhat eroded after his long years of service to his country, but it got stronger when he was trying to make a point. He stopped the car, switched on the hazard lights, flashed up the satnav and tapped out the postcode for Repton Manor.

"We should have used this at the beginning, you daft Jock bastard."

"No, mate, old-style navigation is the way ahead." Scottie was looking at a road map with a red-filtered penlight torch. He always preferred to use personal skills rather than machines.

The screen on the satnav lit up and a woman's voice said, "You are approaching your destination."

Scottie smiled. "There you go, Pat."

"Just bootneck luck," said Pat with a sigh of resignation, as he swiped the phone to call Samantha.

"Hello, Pat."

"Yeah, Sam – two minutes."

"Roger that," answered Sam, and hung up.

The gate was open when they arrived, and the Jaguar compressed the gravel as it crunched to a halt on the drive. The house's security lights clicked on with a blinding glare as the cameras inside the stone-colonnaded portico vectored onto their vehicle to scrutinise Repton's latest visitors. Scottie looked across at the outlines of the other vehicles parked at the front of the old house. A new, dark-shaded BMW M4 was nestled in beside the entrance, alongside an RAC recovery vehicle.

"That's Danny's M4," he said.

"Yeah, and it looks like this job will involve some technical stuff." The recovery vehicle was the mobile workshop owned by the team's tech-guru, Jimmy Cohen.

"I wonder when Jimmy got back." Pat looked up at the house and could see light through the windows in several places. "Looks like all the crew's together again." Pat was smiling as the door to Repton Manor opened and the burly shape of Taff appeared.

"What time do you call this?" said Taff, pointing at his watch with his broadest smile.

"What can I say, mate? A bootneck navigator," Pat replied, as he opened the car door. Scottie feigned a look of shock-horror as he reacted.

"Hey, you're the one that took the wrong exit off the M25. It was only my superior map reading skills that saved the day."

Scottie prided himself on the unique skill that had been developed by the covert operators of 14th Intelligence Company in Northern Ireland: the spooky ability to drive at speed on a minor road in the darkest country areas of Ulster, while reading a map book upside down and paralleling a target.

The quick-quipping military banter belied their long bond of comradeship. Their previous missions had forged them into a team, both operationally and emotionally, as they engaged in a group hug.

"For fuck's sake, Taff, what have you been doing in Canada? Have you been teaching pie-eating techniques?"

"Mate, what have you been doing?" Taff responded. "Not much phys, obviously."

"You both could do with doing more," said Scottie.

"Cheeky fucker," said Taff and Pat together, and laughed at the synchronised response.

"OK, here's the crack," said Taff in a more serious voice. "We have about twelve hours to prep this place for a training task."

"Not much time," said Pat.

"How many students?" Scottie added.

"Yeah, it's a strange one, lads. Danny is waiting to brief, so I won't steal his thunder too much, but there's only one student and we collect him tomorrow." A sceptical glance passed between the two new joiners.

"A bit of an overuse of manpower? "Scottie said, with a slight crinkling of his brow.

"Danny Mac will explain, guys." Taff turned towards the imposing entrance of Repton Manor.

"Grab your kit and follow me, lads. The briefing is in one hour.

The new arrivals looked around as they entered the reception room of the old hall. It had that faded safe house look, a unique styling quality found only in rarely used MOD properties. Everything, apart from the original Tudor beams, had been adapted or industrialised. The house was functional, not at all quaint or pretty, and totally untouched by the experts at English Heritage. Scottie looked at the hallway wall. A lined expanse of white plastic was secured by screws to a sixteenth-century oak beam.

"Haven't seen one of them for a while," he said, in his light Highland burr.

It was an old booking-out board, probably not used since the 1990s: a whiteboard with a lined outline for names, call signs, places and intended locations.

"That brings back some memories," said Pat.

"Yeah, before mobile phone fixes and automatic locator beacons."

Taff pointed towards the double staircase that swept down at the sides of the hall.

"You're both on the first floor, rooms 3 and 5," he said, as he handed out some fairly ancient-looking keys. "Dump your kit and have a look around the place. It's been used as a training centre in the past. Check out the barn and the 25-metre range at the back. We will meet in the old Ops Room down here in an hour. I will come and find you when Danny and Sam are ready to brief."

"OK, Taff," Scottie said, as he turned towards the door. "Let's go for a recce."

"Sounds like a plan," said Pat, following him.

Almost directly to the left of the main building stood a structure that clashed uneasily with the faded grandeur of the Manor: a tall, oblong building that glistened in greenish galvanised steel. It was about fifty feet in length and separated from the Manor by a wide concrete walkway. A large tractor tyre seemed to have been abandoned on the path. Scottie eased open the double doors that opened inwards and stepped into semi-darkness.

"Look for a light switch, Pat."

"Got it," Pat said, as he ran his hand over a bank of switches on the wall inside.

Rows of fluorescent lights flashed on, illuminating a decade of neglect. The inside of the barn looked like it had been sealed up in a hurry in the '90s. Various pieces of gym equipment lay discarded on the floor, and a dusty boxing glove nestled up alongside an equally forlorn medicine ball, the two connected by the intricate pattern of an old spider's web. Four large, heavy boxing bags hung over four other large medicine balls at the end of the room.

"It looks like the place was set up for a GLF session," the SAS man said.

"Yeah," replied Scottie, almost reverently. Both had experienced the torture of a full GLF session during their own Special Forces training. GLF was the polite abbreviation of a functional military martial art called 'Go Like Fuck'. Exponents of the system valued its simplicity; it trained operators of both sexes in the ability to effectively strike at multiple assailants, so that they could create the space to draw their weapons – first the 9mm H&K MP5 Kurz machine pistol and then, in those days, the Browning high-power pistol of the same calibre. Each session started with simple technique training and developed into a daily progression that varied in intensity over the period of a CQB (Close Quarter Battle) course.

The student first learned to punch with both hands, then progressed to other 'dirty tricks' like using the heel of the hand to smash an assailant's chin, or the inside 'vee' of the forefinger and thumb to crush his larynx. Each day of the course taught another aspect of effective self-defence. It was a basic mixture of boxing, Muay Thai and fitness training that was mixed up with extreme cardio sessions to achieve a supreme level of fight fitness.

Both operators could remember their training sessions, sprinting with a 20-kilo medicine ball for varying lengths of time while your partner in the workout hammered the heavy bag. Your punching partner would then shout "break right" when the bell rang, and you handed him the medicine ball. A GLF session always lasted over an hour and ended with what the trainers called 'a mad minute' where you had to hit the bag as many times and as hard as you could until the bell rang. It had always seemed like the lung-busting 'mad minute' lasted well over sixty seconds.

"Hey, even after twenty years I can still feel the pain," said Pat.

"Yeah," said Scottie, knowing exactly what the SAS man meant. "What do you think about the training you had?"

"What – P Company or Selection?"

"Both."

"Loved it. I had nothing else, mate. As a Barnardo's boy it was the first proper family I had." Pat looked at his old friend from Iraq. "What about you?"

"I needed it." Scottie looked as if he was searching his memory banks. "I was a farm labourer, no education; I had to go to night school to learn to read and write properly so I could pass the entrance exam." He looked towards the heavy punch bags hanging at the end of the room.

"I had about as much chance in life as those fuckers." He walked towards the nearest bag and punched it; the whole place reverberated with the noise. "The Royal Marines gave me a home and a reason to improve myself. I was the youngest guy ever to pass SBS selection."

"Yeah, I suppose that this place brings back those emotions," Pat said.

"There's something about a training establishment like this that reminds you that we passed."

"Yeah." Scottie looked around. "That 'I don't give a fuck whether you pass or fail' attitude from those old training teams still hangs around this dusty old place."

"I hope this kid can cope," Pat said.

"Well, if he can't, he will suffer quite badly before he gets binned," Scottie said almost mournfully. He looked at the knuckles of his right hand: he had scraped the skin.

"I'm getting weak, mate," he smiled. His hands were usually hardened by constant bag work.

"Let's hope our new student's skin is thicker," quipped Pat, "or we'll all be back in London next week."

There was a creak from the old doors at their backs and Danny Mac, flanked by Samantha and Taff, entered the barn.

"The old Ops Room is still locked," said a smiling Danny Mac.

"Need to check those keys Taff gave you guys," Samantha added. "One of them is for the Ops Room."

"All the keys look the same," Taff said.

"Never trust a dumb bootneck," Pat quipped.

"I resemble that remark," Taff retorted.

"Hey, guys, this place is as good as any for a brief." Danny pointed towards a couple of exercise benches and the slightly rusted remains of an old multigym. "I have another meeting with the client in London when I get back, and then I can let you know more, but at the moment it's a training task. Jimmy is sorting the comms out; I will brief him later."

"Sounds like a plan," said Scottie. The team tried to make themselves comfortable amongst the ingrained dust of the old training facility. They sat in a collective huddle, leaving the bench of the multigym to Danny. He wiped the dust with a handkerchief and faced the team.

"I was DS (directing staff) in this place nearly forty years ago," he said in an almost wistful way. "Repton turned out some good operators." He paused as if remembering. "This was the finishing school for the Research and Surveillance branches when the Corps (the Intelligence Corps) was based at Templer Barracks in

Ashford." He cupped his chin in thought and slightly tilted his head, as if summoning up some vintage Danny Mac wisdom.

"And that's what we need to do again." He paused and shifted his position slightly. "First of all, I'm going to introduce you to the single student we have arriving, and then I'll explain how we will attempt to equip him with the skills our client requires." Danny's voice was low, almost a whisper, as he looked around the team. "The young man's name is Richard Miller, and you collect him from Wandsworth Prison tomorrow."

The team exchanged glances.

"Well, *that's* different," said Scottie.

***

London, early morning

The streets of inner London were almost deserted as the dark blue van made its way towards the prison. The streetlights were still on as the first signs appeared of the urban dawning of a new day. The lights in the shops, too, were beginning to flash on as night alarms were disabled. Taff spotted a paper seller readying his pitch by a Tube station; inner-city London seemed to be stretching itself and preparing for work. He checked his watch; they were still on time.

"So, what do we know about this guy?" Taff shot Sam his 'questioning look' from the driver's side of the van.

"Only what we've read on his file." Samantha was scrolling through her iPhone trying to locate Lou's number.

"And that was pretty basic. We know that he was originally recruited under duress and that's usually not a good start, but in this case, I think it might be better not to know too much," she said, as she found the number.

"What do you mean, a sort of need-to-know thing?" Taff checked the rear-view mirror, spotting the distinctive headlights of the Jag behind. Scottie and Pat were providing the rear cover as the van's V8 engine purred through the early-morning streets. Jimmy was sitting on the bench seats in the darkness of the back of the vehicle.

"No, not really, but it's just a matter of taking one thing at a time. Our collective team job is to train him as best we can, in the time we have, and then make an assessment." Sam took a lipstick from her bag and applied it, looking into the same mirror that he had just used. Taff saw her check, almost subliminally, the traffic to the rear.

It's bizarre, thought Taff. His wife's anti-surveillance tradecraft was so deeply ingrained in her everyday behaviour that she sometimes did not even realise she was practising it. She replaced the lipstick, snapped the bag shut and carried on the conversation.

"He's a Joint Task Force asset, so his final destination and mission will in all probability have very little to do with us."

"Yeah, I get that, but if we don't know the task we are training him for, how can we assess him?"

"Same way they trained us, Nigel: for capability, reliability, motivation, resilience and mental attitude."

"Yeah, I get that, too," said Taff. "I'm just not sure whether we will have time to assess the most important of those, the reliability thing. Even from the sketchy pen picture in his file, we know that this lad has a criminal past and that he's just been sprung from inside a radical Islamist organisation. My risk-management spider sense is tingling, and I just don't like it."

Samantha looked towards him. "What's your main worry?"

"Well, picking up our man at a prison gate means that his vetting procedure might have been slightly lax," he smiled.

"Yes, I can appreciate your concerns, but try and not be too judgemental from the outset." Sam placed her hand on Taff's shoulder. "Remember that we are all products of our environments; maybe if you'd been born on a shit council estate in London, you might have turned out the same."

"I disagree," said Taff, as if Sam had touched a raw nerve. "All people want to do now is make excuses for themselves and others. I came from a South Wales pit village with no pit, where we could only have dreamed about the help that London's inner-city bad lads get. There's a whole industry of people trained at uni in half-arsed 'isms' and 'ologies' just making excuses for them. I look at it in a different way: there are just some bad bastards out there. Inner-city deprivation my arse. They should try living where I did."

Sam was surprised: her normally placid and supportive husband had another side to him. She decided to move on.

"OK, I understand it's all a bit quick and that we've been crashed into this task, but I'm going to trust his handler's judgement, and all I ask is that you give the guy a chance."

"Yeah, he's got it," Taff said, almost grudgingly.

Sam dialled the number as she checked the satnav. They had just turned onto Wandsworth Bridge Road as Lou answered the phone.

"Yeah."

"RV ten minutes," Sam replied.

"Roger that." Lou, Coco and three black-clad Tornado Team heavies were still waiting in the Hobbit Shop. Lou closed the phone.

"We move out in ten." He picked up his black ops bag. Coco moved to pick up his own possessions, gathered in a heavy black bin-liner with a large white sticky label saying, 'Miller R, 237755T', but the Tornado Team leader grabbed it from him.

"I'll look after that, son," he said as he opened the door. They walked quickly and soundlessly along the corridor towards the prison's family visiting area and the main gate beyond.

The Team leader spoke into his Motorola handheld: "In five." In five minutes, all the CCTV cameras on the outside wall of the prison would be stalled for ten minutes and then restarted.

Lou was within whispering distance of Coco as they moved towards the gate.

"You are going to meet the people that you'll have to impress if you want to work for us, kid. Do you understand?"

"Yeah, sort of," he replied, in a rather confused way.

"Be aware: they are much, much harder than anybody you have ever met in your gang days. These are all ex British Special Forces, and they have been that for the period of your whole life. Just try and listen and learn. The boss is a blonde girl, but don't let the looks fool you: she is the hardest person you'll ever meet. The bad guys called her the Angel of Death."

Coco was quiet for a minute.

"I only want a chance."

"You're getting it," said Lou, as the electric door clicked and they could see the inside of the main gates. Lou called Samantha's number four times and rang off.

Sam checked her phone.

"That's them to pick up," she said to Taff.

"That's a roger," he replied, as the main gates of the Hate Factory appeared just as the sun started to illuminate them. They were a forbidding sight, with the canopied double gates, nestled between mock-medieval twin towers, creating a portcullis effect. The prison was stone-built, stained with urban grime and grim.

"This place was built when prisons were supposed to scare you," Taff said, as he indicated right towards the gate.

"Yeah," Sam agreed. "Well, it definitely works for me."

The right-hand main door was just opening as the van pulled up, revealing four guys in black and their 'passenger' in a tight group.

Taff tapped the inside of the cab in the front and Jimmy opened the rear doors. Coco immediately clambered into the back, followed by the black-clad Lou. Coco's belongings were then passed into the van and the rear doors slammed shut.

"Good morning," Coco muttered to Jimmy, as he sat on the bench seat as if it were the most natural thing in the world.

"Good morning, bruv," said Jimmy with a big smile. "Hope you have a nice stay."

Chapter Thirteen

Repton Manor: The Six-Miler

He ducked his head; the sweat stung his eyes as he passed at a sprint under a low branch of an elder tree. He was on the early morning run through what the training team called The Warren, a heavily tracked and hilly piece of spindly wood two miles from the Manor. He snapped his head up, drew a gasping breath into his lungs and refocused on the task of catching the fleeting form of a man who he knew was at least twice his age. Big Taff seemed to lope along, with Coco's former handler Lou slightly behind, running fast but chatting like they had just started a stroll down to the pub.

"Ricky, KEEP UP!" the blonde girl shouted. She was the rear marker, and if he fell behind her on this physical fitness test it would be considered a failure.

He was no longer called Coco. Such a name didn't fit into the modern MI5 lexicon of Newspeak, so he had lost the nickname that he'd had since primary school. He was now just Ricky to the team. And Ricky Miller, the trainee agent handler and junior MI6 man, was tired, worn out in a way that he had never experienced before. It was a deep inner feeling of utter exhaustion that affected him mentally and physically, but It was also brought with it a strange type of elation.

Repton had managed to both stretch him and excite him simultaneously. He couldn't believe that he had only arrived a week before; the pace of training had been relentless. He had been taught by everybody on the team at various times, with no discernible breaks in a constant pattern of instruction.

That week had been a blur, with the trainers rotating constantly, a never-ending series of subjects, each carefully taught by a person specialising in that particular skill. The day started at zero six hundred with a physical training circuit, usually a run or GLF session, and finished in abject weariness with the last lesson in the evening. There was no declared training programme for him to follow, so the next lesson was always a surprise. He ate when he could, with snatched breakfasts and packed lunches. He had an hour off at midday that he used for revising some vital piece of information or lying on his bed preparing for the next taxing download. His evening meal was chosen from a standard fast-food menu and always eaten, hurriedly and alone, before bed. Time had vanished in a haze, a constant mayhem of activity that was both exhausting and strangely satisfying. Although he always felt tired, he also knew that he was getting stronger and not weaker.

The ground rules of the Manor were simple. There was quiet encouragement to make the grade, but nothing that was excessively verbal and with none of the shouting or screaming that civilians associate with the military. The only discipline was self-discipline, and he had to drive himself. He was told before he started, and while he was actually signing the Official Secrets Act, that although everything on the course was classified Secret and therefore subject to the full strictures of the law, it was also an entirely voluntary course. That meant that failure brought no group shame, no animosity, no ringing of bells or stepping across a line in the sand. If ever he wanted to quit, he only needed a quick whisper to whoever was training him at the time, and a simple. "I've had enough" would suffice, with the option of a generous resettlement package for his work so far.

But he had put failure out of his mind, and the idea of being a volunteer fuelled his determination to succeed. He thought he had fitted in well. It had taken a while to sort out the dynamics within the team that were training him. They were obviously very close, with that innate brotherhood that automatically excluded interlopers. He was, after all, in their manor, both figuratively and literally. The blonde girl was the boss – and stunning. He had to try and not really focus on her too much during the phys sessions. She was married to Taff, and he thought that maybe, just once, Taff had caught him looking at her a bit too closely. There had been nothing too much, just a quick steely glance that seemed like a warning. Very little worried him, but he had to admit that the big Welsh ex-Marine did.

Apart from that, he was enjoying the challenge. During his entire life, a succession of teachers and social workers had told him how society had failed him, and how his failures and lifestyle had been forced on him. He realised that the training at Repton Manor was the first thing that he had tried that was actually 'pass or fail'. It was liberating; he could finally chart his own course. He thought about it: *I've spent my entire life force-fed by failure.*

He soaked up the knowledge and was learning all the time. The trainers were good at what they did, and the simple system of instruction was explained to him by Taff. "We simply call it EDI, which is really how all military and intelligence skills are imparted, just a basic format for learning: Explanation, Demonstration and Imitation. First, I'm going to explain it. Then you'll see it happen, with me doing it, and then you'll have a go. And then, after you've done it correctly, we practise it until it's almost second nature to you."

Ricky knew it was an effective training method. Taff had taught him to handle a pistol using it, and he remembered his first day on the 25-metre range. There were just three full-size enemy targets, what the team called Figure Elevens. They still looked alarmingly like German stormtroopers nearly eighty years after World War Two, but there they were, the same eternal bad guys, propped sternly upright in their frames against a sandbagged backdrop, in German-style coal scuttle helmets, with their faces transfixed in the permanent scowl of an ancient war cry. Taff was about ten metres away from the targets and was casually chatting when he said, "OK, Ricky, Amplivox (ear defenders) on." Taff waited as he secured his own set and checked that his student was properly protected. "I'm going to show you how effective this deadly piece of Tupperware and steel is. It can always fuck up a bad guy's day, and it's an agent's best friend."

As soon as he finished the last word Taff drew his Glock 19 pistol from a hidden covert spring holster on his right hip. His blindingly quick hands morphed seamlessly into a firing grip as he engaged the three targets from left to right in a blur of movement. He had placed two closely grouped 9mm rounds into the head of each target within what seemed like a millisecond. Ricky was spellbound. "You ever done that for real, bruv?" were the first words that left his lips. Taff had just looked at him slightly askance; Ricky immediately realised that the comment made him seem immature, and had been one of those 'I wish I hadn't said that' moments. The big Welshman just moved on.

"Have a close look at the targets." Ricky moved slightly forward. At first, it looked like there was just a single hole in the centre of the head of each target, located with uncanny precision right between the eyes. On closer inspection, though, the trainee agent realised that each 'single' hole was in fact two, almost intersecting.

"It's called a double tap," Taff said. He had already slid the weapon back into its holster as he pointed his index finger towards one of the targets.

"The idea is simple. One is good, two is better. The head is always the preferred target for two reasons. First, the bad guys generally wear body armour and, second, because the brain controls the body." He looked towards his student and sensed his doubt.

"It's a hard concept, I know." Taff paused. "Human life is precious to us all, but sometimes you have to take it to protect your own and the lives of others." He held his student's gaze. "And remember, it isn't gangland any more. When you are working for the government it's not the pictures, you don't have a licence to kill. You are always held accountable and you will always have to justify your actions." With that statement the big ex-Marine had answered his student's earlier question.

"The first thing I'm going to do is teach you how to hold the weapon properly. Just clear your mind of all that Hollywood movie bollocks and the numerous video games that you've played, and we'll start with the basics."

All the instruction was imparted in the same methodical manner. The quiet-speaking Scot and Pat, the hard-looking older guy from Yorkshire, taught him all the tradecraft, and the blonde girl supervised everything. The cockney guy taught him all the technical computer and phone stuff.

All the training was delivered with quiet good humour. Nobody shouted when he got things wrong, they just told him where the fault lay and moved on. The memory tests were a constant feature of the start and finish of every lesson at the Manor. There was always the same light canvas camouflage cover laid on the ground as he met the next instructor. The cover concealed a number of varied objects. The instructors all called it Kim's Game, after a character in a Rudyard Kipling story.

"OK, Ricky, you have one minute to look at these twelve different objects," and then the canvas cover was pulled back for those sixty seconds before being replaced. At first it was acceptable to only list what lay under the cover, but that skill of basic memory was quickly developed into describing each object in fine detail. In the first lesson, a notebook could be described simply as 'a notebook', but after a week it was as 'a small red notebook, held closed with a dark blue elastic band and with a torn upper right corner'.

He was taught very simple ways to memorise letters and numbers, cars and faces. They also demonstrated various types of foreign weapons, and he got to actually try some of them on the Repton Manor range.

He had learned a lot. But not all of it from Repton.

The training team noticed that he seemed to know his way around the Czech vz.61 Skorpion machine pistol particularly well, and he found the tradecraft especially interesting.

"Today, we are going to look at using a dead letter box," or "Watch the demonstration, Ricky, this is what we call a brush contact." Some of the tradecraft was very familiar to the former London gangster. The brush contact was a carbon copy of what he had constantly seen around Frobisher Heights: it ensured that a dealer could always place a new wrap of crack cocaine into a punter's hand with seamless ease.

He began to realise that his previous profession had probably already given him some of the necessary skills he needed in this new venture. He had made his first brush contact when he was about ten, and he'd used dead letter boxes for drugs, weapons and money all around his postcode. As far as he was concerned, the skills he was acquiring at Repton were not that dissimilar to those he had needed in his drug-gang days. He was beginning to realise that the same pressures would also be there. The constant fear of compromise or betrayal, the need to be constantly planning to keep one step ahead. A poor piece of tradecraft or a lack of concentration could get you killed, and he knew that he was involved in a very risky game; for him, Ricky Miller, alias Coco, it was a more dangerous game than even the training team realised. He was a different person now that he was finally out of prison, and he had totally different loyalties. He also knew that he would eventually have to ply his new trade in exactly the same places he had worked in before he got banged up. If he passed this course he would still be operating in the shadows, in London's darker places like his own estate, or maybe even his ex-abode, Her Majesty's Prison Wandsworth.

He wondered who was truly in charge of his destiny. If he passed the course, what would the mission be? And would the mission meet his higher ambitions? The trouble with an organisation wedded to the principle of 'Need to Know 'and obsessed with the so-called 'Circle of Knowledge', was that he wasn't in the circle and, at this stage, they obviously thought he didn't need to know.

Room 11, Repton Manor

Samantha and Taff lay together on the small sofa in room 11. It was typical Ministry of Defence accommodation with bright magnolia walls and cheap carpets, furnished with the throw-outs from old British Army married quarters. There were the same high-backed floral design chairs from the 1980s and the same type of whitewood coffee table, with matching lamp, that you would have seen in every married soldier's house in the 1990s. It could have been any one of the rooms in the house, as they were all decorated in the same way, supplied by the same MoD warehouse. The light was beginning to fade after a long day. They had just eaten: a frozen pizza and microwaved chips. Taff stretched and yawned.

"I'd forgotten how tiring a twelve-hours training day is," he said.

"Yeah, and that's when you're the DS. Maybe our guest is a wee bit more so."

Samantha moved in closer towards her husband. Taff's big arm was wrapped around her and the combination of both the warmth and the slight tang of gun smoke that clung to his clothes lit up her lower insides.

She tried to put the thought to the back of her mind.

"How did he do today?" she asked.

"Good, but a bit too good."

"What do you mean?"

"I can't put my finger on it, just a sort of feeling."

"What did you cover?"

"Some fairly advanced stuff: covert carriage, engaging from the turn. Got through two thousand Luger 9 mill."

"Any problems?"

"No, he's a quick learner. But there is something bothering me about the kid."

"Explain?"

"He just seems a little bit too good. I mean, I think he's had training before."

"Maybe it's just his previous lifestyle."

"No, it's more than that." Taff picked up the remote control on the small table and the TV flashed into life.

"There's something not right," he said, as he surfed through the channels. "He's either a real natural for anything or…"

"What?"

"Or he has his own agenda." Taff increased the volume.

"Do you really want to watch the telly?" said Sam, in her best sexy voice.

"No, I just want to drown out the noise." Taff turned and kissed her.

"So, you have your own agenda as well?"

"Get your clothes off."

"I thought you'd never ask," Sam said with a smile, as she started to undress.

Room 8

"For fuck's sake," said Scottie. "Taff and his TV, here we go again."

He was sharing a can of beer with Pat and Jimmy.

"I'm sure the fucker's deaf." Pat took another sip.

"Maybe he has ulterior motives," Jimmy smiled. "I'm sure if I was with my Mrs, my TV might be cranked up a bit as well."

"Never thought of that; fair one, it's a possibility." Scottie smiled.

The guys always got together in the evenings just to do what they called 'shoot the shit'. The saying was a shameless Americanism for their own unofficial debrief on the day, mixed in with the odd joke and war story.

"What do you think about our lad?" Pat said.

"Don't know yet." Jimmy's brow was creased in his thinking mode. "He isn't getting particularly stretched by anything we've chucked at him so far."

"Yeah, he's nailing some stuff really quickly, and he's got an almost photographic memory."

"Yep," Scottie agreed. He was charged with teaching foot and mobile surveillance techniques. "We were in the cars yesterday, trying to get in front of the target. He was well on form, like a veteran Det guy. He was in the zone, map-reading upside down from a map book, driving fast and working out a route while shouting out the spots for the radio." Scottie moved a big hand and stroked his chin in thought.

"And when I asked him who we had passed at the garage, he described two guys and even had the first three of the number plate."

"That's good," said Pat.

"Yeah, a bit too good," Jimmy said.

"Hey, let's give the kid a chance," said Pat. "We all know what it's like to learn on the job. The lad's come out of a rough part of the Smoke and might have needed to develop some of this same stuff to survive. We've all read his file: gangs, robbery and guns. And a spell in Wandsworth will always tend to increase your learning curve."

"Yeah, point taken," said Jimmy, still looking thoughtful.

CHAPTER FOURTEEN

London, Park Lane. Same time

As the three operators continued to discuss their day, a senior civil servant was walking along a prestigious London street to meet his source. Park Lane was about as far as you could get from Ricky's area of London on a cultural scale, but that was where on a late summer's evening the MI6 officer who spun all the plates at the Middle East desk was going. Not all intelligence operations are conducted in the shadows, and as you move up the ladder of Britain's security services the locations upgrade accordingly. Human Intelligence operations are sometimes conducted in plain sight, at a place that reflects the natural pattern of life of both the agent and his handler.

A meeting could still be covert and almost unseen amongst normal human interaction. The contact could still be met, debriefed and paid without compromise if you chose the right place, and that's where he was now heading. Nobu, an upmarket restaurant overlooking Hyde Park, would serve his purposes very well. The SIS man knew, though, that money wouldn't interest the person he was meeting and even if it did, he could never get the bean-counters at VX to provide enough to even faintly interest his Arab contact.

Sheikh Mohammad bin Jabber was immensely rich and was therefore dressed in the finest that London's Savile Row could offer, wearing a dark grey suit with a tastefully patterned handmade silk tie. He loved London, and he especially liked the large chunks of it that he and his family owned. He was, unlike many rich Arabs that sheltered in the city, a true Anglophile at heart. The five years that he had spent at Oxford, followed by the British Army's military academy at Sandhurst, had given him both a cut-glass English accent and an admiration for most things British. He was deep in thought as he observed a darkening Hyde Park from his special table by the restaurant's window. He tapped his hand nervously on the table as he considered the problem he needed to discuss. It took his mind to a dustier, dirtier and far more dangerous time, in a place that the Tajiks of Afghanistan call the 'Valley of the Five Lions'. It was there that he had first met the MI6 man he was going to have supper with, the man that had quite literally saved his life. They had worked together during the glory days of his first assignment, in the Soviet-Afghan War.

The so-called godless Russians were Allah's gift to all.

Qatar's immense oil and gas reserves had allowed it to use its largesse to make life uncomfortable for the Soviet occupiers of Afghanistan. Qatar at all times fully subscribed to the Arab maxim that *'the enemy of my enemy is my friend'*, although, he thought, from a personal perspective his country's policy stretched the credulity of even the most partisan observer at times.

He was a member of the governing elite of the little state. He also secretly thought that he was more part of its historical past rather than its very uncertain future. Oil-rich, good-time Arabs like himself had been doing very well until some over-enthusiastic Saudis from the younger generation truly upset the apple cart on 9/11. This one savage act had immediately undermined the easy relationship Qatar had developed with the USA and the Western world. He thought of the myriad problems in the Middle East as one giant Russian babushka doll. Each problem was wrapped sequentially and snapped inside the next until they made up the whole of the disastrous mess, and it was this toxic blend of religion, history, ideology and the abuse of power that was finally about to implode.

The outer shell was the most obvious. The failed Bush/Blair policy of somehow trying to impose a liberal democratic order by military force had produced the opposite and inverse effect. It had destabilised both Iraq and Syria, which, despite being run by tyrannical dictators, had been largely secular countries before the West's attempts at regime change. Most modern historians agreed that this had led directly to the formation of ISIS, although Qatar had also played a very strong card here.

But not the right one, he thought. *It had played both sides against the middle, by financing not only the FSA (Free Syrian Army) but also ISIS and the equally radical Al Nusra Front.*

The Sheikh thought that the Qatari and Saudi Arabian policies were almost sure to backfire.

Surely, if you use your money to destabilise some countries, you encourage others to destabilise yours.

The next level of complexity was the complicated political posturing between Russia, NATO and the USA: just a revamp of the old Cold War. The two leading contenders in the ring were a resurgent Russia under Vladimir Putin and, in the opposite corner, the United States under its untried President Biden. Qatar had always looked to the USA for its military support; the largest US base in the Middle East was situated in its desert wastes. This was because the recent history of the Middle East had taught the Qataris that money alone couldn't magic up an efficient military machine. Arab armies had spent billions on hardware and training but still struggled with the basics. Mohammad smiled wryly as he remembered the saying his Colour Sergeant instructor had used at Sandhurst: Arab armies, as far as he was concerned, always had *"all the gear, but no idea"*.

Once that level was peeled away, the next smaller but more dangerous doll popped out, and it was the underlying cause of most of the political struggle in the Middle East. Israel, like a champion but very battered boxer, was in its corner of the ring, but in the other was the ancient schism between the two main branches of Islam, Sunni and Shi'a, and they were battering each other to the death in the opposite corner. The one thing they could agree on was their joint hatred of the Jews, but they hated each other much more! The two traditions of Islam grated together like seismic plates in an earthquake zone and were engaged in proxy wars all over the Islamic world, from Baghdad to Birmingham.

Inside that struggle was the third doll – the even more dangerous situation that had led to his meeting with MI6: the battle taking place between the old guard and the new, angry opposition in Saudi Arabia itself. Between the pro-Western political pragmatists, that he and his type of Arab represented, and the new breed of Saudi religious fanatics now gaining a foothold in the Kingdom. This is why he had to ask MI6 for help; the genie was well and truly out of the bottle and the time for petty squabbles between intelligence agencies was over. How would he let the British know about this latest threat to the West? His friend from his Afghan days, known as 'Mac', was now a senior MI6 man.

They had initially met at the operational level, but now they were both London-based senior diplomats. He knew Mac was someone that he could trust with the source of his information. As he gazed over the London he had grown to love, he thought back to that hard and brutal afternoon in Afghanistan's Panjshir Valley, when Mac had saved his life.

Repton Manor, same evening

On the final day of the first week, Ricky had a scheduled meeting with his former MI5 handler, Lou. There were only the two of them in Repton Manor's old 'Operations Room'. The place looked like it had been mothballed in the 1990s, as indeed it had. The cursory clean-up hadn't quite removed ten years' worth of glistening spiders' webs that interlocked in the corners of the room. A weak light strained through the bird shit on the glass of the only window.

"So, how do you think you are doing, Ricky?" Lou asked in a friendly manner. Pointing to a white plastic chair, he said "Sit down, bruv," as he took a seat himself in front of a single whiteboard.

"OK, I think?"

"Yeah, you're doing OK. You seem to be quite quick at picking things up, which is a huge advantage in this business. But you will need to stay on your game, mate." He stood up. "Because things start to get a bit more demanding next week, with some of the exercises outside." Lou picked up a marker pen from the board.

"Let me explain where you are and where you need to be." He pointed towards the whiteboard where, in bold writing, was the heading, "The Intelligence Cycle" over a circular diagram. Each word had an arrow which directed it to another word, and Ricky immediately understood the concept. The first word said, "Direction".

"OK, buddy, the direction bit is our bosses asking us to collect certain information that they call 'intelligence requirements', and that's how we first met, if you remember." Lou shifted uneasily on his feet, as if slightly embarrassed. "It was my job to identify you as what we call a POI, or a person of interest, and recruit you for our organisation."

"Why me?" Ricky asked, although he knew the answer already. His life of crime had hardened him to some of the negative aspects of human nature, and it was a question generated by genuine interest rather than any sense of victimhood. What had happened to him mirrored the world that he was part of: winners and losers, the predator and the prey. He had recruited lots of kids, especially young ones, to work for him running drugs outside London to smaller towns in what the police called 'county lines' drug links, so he supposed that this had given him experience for his new job (*and maybe my own recruitment has been a little bit of payback for that*).

"There are several reasons, Ricky. First of all, you were in the right age group and living where half the ISIS suspects in South London also live. You were also a known gangster; that meant that you would always end up in the shit with the feds, and that would give us an opportunity to help you. So, in short, mate, you had what we call ACM and that stands for access, capability and motivation, and they are the three things that you will start to look for in a potential source when you are doing my job."

It was Lou's intention to be truthful. If you wanted to develop an 'eyes and ears' agent into a real intelligence operator then he needed to know that, in the end, everybody eventually gets used. The Intelligence Cycle spiralled around and built up speed as more and more information arrived, and sometimes ordinary people just got sucked into its vortex and were smashed around in it.

Lou pointed again towards "Direction", and then to the scrawled arrow that led towards the next word: "Collection".

"This is where we were." Lou pointed a brawny index finger to "Collection" and flashed a smile.

"This is where we both worked, the sweet spot between Direction and Collection. My bosses direct me and both of us work together in that phase. You collected the raw information and I debriefed you and tapped out the reports that are directly fed into this next part of the chain, here.

"In 'Analysis', all those items of information are collated: in other words, compared and contrasted with each other, and with that which has gone before in the same field of requirement. The degree of proven reliability (or otherwise) of each source of information is also factored in. The carefully assessed result of all this is then computerised and cross-checked for anomalies, or other apparent faults. When all this has been done, you have Intelligence. The refined product then goes to the end user and that's called" – a big finger pointed to the next word – "'Dissemination'. Once it ends up with the end user, they look to see what's missing, or what else they now need to know as a result of what you've just given them and raise another IR (Information Requirement) and feed it back into the circle." Lou smiled. "Any questions?"

"No, seems logical," Ricky said, his eyes moving over the cyclical diagram and nodding slowly.

"Yeah," Lou looked directly at his former agent, "but this wheel never stops spinning, and it always needs feeding, but it isn't the machine of the James Bond shite you see at the movies. It's always dangerous but never very glamorous. The primary job as a source handler is to find out what the bad guys are up to and report it. A good handler focuses on saving innocent life, and he must consider that at all times."

"Does that mean I've passed the course?" It was Ricky's turn to smile.

"No idea." Lou sounded sincere. "I don't even know how long the course is; it all depends on the final deployment. I will probably know when you do." Lou moved from in front of the board and sat directly opposite his agent, whose eyes reflected his worry.

"That's the other thing to get used to in our world. You don't control the Intelligence Cycle – it controls you. Somewhere, someone is gathering information that will decide where and when we deploy and what we do. Always remember that what some people call the Great Game isn't a game at all, it's life or death, and you can never just cheer from the sidelines. We are all just small cogs in the ever-spinning machine called the security services, and like all small cogs we just have to wait to get direction from a bigger one." He pointed back to the board.

"Remember the first part of the cycle: *Direction*. We'll soon know, Ricky. Once we have the Direction, we'll know!"

Chapter Fifteen

Nobu

The source liked to eat at Nobu, and he had missed his weekly visits during last year's lockdown. He was now seated at his favourite table in the London restaurant, and the table was set for two. The venue had many advantages. It served great food at prices set at a level that meant that poor people of any kind wouldn't disturb him. It was also a place that blended with both men's pattern of life. The restaurant's central theme was subtle minimalism, with lots of white and light-coloured woods and natural stone. It also reeked of wealth. The subtle perfume from expensively dressed women mixed delicately with the bouquet of the finest seafood available in London. The place altogether smelled of money, and he felt at home.

Mac, and what had happened in the Valley of the Five Lions, was the key to it all.

He had met Christian McCann at the height of the Soviet-Afghan war, when they were both field operatives in their respective intelligence agencies. It had been a period of unwavering British and US support for the Afghan Mujahadeen; it seemed a long time ago now. Mac's first name, Christian, and his Para and SAS nickname, Genghis, were equally guaranteed to risk causing offence while supporting an Islamic insurgency, so they had simply called him Mac. He was then one of the MI6-supplied military advisors to Ahmad Shah Massoud, known throughout Afghanistan as the Lion of Panjshir.

The Sheikh remembered the Valley of the Five Lions for many reasons. There was a particular wild savagery about it that he could never forget; the Panjshir River had carved the valley from the rock of the Hindu Kush. It was a beautiful but unforgiving place, and in the mid-eighties it had been the centre of an armed insurgency against the Red Army. It was there, on a hot, cinder-dry afternoon, that Mac had saved his life, and his thoughts drifted to that rough day on the mountain.

He had clambered ever upward, the stored heat radiating from the rocks onto his sunburned face. He remembered the dry smell of dust, and the eerily ominous silence that had enveloped them, just before they heard the alarm bell from the valley below. The Soviets had arrived! He had his AK-47 inverted, Mujahadeen-style, and hung from a sling in the middle of his back. The banana-shaped magazine had chafed his skin; it hurt, and he was tired. He was scrambling up the small smooth rocks of one of the many scree runs that were a feature of the mountainside. Mac was in front of him, upright and almost loping along, holding his British Lee Enfield rifle, with its telescopic scope, cradled in the crook of his left arm. Sheikh Mohammad remembered looking down and admiring the beauty of the bluish-green ribbon of the Panjshir River shimmering in the sun. That was when they had first heard the distant drone of a Russian helicopter.

Mac had been the first to identify it. "Shaitan-Arba" (The Devil's Chariot), he had shouted over his shoulder, with a worried look. It was the Afghan name for the Soviet Army's latest helicopter gunship. They frantically managed to half-scramble and half-fall down the scree run, dislodging boulders in a mini-avalanche in their haste to take cover. They crawled, just in time, into one of the small storage caves overlooking the village. The hovering Soviet war machine was hunting them.

He remembered his fear as the giant shadow of the craft moved over the entrance, blocking the sun. He felt again the violent downdraught of the rotor blades and smelt the pungent tang of used aviation fuel as the demonic-looking machine hung over him. The Mil MI-27 armoured helicopter hovered, slowly turning on its axis as if to get its bearings. In that brief glimpse of the Russian killing machine, Mac had understood the nature of the threat. He had seen by the unit markings that this helicopter was a Soviet Special Forces one, and he was aware that they did things differently.

For a young Arab straight off the plane from Doha, the camouflaged flying monster was a terrifying sight. Its front consisted of a double glass bubble that housed the pilot and the front gunner and resembled a shimmering giant bug-eye that seemed to be searching for them. He could clearly see the pink face of the young gunner as he peered into the cave. The large craft then rose and turned almost lethargically as the giant rotors strained and screamed in the thin mountain air. The nose dropped, the rotors accelerated and then it disappeared over a rise in the ground about a kilometre from the cave.

"Let's move," Mohammad had suggested. There was the slightest hint of fear in his voice. "We need to get back to the village."

"No, not yet Mo." Mac gripped his arm and switched to English, using his nickname for the young Arab in a broad Newcastle accent. "I think that's where they're going." Mac quickly checked his rifle, worked the bolt and put a round into its chamber. "They're dropping off troops, and the crocodile will stay airborne to support them." Mac used the Soviet Army term for the machine. "They probably know there are Arabs in the village," he added. "Someone's talked."

He pointed up towards the group of little buildings and mud huts that was Khanez village. They could clearly see the occupants, mainly women and children, scurrying around and streaming towards the shelter of the mosque. Most of the men were in the mountains with Massoud. Mac was looking through his British Army issue binoculars. They were wrapped in an old dark green 'cam' scarf to shield the lenses from the sun – a tell-tale glint of light from inside the cold darkness of the cave could have had dire consequences. He turned the glasses from the village, scanned the next rise of the hill and immediately located them. They looked initially like eight little black ants on the skyline, then gradually morphed into human shape as they got closer. They were moving quickly – far too quickly for regular troops.

As they got nearer, the details became clearer. They were all dressed in their light brown 'Afghanzy' summer uniform, with the dark outline of chest webbing strung across their torsos. With their AK 74s, the newest Soviet assault rifle, in their shoulders they were using what soldiers call 'Fire and Movement', moving in tandem, with one guy covering the other in short rushes, using the rocks as cover. As an ex- paratrooper, Mac knew how well-trained soldiers covered ground. These men were good.

He continued to track their progress with the binoculars. The AK 74s all had 60-millimetre grenade launchers protruding ominously beneath the barrels. This was the latest variant, issued only to Soviet Airborne and Special Forces. The underslung launcher could fire a grenade accurately over three hundred metres.

"What's happening? Let's go to the village now." Mohammad was scared. He was being hunted for the first time.

"Not a fucking good idea, old mate; that's where they're going," said Mac. "They're looking for something, and I think it might be us. We stay here," he whispered into Mo's ear. And then:

BOOM!

The loudest noise he had ever heard reverberated around the confines of their refuge. A grenade fired by the approaching Russian Special Forces team exploded within twenty feet of the cave. It was briefly followed by total silence and then, only when the ear-ringing blast had subsided, a Newcastle accent.

"Fuck that!" The grenade had been launched over the full extent of its three-hundred-metre range. "They've got the range straight away; they're good."

Mac half shouted the compliment as he gripped Mo's arm and pulled him deeper into the cave. Then followed the multiple cracks and thumps and angry buzz of 'incoming', as the Spetsnaz team opened up. Short, concise, three-round bursts of high velocity bullets rattled into their refuge, spattering them in shards of rock.

BOOM!

Another 60-mill grenade landed with the same unnerving accuracy, and Mohammad felt the overpressure of the explosion. *I'm going to die.*

He then heard Mac's clear voice over the noise of incoming rounds.

"They know we're here; we've got to move."

The younger man was unable to focus, his ears still ringing from the blast. He wiped the fine dust of the explosion from his eyes and looked towards Mac but saw only a blurred outline. He tried to move, felt pain, and collapsed as the hard floor of the cave rushed up to meet him.

"You're going to be OK, buddy," he remembered Mac saying.

It was almost as if he were suspended above himself, seemingly detached from his own body, and looking down at the bright red stream of blood spurting from his thigh. A thin, laser-like pencil of Afghan sun pierced the darkness of the cave and intersected with it; it made the blood shine and glitter.

It was almost a beautiful thing, nearly as bright as the Panjshir River below.

He looked down at Mac, who was working feverishly to save him. He had twisted his shemagh (scarf) into a tourniquet and wrapped it around Mo's upper leg. He took the cleaning rod from the butt of Mo's AK-47 and twisted it into the scarf to increase the leverage. As Mac turned the tourniquet in a deliberate, slow, clockwise manner, the glittering blood stopped, and that was the last thing he could remember. He woke up in the village mosque later, being attended to by a French doctor. Later still, he learned that they had evaded the Russians by Mac's dragging him deeper into the cave system. He had then physically carried him over his shoulder to the village, after the raid.

The Sheikh's thoughts were abruptly dragged back into the present by one of his bodyguards.

"Your guest has arrived, sir."

He looked across to the entrance of the restaurant and instantly recognised him. Mac looked the same, a lean, hard-looking man, late-fifties, middle height, with the build of a mountain climber. He maybe seemed a little older, but not by much. He wore a smart business suit with a Parachute Regiment tie. Mac raised his hand in recognition and smiled. As the Sheikh stood, his two British bodyguards also rose to their feet. He gestured for them to stay seated and beckoned Mac over.

Mac looked around the restaurant, making a quick mental note of who was where. It was the usual mix of the wealthy: such A-list places were normally ideal for quiet diplomatic meetings. Rich people are never too inquisitive, just in case others notice with whom they are sitting. London's elite might eat at Nobu, but not necessarily with their current spouses or partners. He walked across at his usual confident loping pace and joined the table. They exchanged a warm handshake. Before sitting down, Mac took a large silver coin from his pocket and flicked it expertly with his thumb. The coin tumbled upward, glittered briefly in the candlelight and was caught with precision in the palm of his right hand. He then slapped it onto the sparkling white tablecloth. He laughed. "You still got your coin, Mo?"

The Sheikh reached into the right ticket pocket of his immaculately cut jacket and removed an identical coin, flicked it in the same manner and slapped it down next to the one Mac had produced. "Yes, Mac. Is yours genuine?" He smiled.

"Yeah, look at the date – it says 1780." Mac pointed to his coin and both men laughed. It was their private joke.

Both coins were Maria Theresa thaler silver crowns that Shah Ahmad Massoud had given them on the same day. This silver coin has been used throughout the Arab world as a universal currency for over two centuries. Those on the table were beautiful coins but far from unique; over 800 million had been minted from 1780 to the year 2000, but, bizarrely, were always dated 1780. The Sheikh gestured at the seat opposite, removed the crisp white napkin from its ring and placed it deftly on his lap with a flourish.

"Let us talk while we eat, my old friend."

"Yeah, it's always good to reinforce a cover story," Mac said, pulling out his chair. "Especially when your firm is paying the bill."

The Sheikh smiled, picked up the menu, scanned it and selected his favourite offering.

"May I recommend the shrimp and lobster with spicy lemon dressing, accompanied by the 2009 Pavillon Blanc? It's a great combination."

"Yeah, sounds good; I always go with local knowledge, old mate." Mac glanced up and made direct eye contact with his old friend from the mountains. He sensed Mohammad was searching for the right words. Mac quickly glanced at his watch.

"Just in case we run out of time with the small talk, what have you got for me, Mo?" The Arab diplomat met his gaze; the MI6 man thought he detected concern in his face. "I have a present from the Qatar Security Service in the normal place," he said quietly. Mac searched the underside of the table with the fingers of his right hand, directly under where his still empty wine glass glistened. It was there: a small USB computer stick pressed into place with a piece of Blu Tack.

The old methods are sometimes the best. He placed the thumb drive into his right trouser pocket.

"What's the urgency of this?"

"It's frightfully urgent." The Arab intelligence officer spoke slowly and very quietly, with an added nervous tremor.

"Mac, what do you know about why the date of the eleventh of September was chosen for the Twin Towers attack in New York?" he suddenly asked.

Mac's eyebrows rose. "What a strange and worrying question, old mate. I hope this is not the Afghan reunion Quiz Night?"

The Sheikh laughed. *Typical Geordie Mac, he was very undiplomatic at times and brooked no small talk.* "There are a couple of theories, my old battle buddy." Mac picked up his silver coin, again flipped it, palmed it and made it disappear. It was an old magic trick that had always amused the Afghans.

"The first one is the one most commonly believed." He now looked more serious. "Although I think that crediting Al Qaeda with any thoughts apart from murderous ones is over-valuing their humanity. The most commonly held version is that this date was chosen as the anniversary of September the eleventh, 1683, when the knights of the Polish King Jan Sobieski arrived at the gates of Vienna, looking to give the invading armies of the Ottoman Empire a good kicking. Some academics actually think that this was the pivotal moment when the momentum of history changed in favour of the West. Other people say that choosing the date was just a cruel joke by Osama, 911 being the USA's emergency telephone number."

Sheikh Mohammad looked mournful. "It's irrelevant; it doesn't really matter why the date was chosen, or even whether it was intended or entirely fortuitous. What does matter is ..." he paused to add emphasis, "that it's now a very important date in the ISIS calendar, and we are picking up reports that they intend to use this same date for the mother of all attacks. And it's about to start. Your organisation and the Americans are the only people that can stop this now."

"OK, I get the date, just tell me what else you know," said Mac.

The Sheikh paused, as if nervous about what the reaction would be, and then rapidly blurted it out.

"There is a portable atomic device missing from the Pakistani Army." There was silence from Mac as he processed this information.

"We were tracking it, but we've lost control, and it's now with an anti-government faction in Saudi Arabia." He added a rugby analogy. "The ball is loose in the scrum, my old friend, and it needs to be controlled."

The MI6 man flashed him a look, not really believing that the normally cool diplomat could be so upfront. "And what does Qatar Security hope my organisation can do about it now?" he said. "You should have let us know sooner; you guys have fucked up."

"Yes, I'm totally aware of that, Mac, this has blindsided us. Just try to control this nightmare, my friend; we've tried, and failed. We don't have the right people, the equipment or the global reach." Mac knew Mohammad and knew that he never exaggerated. He was genuinely worried, or even scared.

"We are meeting a source from the Saudi GID (the General Intelligence Directorate of Saudi Intelligence)." The whisper grew quieter. "We are agreeing a price for the information, and as soon as we have the name of who stole the warhead, I will pass it on. When you get it, you must promise me that this stays only between the two of us. It's a very finite circle of knowledge and my life and the lives of my family are at stake."

"You have my assurance," Mac said. He caught the Sheikh's gaze, remembered the moments of extreme danger they had endured together and said, "Just trust me and tell me everything you know." He settled down to listen to the story in the time-honoured way agent handlers always do. His former comrade from the Soviet-Afghan war would tell him the whole thing, then Mac would recap the main points and ask his own questions. At the end of the meeting Mac would know everything that there was to know, apart from the name of the man who had stolen the nuclear device.

CHAPTER SIXTEEN

The Black Site in Eastern Europe.

The doctor looked into the cell. The man was still suspended, still cold, and still lost. He could almost feel the despair permeate through the toughened glass that doubled up as a one-way mirror. *It's nearly time!* he thought, as he looked at his watch. The doctor was unemotional and dispassionate; he didn't hate the terrorist that had planned to kill his countrymen, as he had long ago learned that negative emotions disturbed the rhythm of his work. He looked through the glass much as a diligent cook would observe a roasting chicken. He had had to wait until the time was right, and that time was now. He watched as the door to the darkened cell opened and the prison orderly with the syringe entered. The hooded figure stayed slumped as the injection was efficiently administered. The doctor looked on as the orderly walked out and passed the two other guards with the army-style stretcher. They unclipped Cyclone and carefully, almost tenderly, placed him on the green canvas and carried him out. Doctor Jacob returned to his desk and jotted down some notes. He checked them and looked at his watch.

"Two hundred milligrams of Scopolamine at zero five thirty," he said aloud, so his colleagues could hear in the main office. The injection wouldn't be just Scopolamine, the infamous truth drug and the basic herbal extract of the henbane family. The doctor always experimented with newer compounds and always put his own spin on it.

"The patient will be ready to talk in two hours. Please get the room ready."

"OK, doctor," a disembodied anonymous female voice said from the wall.

He gathered his notes, shuffled them into an acceptable pile and moved towards the office shredder. He was smiling. Interrogation was like a very entertaining game of chess: you had to out-think your opponent at every step and always know where you thought he would move next. Doctor J knew that his subject was broken, disconnected, and beyond hope. Now was the time to question him, but he would take a nap first. *At zero seven thirty he would start to talk to him and at zero seven thirty-five he would learn all his secrets.*

0730

Cyclone was awake. He was dressed in the same clothes that he had worn back in the safe house in Scotland. The surroundings were familiar. There was the dark teak desk with his laptops. The very ugly standard lamp was the same, with the same dim light fighting to get through its faded satin shade. An empty teacup was on the small coffee table along with the wrapper of the KitKat that he had eaten. He then started to notice what was different. He couldn't lift his arms yet, but he could wiggle his fingers. He felt like his head was transfixed onto the Scottish tartan of the large armchair. Could he speak?

"Where am I?" He recognised his own voice. *Yes, I can.*

He looked again at his surroundings. Something wasn't right. The safe house in Glasgow had had a window that he had shuttered.

No windows!
The room is smaller!
There's only one door!
And it's a cell door?
At that final moment of recognition, the handle clanked on the door and an apparition in white appeared. A beautiful blonde woman entered the room and turned towards him. She was dressed in a white forensic suit, spattered in blood. She smiled radiantly, picked up an empty teacup and walked out of the room.
It's not the same woman, is it?
She was immediately replaced by a tall, white-coated man with a stethoscope dangling from his neck.
"Hi," the man said. "Don't worry, you're safe now." He took a packet of cigarettes from his pocket and flipped open the lid.
"I'm Doctor Jacob, and I want you to tell me everything so that I can help you."
The Doctor placed a cigarette in the prisoner's mouth and lit it with his own silver Zippo lighter. The smoke drifted into the prisoner's lungs and the nicotine hit, but he had difficulty lifting his right arm to control the cigarette. Objective Cyclone, the jihadist mass murderer, took another long drag on the cigarette and smiled.
"So, I'm really impressed with what you have managed to achieve," the doctor began. "What do you think is your finest achievement?"
"It's the secret." The terrorist smiled again. "Something that the kuffar will never find out." He felt elated, joyous.
"What?"
"If I told you, you couldn't comprehend its enormity." Doctor Jacob knew that this was the time, that subtle moment when a man snatches at what he can. When a man who is trying to cling to his sanity must unburden the secrets he has hidden, when he has to verbalise his thoughts, just to hear the sound of his own voice.

When he finds the silence deafening. "It's the final attack that will burn the Crusader army at Dabiq."

"Dabiq?" said Jacob. He needed just one more turn of the key to unlock the secrets concealed in Objective Cyclone's limbic system. To finally expose the thoughts hidden in the deep, dark recesses of the hippocampus.

"Tell me about it," said the doctor. The prisoner's seemed to open his mouth to answer and then with a visible effort clenched it shut. The doctor waited, but there was only silence.

***

Vauxhall Cross (VX)

As Danny entered the conference room, he saw Tim and Collette Brown, a senior MI6 officer, on one side of a shiny modernist teak conference desk, chatting to somebody he recognised as a CIA spook. Collette was stylishly dressed and impeccably made up, as usual. She flicked her hair in a girlish way and beamed a smile.

"Come and join us. We are just waiting for one more colleague before we start work."

Collette was the MI6 Head of Operations and one of the reasons why Danny had committed his company to the last mission. She was known both for her uncompromising attitude to Britain's enemies and the support she gave to friends. She was the woman most likely to be the next 'C', or Chief, of the SIS (Secret Intelligence Service).

"Danny, good to see you again." The smile continued. "I think you know Alex."

"Yes, very well," Danny smiled.

"Yeah, Baghdad, wasn't it?" said Tim.

"When the bad guys were worried," Alex added.

Alex was officially a diplomat on the US Ambassador's staff, but Danny knew his back story, and he was far from the archetypal 'grey man'. He was a bit too larger than life for that: an ex-Delta operator who looked like one. He was in his mid-forties with a bald, almost bullet-shaped head, and had a livid blue scar, a souvenir of a firefight in Helmand just before the 2010 surge that had been supposed to finish the war. An insurgent's bullet had passed through his face, hitting some rear molars before opening up his left cheek. He now sported what resembled a deep 'Teutonic' duelling scar, a disfiguration that also served to give him an almost permanent wry smile. He had hit his head when he fell, and the guys of the Second Battalion, Sixth Marines, who had been fighting alongside, initially thought he was dead. However, both Alex and the Taliban had proved to be remarkably resilient and were still very much alive, with the Taliban in so-called 'peace negotiations' with the USA, though they were killing more people than ever.

Alex looked across and smiled.

"It's a long time since the Death Star days, buddy."

"Yes," said Danny. "Dark but rewarding times."

"Yeah, the good old days, when people just let us do our jobs!" Alex touched the scar on his face thoughtfully.

The Death Star was the nickname given to the Special Forces bunker on the Balad Air Force base near Baghdad. It was from there that British and American Special Forces had made nightly raids against command-level Al Qaeda targets. Danny and his small unit of British agent handlers had supplied HUMINT for the target packs that fuelled the 'kill or capture' missions. The raids had sometimes provided enough information in seized documents and computer data to lead to other operations, and the bad guys' attrition rate had been off the scale. The SF helicopters took off all through the dark hours, bringing a little bit of Dante's Inferno to what Al Qaeda thought were 'safe' houses.

As Danny sat opposite him, the automatic door swished open again and another man from that harsh, rough time and place in counter-insurgency history appeared. It was Mac McCann, the MI6 guy that Danny had worked with during the Baghdad days. All three men had once shared an excellent bottle of Irish single malt whiskey after a particularly successful raid. The whiskey, from a particularly famous distillery, came with an interesting history: it had once belonged to Uday Hussein, one of Saddam's brutal sons, and Australian SAS guys had liberated one hundred bottles of it from his cellar after the fall of Baghdad in 2003. The bottle had been used to celebrate the Seal Team task that had finally finished the murderous reign of Abu Musab al-Zarqawi, the 'Emir' of Al Qaeda in Iraq.

Mac smiled as he entered the room, and Danny now knew that something unusually serious was going to be discussed. Mac was a senior MI6 man who sometimes had an unofficial chair at COBRA meetings. Alex fulfilled more or less the same role for the CIA. *It's going to be interesting,* Danny thought.

There was no time for further recollection; a quick shake of hands took place before Tim Broughton spoke.

"Gentlemen, as you have no doubt ascertained, things have changed quite drastically over the past few days." He paused and slowly looked around the room. "I will firstly give Mac the floor, to explain the political developments in Saudi Arabia that have led to the current spike in the threat level." Mac moved towards the small podium in front of the PowerPoint screen.

"Guys, we are all familiar with contemporary politics in the Middle East, we have all worked within its Machiavellian sphere, and we all know that sometimes things on the surface do not actually reflect what is happening at depth." He paused and looked around the room.

"Saudi politics is in a dangerous state of flux, and things are going badly for the royal family. They are now realising that they have bitten off more than they can chew in Yemen, and that you can't just butcher any journalist, even a Saudi one, simply because you don't particularly like them. They have also steered pretty close to the wind in their ties with the Russians in Syria, and in their increasingly heated relationship with the USA under the new Biden administration.

"All this has provoked a backlash from some of the more severely Islamist elements in the kingdom, who have formed an anti-government group. It calls itself 'The Guardians of Dabiq', a name taken from a town in northern Syria mentioned in a hadith about Armageddon, because they believe that that is where the final battle with Christendom will take place. They think it can only happen after another act of mass slaughter, and that a targeted attack on the scale of 9/11 will elicit an extreme reaction from the West and spark their long-hoped-for Holy War."

Mac clicked the projector button and a large network chart flashed onto the screen, showing links between ISIS and the Guardians.

"Stranger still, some members of the Saudi royal family are also involved with this group.

He looked around the room. "And how can they achieve this?"

"The group intends to use ISIS as its instrument to deliver such a blow. We have received information from a proven and reliable source that both Britain and the USA are about to be attacked." Mac again paused, an almost pained expression on his face.

"We also believe that this Saudi group has supplied, or is about to supply, ISIS with the nuclear tip of a newly-acquired battlefield tactical nuclear weapon, stolen from the Pakistani military." His audience exchanged quick worried glances as he continued.

"The nuclear tip itself is portable, and that's why it went missing. It could be concealed within a car, or even a small crate on a cargo ship. It could be in any one of the thousands of containers that arrive in our docks every day. It could even be in someone's luggage on the Eurostar. We have assessed that there are over two hundred potential targets that could be the terrorists' preferred objectives, but the method of delivery is unknown to us at this time."

Mac flashed up a slide of targets in order of probability. The first line listed the predictable targets that remained constantly under threat: The White House, The Pentagon, The Houses of Parliament and Buckingham Palace.

The next line was devoted to infrastructure targets. The Eurostar, Cross-Channel ferries, Heathrow, Gatwick, Dover.

The next line was devoted to targets further out like vulnerable ships, oil tankers, liquid gas tankers and passenger planes.

"Each of these targets is potentially vulnerable and, in principle, has to be protected, but we haven't sufficient assets to achieve that. The only good news is that we have got some HUMINT coverage at the London end and some technical means in play."

Danny was the first to break the stunned silence. "How did we find this out?"

Tim shifted uneasily and took the question. "Unfortunately, that's still close hold and source-sensitive information."

Danny's face reflected his feelings. *A nuclear bomb plot? A bit late for 'Need to Know'!*

Tim continued. "Our analysts believe that ISIS think the time is right. They have a new weapon and the continuing migrant crisis in Europe has empowered extreme right-wing elements. They think that, if there was ever a day to trigger an apocalyptic religious war, it's now, especially with a Biden administration in the White

House that has only served to further enrage the extreme right of American politics. The CIA has picked up significant ISIS-related chatter on the dark web that something big is about to happen."

Danny raised his hand. "Anything on the potential target?"

"No specific target. Their security is tight on this. We think they may have outsourced the attack to a 'clean skin', or previously unknown operator or organisation," said Tim, shifting uneasily on his feet.

"There is also a possibility that elements of Pakistan's Inter-Services Intelligence agency might be complicit in some wider aspects of the plot."

"Are you sure about that?" Danny asked.

"No, it's not confirmed Danny, it's just difficult to believe that the Pakistani military could have lost control of a nuclear device unless someone at a high level in the ISI turned a blind eye." Tim looked worried at the theory he was about to suggest.

"But the really worrying thing is that all this is happening just before the anniversary of *this*."

The iconic slide was known to all; it was seared into their collective memory and had been the driving force behind their careers for almost twenty years. The slide pictured the 2001 terrorist attack on New York's World Trade Center, at the moment when the second aircraft smashed into the reinforced concrete and glass of the south tower. The next September the eleventh, in a few weeks' time, would be the twentieth anniversary of the attack.

"So, something as bad as that?" Danny said.

"We don't know, there's nothing definite but we will have to prepare for the worst. Firstly, protect the population centres as best we can, and then spread things out to the likely targets on the peripheries." Tim looked towards Collette. "What do you think?"

Collette considered the question.

"Two points. First, a viable improvised nuclear device is a relatively easy thing to move around, but it's a lot harder to detonate without specialist knowledge," she said, as she stood and turned towards the rest of the company.

"And if there *is* a bomb plot, and if it's due to happen on the anniversary of 9/11, then the terrorists have already moved from the planning to the operational stage."

She paused, and again brushed her very expensively styled hair to the side. "And if the device is moving and they are also communicating, that's when they're at their most vulnerable. We have to organise concentric rings of security to stop this thing coming in, while using every intelligence asset we have to identify and disrupt the plot."

Collette turned towards Danny. She knew of his track record in Ulster, Iraq and Afghanistan, and of his intelligence work during the Cold War with the USSR. "What do you think?"

Danny shifted uneasily in his chair.

"As you know, Collette, the Soviets developed portable nuclear devices in the early days of the Cold War. I was working as a case officer on this stuff before the Wall came down,"

He paused, adopting what Tim recognised as his old friend's meditative pose, before he continued, his weathered chin cupped in his right hand. "The thing is, the Russians were a logical bunch compared to these ISIS monsters. The KGB worked against us, and we worked against them. It was a dangerous game, but it was almost civilised compared to how it's played now."

"Yes, they called it MAD then," Collette said. "Mutually Assured Destruction, and that worked. No sane government, communist or otherwise, would push the button knowing that it guaranteed the incineration of its own population."

"Yes, that sort of summed it up," Danny said. "Although things are vastly different with these ISIS wankers." His shoulders slumped as he remembered the 'bad old, good old days' of the Cold War. During those terrifying times both the US and the Soviets had developed portable nuclear weapons as easily smuggled suitcase-sized devices. It was fairly easy to do: the smallest and lightest American nuclear warhead ever designed was intended for a 120mm recoilless anti-tank gun, which in those days was not even considered artillery.

"In other words, they were as scared of things going nuclear as we were." He paused in thought as he reflected on the horror of how things could have been.

"And in those days, we were scared absolutely shitless. I can remember that quote from the Soviet leader Nikita Khrushchev from the late sixties. He said that *'even the survivors of a nuclear war would envy the dead'*. The main threat then was the smuggling in of a suitcase bomb, a portable nuclear device that could be carried to its target. We must assume that this device is equally adaptable."

"Yeah, and if they have it already, it's a real game changer," Collette said. "These evil bastards have no such checks or balances; their ideology means they are unencumbered by the constraints of rational thought."

"Yes, the Soviets were easy to deal with in comparison," Danny answered. "To know an enemy, you have to understand his thought processes, and that's nearly impossible with the Daesh. When your sole ultimate ambition is your own death and the promise of heaven, with the added bonus of seventy-two virgins, and you actually believe that shit, why bother with life?"

There was silence as Danny was momentarily lost in thought.

How had the Pakistani military lost control of the device? Or was it a deliberate action? The Security Service had been prepared to counter a British mainland mass-casualty attack by a returning ISIS active service unit. The last atrocity, the Paris attack, had been horrific, with 130 innocents slaughtered, but this new threat was something far more deadly. The kill rate of a portable nuclear device could be in the tens of thousands rather than the hundreds. A nuclear device would also leave a toxic legacy of contamination for decades.

"Have we narrowed down what the type of target might be?"

Tim broke the silence. "Nothing firm so far on the possible target, but that's something that our analysts at JTAC have crunched and they have some theories, which are admittedly only *supposition* at the moment."

He deliberately emphasised the intelligence operators' most hated word and smiled. "What does your old unit say about 'supposition', Danny?" Tim already knew the answer.

"The same as assumption: it's the mother of all fuck-ups," Danny said, quite sadly. "But sometimes it's all we've got, my old friend. Finding this bomb will literally be like finding a needle in a haystack. What we need to do is game play where they could deploy this thing without causing a retaliatory nuclear strike against either Saudi Arabia or Pakistan, while still sparking the Armageddon, or Dabiq, that they hope for in the Middle East." He looked towards the PowerPoint projection, where the Twin Towers were again displayed. "But we know what they are capable of." His audience was once more momentarily lost in thought.

Tim again broke the silence. "OK guys, that's the problem, so I suppose this is what you call 'Troops to Task'. Mac and Collette take on the MI6 effort and co-ordinate tasks allocated to the British Special Forces. Alex will handle the overlap with US Special Forces on some of the more likely terrorist targets." He turned and addressed his next statement directly to Danny.

"I need to speak to you, mate; I have a specific task for your team, for a particular reason."

Danny looked up with a slightly bemused look on his face. *What the flying fuck would that be?*

Chapter Seventeen

VX, the fifth floor

The electronic door shut behind them as Tim escorted Danny back to the entrance. As they walked along the long, brightly lit corridor, Danny could sense the all-pervading buzz of urgency that was a familiar feeling for him. An intelligence agency working to an unknown deadline, against a not-yet fully identified target, still generated its own internal energy, a shared sense of purpose. He hadn't realised the seriousness of the threat till now. The current one was bad – a suicide bomb was deadly enough – but there was no realistic protection against a nuclear device. But it was familiar territory for him in one sense: he had worked against the ISI before, when the government of Pakistan had been using British foreign-aid money to develop their nuclear option.

It had been meant to be a clandestine programme, but a secret that too many people shared ceased to be a secret at all. After all, it was relatively old military technology that had been around for a long time.

"What do you think, Danny?"

"I really don't know what to think, Tim. What are your priorities on this one?"

"My priorities have been defined by the government, Danny; I have no latitude for independent action, HMG's main priority is to close down Britain to this device, seal the ports, monitor all passenger movement and place a final protective ring around London. This has meant a huge track-change and a realignment of our insufficient resources. We have earmarked all our Special Forces, and their reserves, to assist. We've even pulled in some gunslingers from the HMSU (Headquarters Mobile Support Unit) in Belfast and have deployed all of the SRR. But I think we've got it wrong, don't you?"

"What do you mean?"

"Let's take a walk."

Danny immediately knew that this was a classic piece of what the security community call firewalling.

They moved in silence along the same corridor towards another office door; Tim applied his electronic pass and the door opened. The office was just one of the many meeting rooms within VX. They all looked the same: off-white walls, comfortable Scandinavian-style interior, pot plants and white wood desks, like IKEA on steroids. The door sealed shut as they moved inside.

"I want to run a theory by you, mate," Tim said, as he slumped onto a small, angular, grey sofa.

"Fire away."

"It's something we are working on at the moment, so the details are still a bit hazy. The worrying thing is that we believe the finance for the operation comes from someone in the Saudi Embassy in Pakistan. We know that they are involved with some of the London-based Islamic State plots, and they have a dodgy track record of supporting Jihadist groups everywhere."

Danny smiled. "Strangely enough, if they are, we have more of a chance of finding out what's going on."

"How?"

"To be honest, Tim, I've worked against the ISI in Helmand, and as an intelligence agency they leak like a sieve. They provided more sources to the British Army than Heinz Tomato, mate!" he said with a beaming smile.

Danny and his unit had worked against covert elements of the ISI in Helmand and knew their dubious track record. The ISI had always paid lip service to the West's 'War on Terror' while simultaneously supplying the logistical support that allowed the Afghan Taliban to operate. They had increased their support to senior figures of the Taliban, or what was known as the Quetta Shura, as Britain and the USA stepped up their joint efforts during the 'Troop Surge' in 2010.

The Pakistani intelligence agency had almost entirely supplied the small Honda 125 motorbikes that made the Taliban so mobile in the early days. They had also provided the weapons, ammunition and cross-border support that had directly led to the deaths of British and American soldiers. Danny therefore knew that the Pakistani ISI were always duplicitous, but they were easy to infiltrate because of their inadequate security procedures. *However, losing control of a tactical nuclear weapon was somewhat sloppy, even by Pakistani military standards!*

"OK, time to be straight with you, mate," said Tim. "And I have Collette and Mac's blessing on this one, by the way."

"Fire away." Danny wondered what had changed in just a few minutes.

"We have confirmed that Saudi money is behind the bomb plot, and our source is well placed within a foreign intelligence agency. The only problem we have lies in believing that any rich Saudi, or any Gulf Arab for that matter, would have any interest in destroying a British mainland target, and especially London, with a nuclear device."

"Yeah, I see," said Danny, as he realised what his MI6 colleague was thinking. "Especially when you own most of it."

"Which leads me to our conclusions about the secondary targets." Tim looked about the room in an involuntary action, almost as if he were checking for other people listening in.

"Floating or flying ones, you mean?"

"Yes." Tim knew that Danny Mac was on the same page.

"JTAC and the analysts have crunched the data. We have twenty different ships and at least two hundred aircraft that will be within striking distance of New York on the anniversary of 9/11, and I want your team to take on the one that we think is most likely – a cruise ship." Tim paused awkwardly. "But we don't have the luxury of time on this one, mate. We need to know whether you and your guys are up for it." He looked at Danny to gauge his reaction. "We need teams to deploy soonest."

Danny was silent and still in receive mode. Tim needed answers. "What do you think, mate?"

"Depends on the task, Tim. But we sort of work for you now. So, I'll check with Sam and the guys, but you're the boss, so I guess it's a yes."

"OK", said Tim. "The training task is finished, and Sam and the team are to deploy soonest."

"What about the student they've been training?"

"He's an MI6 asset; if he's passed the training team's assessment he can deploy as well. I suggest that we use him as an 'eyes and ears' source below decks. I'll get my office to build him a believable cover story."

"You've thought about this, haven't you?" Danny smiled, "What if I had said no?"

"Not possible." It was Tim's turn to smile. "It's what you do. We all know what motivates people, pal, it's our game, and I know you, Danny, and I know the people in your team. You are like me – it's about protecting our country against these murderous bastards." Tim reached into his pocket and said, "Well, are you definitely in?"

"Yes," Danny replied, with the glimmer of a smile. The answer had left his lips before he had even thought about it. This was always the crucial point of any intelligence mission: do you go, or do you say no? Even if it's a decision that you can sometimes regret.

"Excellent," Tim said, and handed Danny a USB thumb drive.

"The task is to assist British Special Forces to protect the passengers on the Cunard ship RMS *Queen Mary 2*, when she leaves Southampton. This is encrypted; I will send you the code when you ring me from your office. The thumb drive has everything you need to know on the task, and also the latest piece of software from our friends at Langley. It's designed to link computer algorithms from intelligence inputs. A very innovative company called Palantile developed it for them."

"OK, but what does that mean in plain speak for an old technophobe like me?"

"More simply put, then, it's called Palantile Expressway. It's a really advanced system for the ultimate in link analysis, the sort you would be used to, but on a global scale. Just punch in a name and it harvests information from every intelligence agency it has links to, including ones where the information 'donors' don't realise they're being hacked.

"It will immediately check a name and biometric details with hundreds of different agencies. This software will give your guys, Jimmy Cohen I suggest, a way to feed details of the passengers and crew into the system, so our analysts here can check their affiliations. It's 'Top Secret, UK/US Eyes Only, by the way. Sam and the team will need this tonight, as they are off to Southampton on Friday."

Danny thoughtfully rubbed the back of his neck as he pondered the problem.

"Sorry, mate, it doesn't leave you a lot of time," Tim added.

"No, not a lot." Tim applied his pass to the door and both men started to walk along the bustling G Branch corridor.

Conference Room

As Danny walked with Tim, he was already starting to calculate all the 'W's. *The who, what, why, when, where and, of course, the how, of any problem. And could it be done?*

"Excuse me, gentlemen." A young G Branch girl, wearing a light blue silk hijab, hurried between the two men. She was carrying a red folder with 'SECRET UK EYES ONLY' stamped on the front.

Some things never change; we had the same folders during the Cold War. It was reassuring that, even in these high-tech days, some of the old methods still co-existed with the new.

They stopped outside another G Branch debriefing room as Tim ran the pass he wore around his neck over the scanner. The glass and steel automatic door opened with what sounded like an intake of air, and Danny followed him in. It was a small, soundproofed conference room: modernist minimalism at its best, and set up for a meeting. The white oval laminate conference table could seat eight, but it held only three standard notebooks and three standard silver propelling pens. A broad-shouldered, stocky-looking guy was sitting in one of the modern-looking leather and stainless-steel chairs. He looked towards them, smiled and stood.

"Danny, I'm not sure if you two have met," Tim said. "May I introduce Gavin Loach, the current head of security for Cunard." Loach stood up with a beaming smile and an outstretched hand.

"I think I know you, Danny."

Danny returned the smile and shook his hand.

"Gavin, we met during the 'Death Star' days, didn't we?"

"Yeah, it was a busy and dangerous time, mate." Gavin grinned. "But a pretty exciting one."

Danny hadn't recognised him immediately. He was ten years older now with a few more grey hairs, but he was still a fit, hard-looking guy. His weathered face reflected a life on the roughest seas, in the smallest boats. He had joined the Marines at the age of sixteen as a Junior Marine, had passed the Commando course at seventeen and made the selection for the Special Boat Service in his twenties. He had left the SBS as a major, twenty-five years later. Tim sat down and pulled in his chair. Danny and Gavin joined him.

"If this operation is approved, Gavin will be the team's link man on board the *Queen Mary 2*," said Tim. "The ship is currently undergoing a minor refit, so that gives us a bit of planning time. We have assessed the vessel as a target because it's highly prestigious and it's going to be in the right place at the right time as far as they are concerned: in US territorial waters on or about the anniversary of 9/11. I want your team on board."

"Their job?" said Danny.

"They will be the onboard liaison officers in case we have to react with pre-deployed Special Forces. I will brief you now."

Danny caught the look on the SBS veteran's face.

"Gavin's already been briefed on the broad outline of the possible threat to the ship."

Both men then looked intently towards Tim.

Danny asked the obvious question "Why not just cancel all transport links?"

"Not possible." Tim looked stressed. "It has political and source protection repercussions and has already been discussed and discarded. For your interest, but not for disclosure, that was my preferred option."

"What was the logic behind refusing your advice?" Danny said.

"It's considered an extreme outside chance, and a bomb on the way out of the country is thought to be a better option than a bomb on its way into London or any other major city."

"One team can't protect a ship that size," Danny said.

"They're not meant to. They are there to supply a watching brief, to gather data on likely terrorist suspects." Tim paused. "We are trying to trace the whereabouts of the device and identify the person who has it. We might track it down before it becomes critical. We have a promising source, and once we get a name, we will fix the device." But he seemed not entirely convinced himself.

"I hope so," said Gav. "I have the responsibility for three thousand souls on board that ship." He looked at his watch, a black issue CW SBS diver's version that had seldom left his wrist since he had passed selection in 1990. "I have to go; I have a meeting at Cunard in an hour."

Tim pressed an intercom and a uniformed security guard appeared at the door.

"Can you take this gentleman back through security?"

Gav stood up, shook hands and prepared to follow the guard out.

"I will meet your team at the jetty; it'll be good to be working with you again, Danny."

"Likewise. Hopefully, it won't be as noisy."

"Yeah, let's hope not." Gav flashed a smile as he left.

There was a moment of silence after Gav left the room. Tim seemed to be momentarily locked within his own thoughts. Then he made eye contact with Danny Mac.

"Do you trust me, Danny?"

"As much as I trust anybody in our line of work, and you more than many." Danny wondered where this was going.

"Yeah, I suppose that's true, but I have to trust you, mate, and that's why I'm going to share this with you."

"OK." The older man nodded.

"And I want your advice," Tim added.

"About what?"

"I want to let you know what's going on in the security agencies at the moment."

"Sounds ominous."

"And it is." Tim took a deep breath, as if he were steeling himself for the ultimate download. "Before I go on, I need to know that this stays between us."

"Fire away; you have my strictest confidence," Danny said, as he felt the full force of Tim's doubts.

"Very well. I have been an intelligence officer for twenty years and I've been working on ISIS for the last ten."

There was a sudden gasp of air from the electronic doors, and the girl in the bright blue hijab appeared in the room.

"I"m sorry, gentlemen; I have this for you, sir."

"Thank you, Fatima." The door gasped again, and she was gone. Tim opened the file and looked at the latest case note from the Cabinet Office.

"Fuck! Just what I thought: they are trying to cancel the maritime task."

"Why?"

"Because Covid 19 has caused more problems than you would think, and really put the idea of Islamist terrorism on the back burner. The world we are living in is changing, mate, and my Service has morphed into something I no longer fully understand.

"There are people at almost all levels now who were too young to have really felt the effects of 9/11. They have an alternative view of what's important and have insisted that the emphasis be placed on the nailing of the pathetic extreme right-wing groups out there, in the hope that it will make the modern security services more acceptable."

Danny listened intently; his chin cradled in his hand. He had picked up the same strange vibrations from his other contacts in the security and intelligence agencies who tended to be approaching retirement stage. Things had changed drastically since his earlier attachment to Thames House. It had been the Ulster problem then, during the death throes of what the IRA called 'the Long War'. He knew that it was a very different place now. The modern Security Service had hitched its trailer to the idea of AI (Artificial Intelligence) collection, which now allowed them to gather what they called 'Sentiment Analysis' just by harvesting data on smart phones. They now had the opportunity to hack every part of a phone's memory, not only to find out where people were, and where they had been, but also, by trawling through millions of social media accounts, what people were actually thinking. Danny thought it was spookily like George Orwell's *1984*.

"Does that mean I stand my team down?"

"No, I have talked at length with Mac, Alex and Collette, and we need coverage on every viable priority target, no matter how."

"What about the SBS?"

"No problems there. M Squadron, in any case, were going to do a forward mount on a ship for a Maritime Intervention exercise as part of their usual training package. Some sealed orders, and they can be stood by for the real thing."

"So, my team goes?" Danny pulled out his iPhone.

"Yes," said Tim, "It's a GO, but you won't be able to use that until you leave the building, old mate. This is an IT-sealed environment."

Danny grimaced. "Yeah, great IT security for really shit decisions."

"Yep," said Tim, almost mournfully. "Welcome to my world!"

CHAPTER EIGHTEEN

Repton Manor, next day

Taff stood by a 1990s-style whiteboard and scrawled 'ABC' in large red letters.

"So, mate, a quick recap. What does ABC stand for?"

Ricky sat on one of the three white plastic chairs in front of the board.

"That's Air, Bleeding and Circulation." He rattled back the answer without hesitation; this was his tenth battlefield First Aid lesson. Teacher and student were again in the old barn, standing amongst a variety of First Aid bits and pieces. An unfurled bandage streamed across an old work bench amongst the detritus of the previous forty-five-minute period of instruction. A 'Resusci Anne', a plastic doll used for CPR training, reclined on the bench and stared blankly up at the ceiling. This was the bit of equipment that he had practised on for the previous nine lessons, and even Anne seemed pissed off. The training always followed the same stages – Explanation, Demonstration, Imitation – and then repetition. *It's the constant endless repetition that pisses me off!*

Ricky was under pressure.

"Yep. Well done mate, good drills." Taff attempted a smile; he was trying to take a professional view of Ricky, but he wasn't feeling the vibes, though he knew it was probably his prejudices, rather than anything tangible, that were influencing him. Taff had developed a stand-offish approach to him and just didn't really know why, but he realised that it was far from professional.

"What we are going to cover now is the treatment of gunshot wounds," said Taff, holding a small green package in his right hand. "Ideally, we should always have access to a decent medical kit like that one." He pointed towards a large black canvas rucksack with EXMED in large capitals, along with the firm's logo, embroidered on the front.

He then tossed the package into the air, caught it and threw it towards Ricky, who caught it instinctively. "But this is what you are more likely to have: a personal gunshot kit. I say personal, because you should always use the casualty's own one if possible; open it up and see what's there, because if you are unlucky enough to get tagged, this is what can save your life." As Ricky placed the kit's components in a line, Taff rattled off each item. "First bit of kit, a thick crepe bandage and a means of fastening it." A large safety pin was holding the bandage closed. "The next very important item is a haemostatic QuikClot dressing." He tossed the dressing towards the student, who again caught it instinctively. Ricky looked at the small oblong package in his hand.

"What's haemostatic?" he said. Taff snatched the QuikClot back from him. "It comes from ancient Greek and means 'stopping blood'. This type of bandage was developed by the Israelis." Taff held it in the palm of his hand. "And it's a life-saver. It contains a chemical called chitosan, harvested from shellfish, that causes a reaction that seals a wound." He ripped the packaging open and took out what looked like a roll of green elasticated bandage.

"And this is it." It had a white plastic clip stitched into the fabric. He opened the bandage and inverted it.

"This is what goes on the wound." There was an off-white patch of bandage in the middle of the wound wrapping.

"The inside is completely sterile, and if you open it like this, and that's the way it stays, it's the part with the chemical magic on it." Taff stopped talking as the old barn door creaked open and Jimmy breezed in.

"Hey, you are practising with the old Israeli dressing," he said proudly. Jimmy had spent some time with the British Parachute Regiment and the Israeli security service. "Top-notch kit," he smiled. "But no time for that now, mate, the boss wants to see us."

"Roger that. What about Ricky?"

Ricky looked at both men. He was always the conversational outsider, it seemed!

"Yeah, I'm sorry, mate." Jimmy seemed in a hurry. "I forgot to say, bruv, Sam says to wait here for Lou." The old door creaked shut as Jimmy and Taff left the barn. There were a couple of minutes of silence and it felt strange. It was the first time in over a week that he hadn't been either eating, working or sleeping. Paranoia started nibbling at his confidence. *Maybe they know more about me than I think!*

Are they talking about me?

I've failed the selection.

What will I do now?

Ricky suddenly felt very much alone. He had time now to look around the place where he had been run ragged for the past week. The cursory clean-up hadn't quite removed the cumulative efforts of industrious spiders, whose webs glistened in the light through the pigeon-stained glass of the skylight. The gloom inside the barn mirrored his feelings. He hadn't really had much time to think since he had left prison, but now he very much felt that he had replaced one prison with another.

He knew he could leave, but he also knew that he had been given a unique chance to do something very special. Then an old saying of his trainer from his boxing days came back to him:

"*When the going gets tough, the tough get going.*"

Ricky sprang to his feet, his doubts forgotten, and walked towards the heavy bags suspended at the end of the barn. He chose his target and put together his best speed combination, finishing with a demonic right hook, his signature punch, that made the bag rattle the barn's old oak rafters.

"Nice," said Lou, as he appeared behind him. "You're good."

"Used to be."

"When?"

"Before drugs, girls and gangs," Ricky said, almost wistfully.

"Yeah, I could have gone the same way."

"Oh, how's that? "Ricky finished on the bag with a quick combination.

"I mean, I could have ended up banged up in Wandsworth if I hadn't joined the Royal Marines."

"Where did you live?"

"Harlesden."

"Whereabouts?"

"Church Road."

Ricky knew the place; it was in north-west London, mainly an Afro-Caribbean postcode, with guys with knives, lots of guns, crack cocaine and very little sense.

"Yeah, one of the Church Road boys got shot there last year," Ricky said.

"Yes, I believe so, but if it was you that did it, don't tell me, son."

Ricky smiled. "No, not me, Lou. It was the fucking Albanians."

"Glad to hear it. My life is complicated enough as it is!"

Lou took a seat in front of the whiteboard and pointed towards the other chair.

"Sit down, bruv. Something has come up with the team and they are going to be talking for a while. Samantha thought it would be a good time for me to have a chat and explain to you what you are getting yourself into."

"I think the training sort of explains itself," said Ricky, pulling up the chair to face his handler. He knew it was time to listen.

"So, how do you think you are doing?"

"OK, I think?"

"Yeah, you're doing OK. You seem to be quick at picking things up, which is a huge advantage. But you will need to stay on your game, mate, because things might start to get a bit more demanding once we know what's going on."

"What do you mean?" Lou could sense the tension in his mentee's voice.

"Not sure myself, mate, but I think another job's just come up."

"Will I be part of it?"

***

Repton, The Ops Room

It was evening, and the old Ops Room at Repton Manor was generating a buzz of activity that it hadn't seen since the final exercise of the last FRU course within its walls, in 1997. Sam had designated specific tasks to everybody in the team. Jimmy was head-down on his MacBook Pro, loading the thumb drive Danny had provided for them, Taff was working on weapons they would need, and

Pat and Scottie on any specialist equipment that the task might require. It was what they had been trained to do: to adapt, improvise and overcome, and they were used to plans changing constantly. HUMINT operations are sometimes like sprinting at full speed across shifting sands, and once again the sands had shifted. The group's dangerous past had moulded them into a very close unit, and they adapted and planned together.

Sam was a good leader, and she knew that she had to harness the team's varied experience to achieve the aim. They had done it before: a lot of what they had achieved during the hostage rescue mission in Iraq, and the recent HUMINT-led and CIA-sponsored operation, had been executed with what the British Army call QBOs or Quick Battle Orders, so they were all familiar with sharp changes in direction. The British Special Forces are known for their ability to think on their feet, and as Samantha looked around her team, she knew that they could make the plan work. There was probably a hundred years' worth of operational experience listening intently to what she had to say. Things were still only at the 'stood to' stage; Samantha had been briefed by Danny in a 'not quite long enough' phone call, and the thumb drive had been delivered by Julian, their own personal MI6 courier and Repton's custodian. All they knew at the moment was only the most basic outline of the task, including the mission statement and the location details, and both were unusual!

"OK, lads" she began. "We have been thrown the ultimate fast ball and we have a deadline." She looked toward Jimmy.

"What have we got on the thumb drive?"

Jimmy was still furiously scrolling down the files.

"This is top-notch," he said, "It's a great piece of software but not very ethical, nor particularly legal." He smiled. "It can steal and analyse algorithms from almost any source if we are chasing somebody down. I also have the task outline; detailed ship plans and direct access to all of Cunard's passenger lists and crew files." Samantha watched his fingers flying across the laptop's keyboard at blinding speed.

"Taff?" she said.

"Yeah, I've worked out what we might need, and we should be able to get the list to Poole once I've checked the other equipment list with the dynamic duo." He pointed towards Pat and Scottie.

"We've almost got that," Scottie said. "It's a wish list rather than essentials, but it's gear that we should have. The lightweight covert body armour is a luxury, but if it goes noisy it would be nice to have."

"What about the trainee?" said Pat.

"Tim wants us to use him." Sam was looking towards Taff and could see a frown forming.

"To do what?" Taff said, as a reciprocal frown started to form on Sam's face.

"This young lad has only got past 'Billy Basic' of the practical side and isn't even properly vetted. He could be a fuck-up waiting to happen."

"Danny thinks he could maybe infiltrate any Jihadist elements of the crew."

"How do we know that similar Jihadist elements might not have already got to him?"

Samantha looked towards Jimmy. He was the go-to guy for the team's more complex intelligence collection scenarios, technical or otherwise. He had actually been a Shin Bet deep cover operative in the Gaza Strip after Hamas had taken control of it, and therefore his opinion was always valued.

Jimmy looked thoughtful for a moment; his eyes magnified by his newest blue-framed acquisition from Specsavers.

"It's a long shot," he said after careful deliberation. "He seems a smart kid, he can look after himself, and I suppose he has gained some relevant experience in Wandsworth. But a deep-cover operative needs week of briefings and a really solid cover story. How's that gonna happen in a few days?"

"Tim and Danny think it's possible," Sam said.

"Yeah, possible," Jimmy flashed back. "But, as I say, a long shot – and very dangerous."

"For him."

"Yeah, but for us as well."

"Will you brief him?" Sam asked Jimmy the question, but immediately registered her husband's negative reaction.

"Yes, OK, give me the cover story and I will run the guy through it, but it's a lot for an undercover operator to soak up in a very short time. I spoke fluent street Arabic and was trained for my mission for two months before I went into Gaza, but I still got blown within two weeks and got this." Jimmy pulled up his old 2 Para tee-shirt and pointed to the livid scar that ran across his chest to his stomach. "Jihadists get pissed off when they find you aren't actually their best buddy," he smiled. "Let's look at putting him into the crew at a safe level, just so he can maybe hear things that the ship's security guys don't."

"OK." Sam looked thoughtful. "It's what Six want and they're the client, but I'm not sure that it's a good idea."

"What's his legend on this one?" Jimmy asked.

Sam handed Jimmy a file. "I've just printed that out. It's also on your thumb drive."

Jimmy quickly leafed through the file; his brow wrinkled in concentration as a thousand different calculations flashed through his mind. A deep cover agent's legend had to be a mixture of the checkable and uncheckable, clinging simultaneously to both half-fact and half-fiction, and protected by a maze of lies, to be successful. As far as was compatible with security, it had to blend with the operator's own life to be believable. Jimmy scanned the pages, making the odd tick or cross on the hard copy. After what seemed longer than it actually was, he asked, "Can this be changed?"

"If it needs to be," replied Sam.

"If I'm going to run his cover, I will need to make changes before we get to the documentation stage."

"Yeah, you have control," Sam said. She was relieved: cover stories were part of any intelligence officer's life, but putting them together, and briefing an operative to live them, were very specialised skills and a different part of the equation. Sam knew that a blown undercover operator was usually a dead one.

"OK, but I will need permission to talk to VX direct and streamline this product, so Ricky stays with me for the next two days. Agreed?"

"Agreed."

"What's the timescale?" Jimmy adjusted his glasses in his characteristic way, with a quick stab of his index finger.

"Two days, max," she said. "We sail in three!"

Repton, later that evening.

Ricky tapped on the old teak door and heard "Come in". The door creaked as he entered.

"Hi, Ricky." Sam pointed towards the chair. She was dressed in an expensive-looking business suit and had her blonde hair tied in a Viking-type plait that hung to one side of her face. It was the second time he had seen her in formal dress. The first had been when he had tried to mug her.

She was sitting at the single desk in Repton's admin office. The only other furniture was a whiteboard and a chair for him to sit in. He didn't know what to expect; Repton was again stretching him out of his comfort zone. The last time he had been in any type of office was when he was discussing his past offences with his social worker.

"Sit down, we need to chat." Sam had a sizeable file on the desk in front of her. The course so far had lasted ten days, and this was the first time that Ricky had ever sat down in the same room as Samantha. He had seen her every day, either joining in with the phys sessions or hovering around during the tradecraft instruction. He supposed that that was her job, a sort of independent arbiter of the course, a tradecraft co-ordinator. Ricky had never met anybody remotely like her. She seemed to glide rather than walk, and had an aura of authority intertwined with unquantifiable charisma that only a few people ever possess.

Not that Ricky trusted the fair sex. He had worked out, very early on in his criminal career, that girlfriends equated to trouble. It was a pretty young girl he had arranged to meet that had triggered the knife attack that had nearly killed him before his eighteenth birthday. He ran his finger over his tee-shirt and could still feel the scar; the jagged serrated edge of the kitchen knife had made a mess, and he could still remember the pretty white, blonde girl laughing as she and his attackers ran away.

She had blue eyes as well. The thought flashed momentarily into his mind as he noticed Sam's.

"OK, Ricky, this isn't a formal interview and it's not even an end-of-course briefing." Sam pointed to the file. "That's just about your whole life up to now." She started leafing through the red folder with 'SECRET, STAFF ONLY' written on the outside.

"This is the only copy we have." She turned another page "All your past is here: the drug stuff, the guns, the knives, and all the source reports that you helped generate in Wandsworth." Sam flashed her eyes up from a page and held Ricky's gaze.

She seemed to be looking straight into him; it felt uncomfortable.

"This is your past, and it could all just disappear." She closed the file.

"It's the only copy of the paperwork, and it could be burned." Sam placed her hand on the top of the file. "We could also erase your entries from every police or online government file or record, if you want to forget your past and concentrate on your future. You make the decision."

Ricky understood immediately that he was getting 'pitched' again.

"So, what do you want from me?"

Sam smiled. "We need your help on our next mission."

"So, I've passed the course?" Ricky smiled.

"Let's call this continuation training," Sam smiled back. "It will concentrate on the practical phase of agent handling in a live environment."

"Is it dangerous?"

"Yes, very!" Sam smiled; she was beginning to warm to the latest member of the team.

"I'm in!" Ricky Miller, Agent CORKSCREW, returned the smile.

Sam picked up the old push-button telephone that was perched on the desk and hit a number; almost instantly there was another knock on the door and Jimmy entered the room.

"You know Jimmy." Sam seemed to look through Ricky with her piercing blue eyes, and a little bit of him melted. "He is the expert on all things covert, and he's going to coach you on your cover story. Learn it well, because inattention to details can get you killed. Best of luck, and welcome to the team."

"Thanks," was all Ricky could think of saying as he looked towards Jimmy's smiling face. He didn't quite know how he felt at that particular moment. It wasn't fear, it wasn't excitement, it was just a strange feeling of continuity, as if one thing had led seamlessly into the other until his own personal preferences no longer mattered. Fate seemed to be propelling him into an even stranger place, where he would have no control. He wasn't angry at the cards he had been dealt; he just marvelled at how completely different his life had become.

A complex life just comes with the new job, I suppose.

CHAPTER NINETEEN

Abbottabad, Pakistan, same time

While Ricky considered his future, another intelligence agent with vastly more experience of the Great Game considered his past. Brigadier Abdul Haq, a recently retired officer of the Pakistani Army, was angry. He looked at the row of family photographs that lined his bedside cabinet. Here was everything that he had tried to protect. The faces of his immediate family smiled out at him. His wife, when she was young, with two small children, a bright-faced boy and a pretty girl. The picture of his own father took pride of place, a colonel of the British Army of India, an imposing man in old-style British officers' service dress, standing ramrod-straight and holding a swagger stick. A more recent military picture caused him pain and pride in equal measure: a smiling young man in Pakistani Army camouflage uniform and carrying an RPG rocket launcher. This was his son Abdulla, martyred by British Special Forces in Afghanistan. He had been a junior ISI case officer with the Taliban.

The brigadier had no photographs of himself and therefore no visual reminders of his military exploits. He thought that an intelligence officer should never leave personal images for his enemies to exploit. He looked back at his life. *He had given everything for his country, but now! However, Allah works in mysterious ways.* He had just got the news that had liberated him. An opened letter lay on the bed where he had discarded it, a terse medical report. He had directed the doctor to be candid, and he had been. It was cancer, probably contracted while working with Pakistan's nuclear testing programme. *He could now concentrate on revenge.*

He thought of his many successes as an officer of the SS Directorate of the ISI. How he and his department had been instrumental in forging the disjointed, disparate and warring Islamist groups in Afghanistan into the unofficial instrument of the Pakistani Government's policy called the 'The Afghan Taliban.' He recalled his long liaison with the CIA and MI6 during the Afghan-Russian War, when he had had to overcome his distaste for the godless kuffar in order to bring money, guns and victory to the Taliban in Afghanistan. He also remembered the covert training he had organised, and the operations he had planned and implemented, in Indian-ruled Kashmir. His hair had turned a silvery white over the last thirty years in the service of Allah and his country, but now he had been discharged from his own army for 'displaying radical extremist tendencies'.

Those tendencies hadn't worried the politicians when he planned the Serena Hotel suicide attack in the Afghan capital of Kabul. He had been ordered to do that!

He had always served two masters: first his religion and then his country. During his thirty-two years of selfless service, this dual loyalty had never once affected his duties. In fact, throughout most of his service career, one had neatly dovetailed into the other. Things had only changed when the Taliban gained dominance in Pakistan's 'Pashtun' tribal areas and the Army had been ordered to destroy them. He knew that this was a basic betrayal of the idea of Ummah, the global solidarity of all Muslims. So, as things began to change, he made his plans. Fortunately, his last job in the Army had been organising the screen of security and disinformation to disguise the fact that the Pakistani Army had developed deployable tactical nuclear weapons.

He looked down at his most treasured possession and his family's retirement plan. He still couldn't quite believe that something so small could be so deadly. It was the tip of a nuclear warhead stolen from a Pakistani Army Nasr Vengeance 4 tactical battlefield missile. The plutonium core was maybe only eight inches long and four wide, but this small cone of death enabled the missile to deliver a nuclear strike of 0.5 to 5.0 kilotons.

He took the nuclear device, cradled it in both hands and closed his eyes as he tried to envisage its awesome power. It was hefty, its weight added to by both its lead covering and, it seemed to him, the grave responsibility of being chosen by God to use it. The exposure to radiation did not worry him; when the time came, the explosion would kill him along with the infidels, and he was dying anyway. He was going to take the war to the Yankee unbelievers' doorstep.

He was on his own personal Jihad and felt blessed. He carefully replaced the container in the piece of luggage they had prepared, a large and very expensive Louis Vuitton trunk with a false bottom. It had been modified with great craftsmanship: he had just to click one small button and the bottom of the trunk popped up, disclosing a foam rubber inset that supplied a cradle for his treasure. He placed his present for the Western world into it, closed the secret compartment and prepared for prayer. The trunk would get to its destination on a Saudia flight, in the care of a minor member of the kingdom's vast royal family. After ritual preparation he prayed, then showered and dressed.

He dressed, as he always did, like an English gentleman. He hated the British but admired the way their elite were attired. His maid had laid out his clothes as instructed: a light Savile Row blazer, a Jermyn Street shirt and tie and smart khaki flannels, all immaculately pressed. Islamabad's morning sun shimmered through the blinds of the bedroom window.

His brown English brogues glittered, polished to perfection. He placed his gold monocle in his right eye and again carefully examined his British Airways ticket. 'First Class', it said, and he smiled. He was looking forward to London; his mission started there. He had been in London many times, sometimes covertly, but this time he had the perfect cover story. As an experienced intelligence officer, he knew that sometimes the best way to hide was in plain sight. He had been invited to a seminar at the Royal United Services Institute. The London based institution was the world's oldest think tank and it had been founded in 1831 by The Duke of Wellington, the victor of Waterloo. He picked up his invitation card:

Security Co-operation Against Radical Islam in Challenging Times

"Interesting subject," he muttered under his breath, and smiled. It was especially ironic, since he had also been asked by his rich Saudi sponsors to review and improve ISIS's current security procedures. They had engineered an invitation for him from a US think tank called The Rand Corporation, with a proper visa and a five-star hotel waiting for him. The Saudi group was footing the bill. It would be a nice way to start his mission, and a sudden thought crossed his mind.

I'm even deeper in the shadows than usual.

He had always lived his life in the shadows, in an alternative paranoid world where he not only thought people were planning to kill him, but where many had actually tried and failed. Therefore, he trusted no one but himself. He, and only he, had put this latest ISIS operation together. He had planned every move and considered every minute detail. The circle of knowledge was small by design: only four people knew the timing and only he, Brigadier Abdul Karim Haq, and one other knew the target.

It was a classic closed-cell operation, and the operatives who would help him were already in place. They were 'sleepers' who, if captured, would know nothing to give away under interrogation, as they would only be activated just before the attack. It was a great plan; the British and Americans would be chasing shadows when Allah's great reckoning cast a really giant shadow that would blot out their wickedness. He had always known that Allah was on his side. Even as a boy of ten he could recite the Koran from memory. Each blessed word of it. He was spiritually warmed by the idea that he would soon be in Jannah (Heaven), with all his earthly sins forgiven. He gently murmured in English a passage from the Koran that he had memorised as a child:

They plan, and Allah plans. And Allah is the best of planners.
Koran (8:30)

Chapter Twenty

Repton Manor

Jimmy had made very few changes to the legend that had been created for the team's latest asset, and it now had all the things a decent cover story needed to be effective. It was, first of all, believable: it matched the asset's profile, and it was not too dissimilar to Ricky's own real story. It needed to be good because he was going in as a deep-cover operative, known as an NOC asset. NOC stood for Non-Official Cover, meaning that part of the deal was that he was a deniable agent. NOC covers were always meant to be BACK (Believable, Accurate, Checkable and Knowledge-based). The process of training an NOC agent was usually a long one; Jimmy himself had been trained for two months by Shin Bet before he had deployed to Gaza. Now, he had just two days to get it right for Ricky.

"That's good," said Jimmy, "but you've got your postcode wrong again. Remember the old saying: *'Cover is like soap - once you rinse it off, you can't put it back on'*. Let's have another look at the place you've lived in for the last five years and try the whole thing again."

Jimmy hit the remote and the screen filled with Google Maps. "OK, Rick, where's this?"

The monitor showed an anonymous bird's eye view of a London council house estate, like the one that Ricky had lived in. Its grey tower blocks vied for space on either side of a main road.

The 1960s had seen the same buildings cloned throughout the city, each replicating the others in its concrete brutalist simplicity. Once a hopeful vision of the future for post-war town planners, who had talked about building homes for living inspired by visionary modern architects like Le Corbusier, they had become just places to save space by stacking poor people on top of each other.

"So, point out your block."

Ricky used the laser pointer. "Here it is, home sweet home – Padstock House."

"OK, what school did you go to?"

"St James's Academy."

"OK, take me from your home to your school." Ricky used the laser pointer to trace the journey for the umpteenth time.

I'm beginning to think I actually live in this shithole, he thought. After another massive download on his fictional past, Jimmy stopped speaking and removed a small black plastic box from a desk drawer. Ricky thought the obvious.

"A gun?"

Jimmy smiled. "No, mate." he said emphatically. "Deep cover operations and personal weapons don't usually mix too well. "He opened the box and removed three items. "But these might."

One object needed no explanation: a battered-looking iPhone 5.

"Does that thing still work?" It was Ricky's turn to smile.

"Yeah, it still works, and it's a bit more than it looks. It's part of the equipment that you will be taking with you." Jimmy lifted up the phone in a frayed black leather cover.

"It looks old for a reason, bro." Jimmy opened the phone's cover.

"This a state-of-the-art transceiver as well as a standard shit-looking iPhone, and it looks old because, below decks, a new iPhone 12 might be a bit too attractive for some of the more

153

light-fingered of the crew. It also has an emergency tracing button for you that can be operated whether the phone is charged or not, and it works with this."

Jimmy smiled as he untangled a thin line of electrical flex, with a tiny black plastic box on one end and what looked like a press stud with a small protruding needle on the other.

"This is a covert camera remote; it's state of the art and worth more than a new iPhone. It uses the camera facility on the phone and directs it to this tiny lens at the end of the press stud."

He pushed the press stud inside his shirt, beside one of the buttons near the collar.

"This line of flex hangs down inside fully extended. The small black piece of plastic is the microphone and transmitter which feeds directly into my laptop." Jimmy buttoned up his shirt and turned the screen of the old iPhone towards Ricky.

"And that's what we have."

Ricky could see a high-resolution image of himself on the screen.

"That's impressive," he said.

"Yeah, made by a good old Israeli firm as well." Jimmy beamed a smile.

"You are the team's eyes and ears below deck, and this kit can work anywhere you need it. It also works in low light and can stream live video," he said, as he passed Ricky a small silver pendant with the sacred *Shahada* ('There is no god but God, and Muhammad is his Prophet') in Arabic in shiny relief on its surface.

"I had one of these when I worked in Gaza." The pendant glittered as he turned it in his hand.

"Wear it around your neck. It's the on-and-off button for the camera and serves as a separate tracking device in case you need it."

"Did you need it?" said Ricky.

"Yeah." Jimmy was straight-faced as he said, "It saved my life." There was a slight glimmer of a smile as he handed the kit over. "Enough war stories for today though, mate. I'm your on-board controller and I'll make sure you're not put in the same position." He extended his hand and Ricky shook it.

"There's a guy outside the office; his name is Julian and it's his job to supply you with what you need and get you onto the ship. Trust him, he's one of us."

"Thanks" Ricky said. "And I mean it!" as he turned towards the door.

Julian, the mysterious MI6 link man-cum driver, held a medium-sized grip bag in his hand.

"Follow me, Ricky," he said cheerily. "We have to go through all this kit, and you have to sign for it."

"Sign for it?"

"Yeah, you work for the MoD now, buddy, and we sign for everything!"

"What is it?"

"Every bit of clothing and equipment you'll need to join the ship."

"When?"

"Tomorrow you become a Cunard employee, mate! Below decks is not too luxurious. I hope you don't mind confined spaces?"

He obviously doesn't know where I've just come from. Ricky beamed a smile.

"No problem, Julian, I'm well used to them!"

***

Sam sat at her desk and opened the red file, turned the first page and looked through the bare bones of Ricky's revised cover story. She tossed the file across the desk to Taff and said, "It looks good." Taff picked it up and glanced through it.

"So, it looks like he'll be working in a useful place. And far enough away from our space that he can work independently."

Taff looked across at Sam with a frown.

"Do you really think that there is a specific threat to the ship?"

"What do you think?" Sam said.

Taff's voice always became a little bit more south Wales when he was trying to make a point.

"I think it's a gigantic arse-covering exercise, to be honest, and this is all overkill."

Sam returned the frown.

"Yeah, well, that may be the case, Nigel, but let's treat the mission as live until we uncover evidence to the contrary. And remember, we are getting paid either way."

"Roger that," said Taff.

"Are we good to go?" Sam asked.

"Yeah, good to go!"

Chapter Twenty-One

London: The Lanesborough Hotel, Hyde Park Corner

Taqiyya is a form of religious dissimulation, or a legal dispensation whereby a believing individual can deny his Islamic faith or commit otherwise illegal or blasphemous acts while they are at risk of significant persecution.

His head throbbed as he struggled to open his eyes. As his vision cleared, the blurred outline of a blindingly white ceiling came into focus. The brigadier was at an age when things were sometimes fuzzy first thing in the morning, but today it was much worse. The room smelled of the previous night's activities, a faint fusion of stale whisky, expensive perfume and the rubbery undertones of used Durex. He reached out his once muscular arms and stretched; he could almost feel them creak with age. His outstretched right hand brushed against something.

CLINK.

The half empty bottle of Johnnie Walker Black Label fell onto its side. He tried to concentrate; he needed to remember what had happened last night, but his eyes crinkled in pain as the hangover fully kicked in. He focused on the delicate Art Deco chandelier and attempted to put the events of the previous evening into some sort of chronological order.

He panicked momentarily. *Where's my wallet?* On the bedside cabinet, next to the bottle now lying on its side, was his old gold Rolex watch, his wallet and his mobile phone. He sighed with relief and checked the wallet first.

All the money was gone. He checked for his credit cards. They were there.

No real damage, only the money.

He then remembered that he had needed to pay Karim an extra two thousand pounds in cash for the girl.

The previous day's activities – and the evening's entertainment – flashed back. He had given his talk at the club and it had gone well; the Royal United Services Institute in Whitehall had hosted the seminar. These so-called Intelligence experts from London and the US had been putty in his hands. The lecture had been about how his old agency, the ISI, was still striving to achieve greater co-operation with the West in what they called 'The War on Terror'.

The War on Terror, kuffar donkeys! They don't know what real terror is. Yet.

He smiled when he thought about what he had actually achieved. He had always outschemed and outmanoeuvred them. He and his agency had actually duped the ever-gullible West and, with Allah's help, used the vast amounts of money donated by the US taxpayer to finance the establishment of the Afghan Taliban. *Of course, it was a war; they were right about that.*

But then, back in the eighties in Afghanistan, only the Saudis knew the truth. The West had actually paid for a religious war designed to bring about the global dominance of Islam and the suppression of every other religion, and that war would only end when all the kuffar were either dead or converted. It would rage until they had all left the house of Dar al-Harb (The House of War) and entered the house of Dar al-Salam (The House of Peace). It would end when the last Christian/Zionist Crusader army was defeated, and all mankind was united in glorious submission to Allah. Then there would be peace.

God had blessed him with a sacred task, and the time was fast approaching.

The blessed Koran allowed him dispensation when he was working against the satanic West. Taqiyya allowed him to indulge in non-Islamic practices, as long as they were used as a subterfuge to confuse Allah's enemies.

He smiled again. *He had enjoyed all the non-Islamic practices so far.*

He picked up his gold monocle and placed it over his weak right eye. On the pillow next to him was a clump of mousey dyed hair that he had ripped from the slut's head. He picked it up and gently felt its texture between his right thumb and forefinger. He felt himself hardening again: that gentle throb of power.

He remembered everything now.
The blonde.
He licked his lips.
She was perfect.
She was just as he liked them.

She had smiled as he approached her. She had gorgeous hair and a trim body, with pert breasts. She had been wearing, as instructed, a short black cocktail dress and spiked heels. He was fussy with his sluts. Captain Karim, the ISI staffer at the Pakistan High Commission, had done well in selecting her.

He remembered being slightly drunk but still confident in his ability to perform, He had recently reinforced that ability with a hundred-mill tablet of Syrian Viagra that he'd swallowed with his whisky. *He was going to enjoy this.* And then the role play began. *She had been such a good actress, demure and retiring one minute, sexy the next.*

Drinks followed: champagne for her, Black Label for him. Then some hot conversation and, finally, the journey to his room for the evening's climax.

She had stripped slowly, teasing.

Skirt first, revealing an expensive low-cut black basque that nipped in her slender waist and pushed her milky white breasts out towards him. Her perfect legs shone with high-cut black silk stockings.

She had then slowly turned her back to him and removed her lacy black thong, revealing a tight backside and a very dark-haired vagina. Then the rage he had been waiting for had begun.

"You cheap fucking kuffar slut," he had grunted, as he grabbed her and physically hurled her across the room. "You're not a proper blonde." He had torn at the blonde wig and ripped it from her head.

"And now you are going to fucking pay."

He had gripped her by the hair with his left hand and slapped her hard with his right. He had then pushed her over the bed and tied her hands with some leather tethers that he had attached to the headboard. He had picked up the riding crop and got to work on her useless, creamy-white kuffar arse.

He had been in a sexual frenzy by now.

She had started to cry.

He liked that.

"No, this has gone too far," she had whimpered.

"NOT FAR ENOUGH, YOU KUFFAR SLUT."

He had held her nose until she opened her bright red lips, and then deftly stuffed her discarded black knickers down her throat.

"NOW, BE FUCKING QUIET, YOU SLUT," he had whispered loudly into her ear.

Then he had begun with the riding crop as she started to gag.

He had thrashed her until he could see the first rivulets of blood escape from the marks he had made. After the frantic effort, just near-silence now, with only the slut's quiet sobbing, and his heavy breathing.

He had stopped to admire his work.

The milky white backside was now striped with the crop.

One of his better designs.

He had regained his breathing and looked down at himself.

He had been excited and ready to finish. He had pushed himself hard against her and whispered into her left ear.

"Now push back, you kuffar slut, or you'll get the crop again."

He had slowly pushed against her from behind, waited, and then smashed deeply into her.

She had cried out in pain as every bit of hate he had for the Western world and Western women was projected with force through his penis. He had emphasised his hate by punching her stomach, kidneys and back.

AHGGGGGG, as he had exploded up her.

YOU FUCKING SLUT.

The girl had been still and whimpering.

He had smiled and gone into the bathroom, to immediately wash off her kuffar stink. He had then phoned the High Commission, with the girl still silently crying in the background.

"Captain Karim, come and collect this piece of shit from my room. I've gone a little too far again, I'm afraid – so sort it out."

"Yes, sir. Does she need the hospital?"

"NO," he had barked. "Not this time, but she will need some extra money; it was a bit rougher than she thought it would be."

He had then paused and looked towards the girl. He had moved towards her, to make sure she could hear.

"Always tell them, Karim, that when these white sluts come for rough play, they should know that Pakistani officers play rough."

Now he had remembered everything.

Another excellent night out in London.

The approach of death had sharpened his appetites.

He liked blondes, and the sponsors could afford it. He didn't have long to wait. The target had been chosen, the planning had been done and the blessed cleansing was approaching.

Chapter Twenty-Two

London, M25. Two days later

Taff was driving, with Sam sitting next to him. They had left Repton Manor early, but not nearly early enough. The blue light on the van was still flashing and the magnetic signage they had attached said 'MEDICARE', but he sounded the siren only occasionally now. The novelty had worn off as he realised that heavy traffic during rush hour on the M25 does not simply dissolve on its application. One of the police cars also flashed on its lights sometimes, just to join in. The two armed-police intervention vehicles were providing an escort to Southampton and had been assigned more for the protection of the weapons and kit in the vehicle than the team's safety. Taff pushed the button to sound the siren again.

"For fuck's sake give it a rest, the lads are trying to get some kip in the back here," Jimmy Cohen said with a chuckle. "It's OK for you, mate, in the front with the lovely Boss Sam, but I'm stuck in the back with these two sleepy old bastards."

The three men were trying to get comfortable among the weapon bags and boxes that had been hastily loaded at the Manor.

"I resent that remark, you cheeky cockney twat," quipped Pat in his broad Yorkshire accent. "Veteran operators like me and the old shaky boats (SBS) guy are only conserving our energy for the mission."

"Enough of the 'old', Pat." Scottie joined in with his light Highland burr. "I think maybe experienced, good-looking fucker is probably a better description."

"Have you looked in the mirror lately, Royal? Gonna drop you off at Specsavers, old mate," Pat said with laugh. "What is it with ex-Marines? You are all victims of your own propaganda."

"What is it with gnarled, old, ugly Paras, Pat?" Scottie answered. "The Royal Marines only exist because paratroopers need heroes, too."

"Fuck right off," said Pat. Both guys grimaced as the siren sounded again, and there was a collective groan from the back of the van.

"Fuck that," said Jimmy. "Taff's new toy."

Taff spoke over his shoulder "Right, guys, I have done with this shit. Let's get our cop mates to make some progress."

He picked up the small handheld Motorola radio and talked to the police car in front.

"Hello Trojan Three, this is Spartan Zero Alpha, over."

"Trojan send," said a rather bored, detached voice from the dark blue BMW 530d in front of them.

"Spartan Zero Alpha. Can we use the hard shoulder to make some progress?" The voice on the other end of the radio brightened.

"Trojan. Sounds like a decent idea, I will get the clearance from the woodentops in Traffic. Give me two minutes."

"Spartan Zero Alpha, roger that, we'll wait out."

Taff turned to Sam, who was lost deep in thought.

"You OK, Samantha?"

Sam smiled. "Yeah, all good, just thinking about the immensity of this particular task."

"Yeah, we seem a bit undermanned for an MCT (Maritime Counter Terrorism) task, "said Taff.

"Yes, you're totally right. Have you ever been on anything this size?"

"No, I've been on a few tubs, but mostly small ones. The only time I've been even near one this big was on HMS *Ocean*, with Forty (40 Commando RM), and that was small compared to the size of this thing."

"Yeah, true fact: the *Queen Mary 2* is actually longer than the Empire State Building laid on its side."

"Where did you get that?" said Taff, not quite believing her.

"Trivial Pursuit, Genus 2008 Edition, and I've never been beaten." Sam smiled and slightly shrugged her shoulders.

"I know that from bitter experience." He returned the smile.

Sam flipped open the passenger mirror, ran her right hand through her hair and checked her lipstick. Taff looked across.

How could such a bright, beautiful, feminine, sexy girl be married to me?

His musings were interrupted as the brake lights of the police escort car in front flashed on as it came to a halt. The driver and passenger momentarily dismounted, and with a rapid slamming of doors swapped places.

"Looks like we got the OK, Sam,'" Taff said.

At that moment the car in front transmitted. They recognised the voice this time: it was Tony, the police team leader.

"Hello Spartan stand by! We have permission to use the hard shoulder."

"Roger that, TL," said Taff.

Tony turned on his flashing lights and siren and indicated left.

"Hey, and Taff, I'm driving," TL said. "So do try to keep up!"

"Cheeky fucker," grinned Taff, and spoke to the guys in the back of the vehicle.

165

"OK lads, strap in."

Pat, Scottie and Jimmy quickly organised themselves and moved from relaxed mode on the floor to strapping themselves into their seats.

"OK, here we go," said Sam, smiling.

They were making good progress now, with the 'blues and twos' on, as they raced along the hard shoulder. The vehicles still stuck in traffic on the inside lane blended into a continuous multicoloured streak as the team's vehicle hit a hundred. Sam felt the gentle pressure of the seatbelt push her into her seat as the van's V8 engine strained to keep pace with the faster lead vehicle. She caught the odd flash of an amazed face as the traffic thinned and they moved into the fast lane, overtaking cars that were already exceeding the speed limit. They were now hitting a hundred and ten, with the noise of the engine straining under the stress and making conversation difficult, but it gave Sam time to think.

Things just seem to be moving too fast for any really detailed planning. The team has just been swept along by the current flow of information.

She had always been a supporter of the military adage drummed into her by her instructors at Chicksands. The extremely grumpy sergeant majors of R Branch had called it "All the fucking Ps". They used it when the students, as they always do, fucked up on a training serial. That military mantra, embodying a soldiering truism, stood for:

Proper Preparation and Planning Prevents Piss-Poor Performance.

The team was, once again, just reacting to situations instead of getting time to plan for an operation. There was still a lot that she couldn't quite understand about the logic behind its latest deployment.

Taff may well be right: deploying the team on board was probably just government arse-covering. They were just one piece of a very large jigsaw puzzle before anybody really knew where it fitted. With the threat so high, so many options to cover, and not enough deployable assets to go around, HMG needed to be seen to be addressing the threat in some way. And the threat was incrementally increasing over time. British Jihadists were now beginning to creep back home after they had tasted blood in Syria and Iraq, though they didn't like the idea of shedding their own. Major terrorist plots were still being uncovered at an alarming rate. This was just one of many that had to be contained. Then, a bizarre thought: for a member of the public in a big city like London, Islamist terror attacks came along almost as often as red buses. If you missed the one meant for you, you could be pretty sure another one would be along soon.

Taff glanced out of the corner of his eye at a pensive-looking Sam.

"What's got you worried, Sam? Not my driving, I hope?"

"No, not that, Nigel." She always used his real name when she was in a contemplative mood. "I'm just trying to get a handle on what's happening, and why we've been deployed."

"And?"

"It's just HMG trying to cover all the bases, I think."

Sam looked over her shoulder and checked the team in the back. Scottie and Pat were locked in conversation, probably about rugby or a new weapon system. Jimmy, looking tense, was frantically tapping away on his MacBook Pro.

"What's happening, Jimmy?"

"I'm just taking another look at this USB Danny got from Tim."

"Any clues on the rationale behind this deployment on there?" Sam said.

"Yeah, this is excellent stuff, and everything we need on the computer investigative side to trace an onboard threat," Jimmy said with enthusiasm. "We need to chat soonest on the best way to employ this system, and we'll need the co-operation of Cunard straight away."

"I'll get everyone together for a briefing when we get on board. I'm glad we have something," Sam said loudly. "Because I'm beginning to think that, since Danny has a Baker Street address, Her Majesty's Government think that his guys can unravel riddles as easily as Sherlock Holmes."

"That's a roger," rebounded around the vehicle.

"Hey, but you know who also had a Baker Street address?" she said.

"No, but surprise me," said Taff.

"Well, it should be a sort of regimental history for you, husband of mine, as an SRR and ex-source handler. During the Second World War the SOE (Special Operations Executive) had an office at number 64."

Taff smiled. "Is that why Danny used the place?"

"No, I think it was just coincidence: right place, right time, and a good deal."

"Yeah, sounds right, Sam. Taff looked across at his wife.

She is smart. If anybody can lead it, she can!

One thing was true, though; this was an investigatory mission rather than a reactive one. If there was a terrorist bomb plot and they managed to uncover it, it would be the conventional security forces that dealt with it. But, if there was a bomb coming aboard, then the clock was already ticking.

Taff's thoughts were interrupted by the radio net.

"Hello Spartan Zero Alpha, this is Trojan Two." Sam picked up the Motorola handset; she recognised TL's voice.

"Send, Tony."

"Hi Sam. Whereabouts for the van switch?"

"I think we'll go for Green Three."

"OK."

He knew what Sam meant. The police escort would turn off their lights and sirens and melt back into the motorway traffic, allowing the team's van to acquire a change of identity before they rolled into Southampton docks. The black V8 van with the large magnetic MEDICARE sign provided excellent cover for speeding along motorways but would stick out 'like a set of racing dog's bollocks' around the terminal for a slower form of transport, and you don't get a much more relaxed form of transport than a Cunard ship. Every covert vehicle used by the MI5 units had alternative identities. The guys had already chosen the signage they needed. As the police escort peeled off, there was one last radio call from Tony in the lead Trojan car.

"Hello Sam, this is Tony. Good luck, guys."

"Roger that, TL, and thanks. OUT." And the team were finally unescorted.

Sam looked at the GPS, watched as the two small green dots of the escort vehicles sped away up the M3 motorway, and felt strangely alone.

"They were good guys to work with," she said to Taff.

"Yeah, top blokes," he replied, his ultimate accolade to other operators, as he picked up the radio handset and transmitted.

"Hello, all stations and Zero, this is Spartan Zero Alpha, from Blue Six to Green Three." The team would now take the A3025 towards Woolston and spot code Green Three. It was a quiet car park on a loop off the main road where the team could change the van's registration plates, switch the Medicare magnetic side panels and replace them with signs that read 'The Baggage Handling Company', featuring a local Southampton firm's logo and its real telephone number. When they eventually rolled into Southampton docks it would blend in with any other vehicles on the quayside.

Sam's iPhone tinged an alert and she glanced down at the screen. It was the GPS co-ordinate for the RV with Gavin, the Cunard security manager. It registered as a green dot on Google Maps. She tapped on the screen, enlarged the map and saw that the co-ordinate was just outside the main baggage terminal on the Cunard jetty. The phone then rang; Sam put it on speaker.

"Hi Samantha, guys, did you get that?" It was Gavin.

"Yeah, roger that, what about security at the gate?"

"All sorted," he replied confidently. "One of my Cunard vehicles will front you in and the barrier will be up."

Sam checked the GPS.

"Roger that, we are ten minutes out."

"Great stuff, look forward to finally meeting you. See you soon."

"Thanks, Gav." Sam ended the call.

She talked loudly so everybody could hear.

"Did you get that?" There was a positive response from all.

"We've got lucky with this guy, I think. I know him from Baggers (Baghdad) in 2006. He was in C Squadron (SBS)."

Taff knew of Gav Loach "If it's the same guy, he's a good bloke. He was C Squadron's sergeant major, then he ended up as the SBS major at DSF (Directorate Special Forces), I think." Sam looked again at Google Maps. "Did you know him personally?"

"No, just by reputation; we operated in different worlds then. We were working on surveillance tasks or covert OPs (Observation Posts), eyes down on some compound that was usually about to get visited by the door-kickers."

"Yeah, as you know, I was doing target packs for those strikes. It was an exciting time but stressful."

Taff smiled. "It was also a fucking scary time, especially just one-up and driving around Fallujah. I still don't know how the fuck we got away with it."

Sam's phone buzzed and she put it on speaker, it was Gav. "Hey guys, SITREP?" (the Army brevity code for 'Situation Report').

"That's us in five minutes," said Sam.

"Roger that, Sam, my guy is waiting. It's a white security van with a Cunard logo, the one that usually does the baggage inspections. It will take you straight outside the baggage processing hangar at the cruise terminal, and I'll see you there."

"Roger that."

Chapter Twenty-Three

Saturday, 4 September. Southampton Docks

The Cunard car flashed its lights as the team's van approached the main gate at Southampton docks. The team glided under the raised barrier and, as they entered the dockyard, got their first look at what they were supposed to be protecting. As they drove towards the Ocean Cruise Terminal the *Queen Mary 2* was preparing to dock and towered behind it. She was a beautiful ship of black-hulled steel, with a white superstructure and glistening glass. A modern cruise ship tends to look more like a floating hotel, but, design-wise, the *Queen Mary 2* was a transatlantic ocean-going liner. The expression 'Queen of the Sea' just about nailed it. She was little short of majestic.

"Look at that beauty," said Taff.

"Yes," said Sam, "that's the second-biggest ocean liner in the world and it was the biggest when they built it. It's thirty-one metres longer than the ill-fated *Titanic* and at nearly twice the tonnage. And before you ask, that's from Trivial Pursuit as well."

"Let's hope this one doesn't sink," said Taff. Sam smiled as they followed the Cunard car towards the Ocean Terminal.

"Best we ensure it doesn't, Nigel, as that's what we are getting paid for." Sam turned and looked back into the rear of the van. "Right, lads, we need to secure this ship as best we can. She sails tomorrow and the clock is ticking."

Sam was only too well aware of the problems involved in trying to ensure the safety of such a massive vessel.

The bigger the target, the harder it is to protect.

Conventional risk-management thinking sought to put consecutive layers of security around any significant target. It was called the 'onion-ring effect', and it ensured that the screening and checks started as far as possible from a terrorist objective. It usually worked well on a land-based high-risk facility, but wasn't quite as effective with a ship, as the nature of the intrusive security measures needed to make it work would be partly counterproductive. When you have up to 2,690 passengers, arriving with their baggage in a limited time window, the concept just doesn't work, and that was even without considering the two thousand-odd members of the crew recruited from maybe ten different countries. Sam had read the outline mission brief and therefore knew that the complexities were mind-boggling.

How do you monitor the movement of the crew when ashore? Do you search them when they come back aboard? Are the crew vetted and, if so, by whom? Even after the end of Covid some people still wear masks, so how do we run them through a photo recognition system? What countries do they come from? Have ISIS a footprint in their countries of origin? The missing tip of the nuclear device was portable and could be hidden in just about anything, from a suitcase to a crate of foodstuffs.

Sam spotted a group of vehicles outside the terminal. As the Cunard car guided the team towards them, she recognised Gav, waving from between two transit vans. She also immediately knew where the vans were from: dark blue V8s with high-speed Pirelli tyres doubled up at the rear, and they just screamed 'SBS' to anybody who had worked down at Poole.

"I bet that's the rest of our kit," said Taff.

"And I guess we have some playmates from the SBS," Sam said, as she turned around in her seat and made eye contact with Jimmy Cohen.

"Jimmy, check out what they've sent. Danny just said it was specialist equipment."

"Roger that. Sounds intriguing, Doctor Watson," said Jimmy, carrying on Sam's Baker Street theme in what, for a cockney lad, was a surprisingly convincing voice. "What we need, though, is not more fucking equipment, but information."

"That's a big roger." said Sam thoughtfully.

Southampton, the Ocean Cruise Terminal

Inside the van closest to Gavin, the ex-SBS major, the four younger SBS men were deep in discussion. They all looked cut from Gavin's own cloth. Major Tom Steel was leant forward, intently explaining a point. The 'Boss' of M Squadron had a tough-looking, weather-beaten face topped with collar-length sandy hair. He was a new type of SBS man, a former Royal Engineer officer from 59 Commando Squadron RE, who had begun the British Special Forces joint selection process at Hereford intending to join the SAS but had then opted for the underwater world of the Special Boat Service after qualification. He had been a diver in the Engineers and therefore had a deep love for the sea, but under it rather than on it. He had also run a counter-IED team in Helmand and was an acknowledged explosives expert.

Tom was explaining to his guys what he knew of the present mission and what he thought was happening. He usually had a knowing half-smile on his face, but today his countenance was solely business-like as he gave his team a quick 'heads up', in hushed tones, behind the blacked-out windows of the Transit. It had been a whirlwind couple of days for the counter-maritime terrorism experts of M Squadron, including a hectic round of 'threat' intelligence briefings from the spooks, the gathering and preparation of mission-related kit and an intense study of the ship's target pack (STP).

Luckily, the most recent STP on the Queen Mary 2 was only a year old. The last two days of operational preparation had culminated in a mad high-speed move down the motorway earlier that day with one of his lads, blue lights on, to get to the meeting quickly. He had thought the near-insane dash worth it, as it gave the guys the opportunity of an 'eyes-on' a prospective target and also a chance to meet the Spartan team, whom they might have to haul out of the 'deep and smelly'.

The four men in the V8 Transit represented the command element of the squadron. They only had another two days before they deployed to their 'Forward Operating Base' on the Royal Navy's latest and largest-ever aircraft carrier, the Queen Elizabeth, that was already deployed in mid-Atlantic. The mission had also been assigned two new Royal Navy Mark 4 Merlin and two Wildcat helicopters from the Commando Brigade Air Squadron.

As Taff pulled the team's vehicle up to where the two SBS vans were parked, Gav Loach rapped on the back door of Tom's van and the doors opened. Four men quickly jumped out, dressed in versions of the ubiquitous training rig of the SBS: dark blue swimmer-canoeist tracksuit smocks, jeans and KSB climbing boots.

All SBS men look just the same, thought Sam. *They are usually compact, broad-shouldered and smiling, which is unusual for some SF guys.*

Taff opened the driver's door as Sam opened hers.

"Fuck me, Taff, long time no see," said Tom Steel.

Taff's face lit up. "Great to see you, old mate. When was the last time, at KAF (Kandahar Airfield, Afghanistan)?"

"In the good old, bad old days, buddy."

"Hoofing times."

"Really hoofing times," Tom said, repeating the Marine-speak term.

Sam was well used to the tribal language created by Commando forces on a loose base of Royal Navy slang, but 'hoofing' was purely bootneck. Her father would have said 'wazzer', but now 'hoofing' was the ultimate word for excellent: a decent weapon was 'a hoofing bit of kit', or a good operator was 'a hoofing bloke'. At the other extreme, if a Marine Commando was downhearted, he was 'threaders'; if he was really fed up, he was 'harry threaders', to be exceeded only by the ultimate in depression, or 'harry turbo-threaders'. Sam was used to it now. Taff was pleased to meet his old comrade from down-range, so he was 'harry hoofers' and smiling broadly as he turned towards his wife.

"Sorry, Sam, I really should have introduced you first. Tom was with 40 Commando in Sangin (Afghanistan), digging out IEDs."

"Nice to finally meet you," said Tom, extending his hand towards Samantha. "I've heard a lot about you."

After a round of introductions Gavin spoke up. "Right, guys, we have to move on quickly here. I want to give you all an idea of the security set-up for the passengers and baggage. Put one of these on."

He handed out some orange Day-Glo jackets with 'Cunard Security' emblazoned across the back. "Not exactly fashionable, I know, but they're big on 'health and safety' here, lads. Don't worry about the staff inside – they're well used to the odd guided tour." He also handed them some dark blue Covid masks with the CUNARD logo.

"Luckily it's still official company policy, and it stops the crew getting too good a look at your faces."

"Every cloud," said Taff, and smiled as he put on his mask.

Gavin was confident. "OK, follow me and prepare to be impressed. This is a huge ship, but she will be crowded once the passengers start to embark. She's just arrived from a minor refit where she's had some cabin improvements, so we don't have to worry about people coming off. This is only our second crossing since Covid 19 and the new passengers don't board till midday, so we've got about two hours."

Gavin then turned and talked to Sam directly. "The pandemic last year gave Cunard time to organise a technical upgrade, both on the ship and shoreside. Take a look at the detection kit – it's probably the most advanced and secure baggage-handling system in the cruise industry. It's better than you get in most modern airports," he added with evident pride.

I bet Gavin has had something to do with putting this together, thought Sam.

The Ocean Cruise Terminal itself was impressive. Sam had failed to recognise just how big it was; it had seemed relatively insignificant compared to the size of the ship looming behind it. She looked up at the roof and tried to gauge the height. *Maybe twenty-five metres?* Stark white walls stretched up to a curved and shiny galvanised steel roof. It had a modernistic look. The cavernous domed building was already busy with employees making sure the mighty liner sailed on time. It rattled and hummed with the sound of forklifts and the occasional clink of metal on metal, accompanied by Cunard's version of lift music. Time was money in the cruise industry, and once the ship was secured alongside it needed to sail again within eleven hours.

Sam found herself looking up at the multi-skylighted roof and down at a vast expanse of polished floor. Seating and waiting areas, vending machines and small shops dotted the terminal. The baggage inspection system looked new, and similar to the sort found in any airport. Numerous conveyor belts looped and snaked all around the building from where she stood at the entry portal, converging separately on three sizeable electronic scanning, sniffing, and inspection machines. Passport Control, and the pedestrian gangway that would eventually be connected to the ship, were beyond that.

As the guided tour continued Samantha turned and looked back at Jimmy Cohen.

"What do you think?"

"Good kit, but not the best." Sam knew that Jimmy was the acknowledged expert on all things technical and had helped put together the security measures on the Gaza checkpoints during his time with Shin Bet.

"A company called Coniscan supplied the machines. It's reliable kit but it hasn't any radiological capacity; we will have to augment it with the kit from Poole."

"What about the facial recognition cameras?" Sam asked, talking over her right shoulder as she walked.

"Yeah, I know where some extra ones might be useful, but it depends on how many people decide to mask up. Could be a problem," he replied.

Later the same day, Queen Mary 2

The guided tour had progressed; Jimmy Cohen was giving a running commentary on the best locations for technical kit as Gav was doing his best to guide them around the biggest ship that Samantha had ever seen. It reminded her of being shepherded around the Natural History Museum when she had been at school. As they crossed the pedestrian bridge that now connected the ship to the terminal, Sam looked down at the bustling quayside and a thought occurred to her. It was swarming with workers in hard hats, driving bright yellow forklifts of various sizes and makes. All were loading the great Queen's provisions for the trip to New York into several different storage bays.

How much goes through a scanning machine? she thought. Sam raised her hand politely and gestured towards the quayside. "Gav, what's the score with checking the kit coming on board over there?"

Gav rubbed his chin in thought. "In all honesty, Sam, sketchy." He walked towards the nearest window, looked down at the quayside and frowned. "It's highly organised chaos down there before the sailing. It doesn't lend itself to a high level of security and there's very little we can do to improve it. The cruise business is exactly that – a business and a commercial enterprise, a money-making concern."

He pointed towards the frantic activity on the quayside. "OK Sam, here's the scale of the problem as it affects the integral security of the ship. You can hold the sailing up and search every passenger's bag twice, but what about the ship's provisions? The average sailing, for instance, gets through eleven thousand bottles of wine and four thousand litres of Pepsi and Coke. The passengers also chomp their way through ten thousand kilos of steak and chicken. To be brutally honest, we are just scratching the surface, with the occasional search as a visible preventative measure."

Gav stopped halfway down the corridor leading to the main atrium. "You'll need these, guys." He took a pile of door key cards from his pocket. "These are access passes for all areas of the ship and will open every room."

He handed them to all the team. He then took another thick pile and handed them to Major Steel. "These will make things much easier," he said with a smile. "Hopefully, they will stop your guys blowing off all the doors of my present employer's ship. Remember, I've done your job. 'P for plenty' to get the door down, but this will give you another option, maybe."

The guided tour then continued into the ship's largest and most magnificent space, the central atrium, a vast expanse of light and elegant furniture interspersed with Art Deco paintings, chandeliers and richly coloured carpets. The soft furnishings were of a similar style. Two elegant stairways, either side of the ship, swept dramatically upward. Shining plate glass enclosed the whole area, ensuring sea views. The place was still a work site, noisy with the steady rhythm of tapping, shouts, and the odd bang of a nail gun. It looked like groups of workers were frantically working to a deadline, trying to finish some trade stands.

"What's going on here?" Sam asked.

"They obviously haven't told you," Gav replied.

Sam looked perplexed. As she waited for Gav to begin his explanation, two uniformed Cunard crew members conveniently unfurled a large banner that now stretched across the stairwell. It simply said, 'Welcome to New York Fashion Week'.

"Gav?" Sam pointed to the banner.

"Yeah, sorry Sam, this further complicates things. This particular crossing happens every year. We dock in New York the day before the city kicks off its Fashion Week. It's an especially big deal this time round because it's the first one for two years that hasn't been a virtual event. It usually happens in February, but they've delayed it until now because of Covid. it's a real money-spinner for the ship and for New York. We have also over four hundred passengers solely from the fashion industry, including everyone from models to buyers; they have all been tested and will be Covid-free when they board. It's going to be a bit like a fashionistas' love fest for the next week, I'm afraid. You will see some of the top designers travelling as well."

Sam looked worried.

"You OK, Sam?" Taff said.

"No Taff, I'm not. I've brought nothing to wear," she said with a smile.

But the levity hid a more profound worry: she was appalled that, yet again, they had been caught flat-footed and forced to play catch-up. She was also annoyed that basic information had simply not been passed on. The most cursory check of the ship's itinerary would have highlighted that one.

In a way, it's an advantage, though. The demographics of passengers on a transatlantic crossing were often on the older side. The average person with both the disposable income and the time to cruise to New York was usually retired and sometimes in their seventies. A group of 'fashionistas', as Gav called them, would at least bring the average age down to a bit more like the team's.

"I suggest we look at where we are locating you guys first, and then we can maybe test and adjust," said Gav. "At the moment I have Sam and Taff in an outside cabin on the sixth deck as a husband and wife. Jimmy is in a staff cabin next to the main communication room as a Cunard technician, and Pat and Scottie I've augmented to my staff as ship's security officers. Your deep cover operative will be employed in the ship's stores. Any questions so far?"

"Just one more, Gav," Sam said, looking around at the ship. "Where has she just come from, and what did she have done in the refit?"

"Nothing too technical, Sam. The pandemic gave us a chance to redecorate and complete a general upgrade. The main rebuild was of one of the main restaurants called the Britannia Grill."

"Where did that happen?" Sam quickly asked.

"The yard that has the contract is the Blohm and Voss shipyard in Hamburg."

"Oh," said Sam, her face registering surprise. "Who looks after the ship's internal security when she's in refit?"

"They do."

Sam remained thoughtful; it was evident that Gav hadn't had access to the latest reports from MI6.

The German city of Hamburg had had a long and painful relationship with Islamic terrorism. The 9/11 attacks had been planned there, with one of the ringleaders, Mohammad Atta, having lived there along with the rest of the so-called Hamburg Cell. Things in the city had also got critical since the recent return of over three hundred Jihadi fighters from Iraq and Syria. The tentacles of the newly reorganised ISIS reached far beyond Hamburg's excellent transport links and now infected the rest of the world. Every current MI6 report on radical Islamism contained at least one mention of the place.

If there was anywhere on Earth where a device could be easily placed on board the QM2, it was Hamburg, thought Sam.

Chapter Twenty-Four

London

Eighty miles away, Mac McCann, the MI6 man and diplomat was staring out of the steamy, rain-streaked window of a London black cab. He held a large silver coin in his right hand, moving it swiftly on the outside of his fist from one finger to another, as if on remote control. He didn't even seem to be aware of it; it was Mac's way of concentrating. He looked at the rain-sodden, crowded pavements as busy people, shrouded and temporarily blinded by umbrellas, jostled and bumped as they competed for space. The heavy rain hammered on the cab's roof, drowning out the hum of traffic and the faint strains of Capital Radio from the confines of the driver's cab.

"That's a fucking miserable day," the cabbie said, a bit too loudly.

"Yeah," said Mac in an automatic response.

It is fucking miserable, this weather. It's still supposed to be summer.

He sometimes missed the warmth of the Middle East.

The weather anyway, not the complicated fuckers that live there.

Mac's mobile phone rang. He quickly checked the screen. *Talk of the devil.*

It was Sheikh Mohammad.

"Hi buddy, what's up?"

"Good afternoon, Habibi (friend). I need to get something to you, Mac." There was a pause, as though the Sheikh was thinking. "Do you remember Uncle Faisal's from the old days?"

"Yeah, certainly do. When?" said Mac.

'Uncle Faisal's' was the codeword they used for what was called, in intelligence circles, a brush contact. Faisal's was one that both men had used in the nineties, when they were on the same side against the Russians. In the old days the package would contain either microfilm or a comm. It was a really old-school method, but was still used sometimes. Before secure phone and computer messaging it had sometimes been the only way to ensure a tight circle of knowledge. The Provisional IRA had adopted the method when their leaders were banged up in the Maze prison, in Northern Ireland, during the 1970s and 1980s following internment They had wrapped their messages in twists of airtight cling-film and sealed them with a cigarette lighter, so the messages could be smuggled in the cheek of a loved one, or in a similarly intimate area, and eventually passed with a kiss at visiting time. Mac and the Sheikh preferred using something more hygienic and less intimate.

Uncle Faisal's was a brush contact using Edgware Tube station on the Northern Line of the London Underground. In the old anti-Soviet days, a suitably dressed Mohammad would enter the 'brush drop' through a screen of his own security guys and jump on the Tube to the next station, Burnt Oak. Mac would time it so that he would be walking down the stairs of the station as Mo was making his way up. The package would be palmed from one operator to the other with no words spoken or looks exchanged. It was old tradecraft, but it was effective and, if done properly, it kept the information tight and safely between the two of them.

"Let's make it soon," said Mo. "It's important you get this quickly."

"OK," said Mac. "Text me a time on my other means."

"OK, old chap," he answered, and immediately rang off. Mac switched lines and his phone tinged. The message simply said: *1130, just like the old days.*

Mac smiled, *I wish things were as simple as in the old days, mate, but they're a bit more fucking complicated now.*

VX, Two hours later.

Mac took the tiny USB stick from the Cohiba Siglo aluminium tube that had once housed a hand-rolled cigar.
He's still got expensive tastes. These are sixty quid a pop.
He also removed a roll of cling film. He carefully opened it with sharp scissors and removed the message, written on folded 'Rizla' cigarette paper in their agreed way. He just as carefully unfolded the paper and examined the tiny, delicately written script with a magnifying glass under a bright lamp. Classic Mo, it read:

> *Just for old times' sake, Habibi! Everything is on the USB stick. Just wanted to know whether you remember life before the Internet. I will text you the encryption code as soon as you text me. May Allah and his Angels protect you and your operators.*

Mac smiled, quickly plugged the stick into his MacBook Pro via the USB cable to speed-read the text. He could tell by the poor grammar that it was a Google translation, but the meaning was crystal clear. It was an ISI document that had been passed to the Qataris.

It was a report on the stolen or missing Vengeance 4 warhead. The circumstances of the loss were as dryly described as if they had mislaid a pair of army binoculars. There was a long diatribe on accountability issues and a report from a board of inquiry. The ordnance had last been seen in 2014, and Mac let out an involuntary groan as he realised that this deadly threat to his country had been missing for seven years. He knew from his time with the Mujahideen that sometimes military hardware went missing via the Pakistani Army.

They thought Admin was a province in China, but losing a nuclear weapon, and not realising it, now that was taking lousy admin to the max; that was just careless!

There was also a list of Pakistani Army personnel that had had access to the device over that time frame. It was a very long list, seemingly endless, ranging from low-ranking logistic guys to very senior officers. The index was compiled in alphabetical order, but it was the Pakistani alphabet, and that didn't quite work with Google Translate. Mac started to scan the list by rank, the most senior military first, and a name he knew from Afghanistan's bloody past just popped out at him:

Brig Abdul Haq of the ISI.

Mac knew the guy; he had been the ISI liaison officer to Gulbuddin Hekmatyar during the time Mac had spent in Panjshir as the MI6 liaison officer with Ahmad Shah Massoud. Hekmatyar had been the most bloodthirsty of all the Islamist commanders ranged against the Soviets, and he had probably killed more Afghans than even they had.

Well, well, well, it's Major Abdul! The murderous bastard! The fucker of Farkhar. Long time no see!

That was the nickname that he and his MI6 colleagues had given the ISI man, and Mac in particular had a personal loathing for him. Major Abdul, as Brigadier Haq had been known then, had organised the murder of thirty of Massoud's top commanders at an ambush spot in what was called the Farkhar Gorge, forty-five miles from the Soviet border. The ISI officer had supervised the killing and finished off the many wounded with a personal touch: an individual bullet to the head.

If this mad bastard is in any way involved in this attack, we have a very serious problem.

Mac also knew that Major Abdul had had a phobia about having his photograph taken. What they needed was the co-operation of the ISI. Could they be pressured at governmental level into handing over his most recent ID card photos or biometric details? Mac didn't think it was at all likely. Islamist radicals had infiltrated the ISI at almost every level, and they would do their best to protect him. Mac knew that, without data for the facial recognition cameras, *it will be like trying to identify a ghost!*

Monday 6 September. Queen Mary 2, At Sea

Brigadier Abdul Haq observed the strange reflection looking back at him. He was attempting to shave as the *Queen Mary 2* ploughed through an increasingly heavy Atlantic swell. Curiously, the person who mirrored his every action looked nothing like his normal self. The thin, longish, grey, brushed-back mane and neatly clipped military moustache were gone. The hair now was close-cropped, US style. His favourite gold monocle had also gone. He put on his thick-framed light blue Armani spectacles, looked at the man staring back at him and smiled at the absurdity of it. A set of gleaming Hollywood teeth beamed back at him.

The bleached teeth summed up all he hated about the venality of the Western world, but they served their purpose: he looked typically American. He was much thinner in the face, too, although he realised that this had more to do with the aggressive form of cancer attacking his pancreas than the excellent disguise.

He also knew that all his background was checkable, with an elaborate, detailed digital cover story of lies in place to protect him and the operation. He had committed the backstory to memory, as he had done on many occasions in the past.

In the event, the Immigration official had accepted his passport without comment, his biometric data had checked out flawlessly, and his baggage from the hotel had arrived safely and was waiting for him in his cabin. He had worn a 'stars and stripes' Covid mask while boarding, which further disguised his identity from the all-intrusive face-collecting cameras. The mask was no longer mandatory, but it was very convenient. He had selected a Second Deck Britannia Premium Balcony Stateroom for a reason. It was on the lowest level of accommodation above the waterline, the one area of the ship guaranteed to cause the most damage on the initial detonation of the warhead.

He locked the cabin door to check whether the device was there. His heart was in his mouth as the new resident of cabin 2004, port side, Deck 2, took a medium sized flat-headed screwdriver from his computer bag and quickly removed the small Art Deco-style panel from the wash basin in the cabin's en suite bathroom. There, concealed in the dim recess under the sink, was the same Louis Vuitton trunk that he remembered from home; crammed in alongside were the three sealed waterproof packages he had also expected to find. He removed the three small parcels and weighed them in his hand; he knew what he had ordered and hoped they had got it right. He placed the packages in the bedside cabinet and then unpacked his clothes. He looked at the suitcase.

I won't need it for the return journey; this is the ultimate one-way trip.

The weapon he had removed from the panel was much heavier than he remembered it. The most recent terrorist technology had weaponised the plutonium core and trigger that he had stolen in Pakistan. The device had copied the design of the EFPs (Explosively Formed Projectiles) that had made moving in vehicles such a deadly hazard during the Iraqi insurgency. The Iranian Quds Force had developed them and tested them on the Israelis, and then given them to Hezbollah and the Iraqi insurgents.

The weapon had been made in laboratory conditions in Pakistan, and he knew its construction had been hugely expensive. It was heavier than he remembered because of the ten kilos of Semtex explosive packed behind the finely machined concaved copper plate on the bottom of the device. The plutonium tip and trigger of the stolen tactical missile were above it, constrained by a titanium steel plate with its complete coded firing chain. The technicians who had constructed it knew that two things would happen when it was triggered. The shaped Semtex charge would cause a superheated molten slug to tear through the hull of the ship at sea level, while simultaneously slamming the trigger of the plutonium core and igniting a limited nuclear detonation.

The tactical nuke itself had been designed to obliterate a full armoured division of the Indian Army while on the move. Abdul Haq thought it more than enough to get the job done, but even if the nuke failed to detonate the radiation generated would probably kill everybody on board anyway.

The prospect did not perturb him at all. After all, innocent people died during any war. What did the US and UK call it? *Collateral Damage*. Well, this was the Holy War between Islam and the Infidel, and the majority of the dead would be unbelievers. All he had to do was stick to the plan; Allah would give him the strength he needed to see it through. He had had no nerves when he had boarded the ship at Southampton. Acting is always part of the spying game, and Abdul Haq had always been a consummate actor. He had played many roles, and now this, his last one, posing as a wealthy Asian-American businessman, wasn't a problem. His passport was faultless and had been issued in New York in the name of

James Singh, a name he had chosen carefully. There are thousands of people called Singh in the New York telephone directory.

In New York there are nearly as many Sikhs called Singh as there are Jews called Cohen.

The Queen Mary, Deck 8, Cunard offices. The same time.

Jimmy Cohen's face was illuminated by the glare from the screen of his MacBook Pro; it gave it an almost translucent glow. He was making the most of the high bandwidth in the Cunard communications room. The sharp brown eyes blinked behind his glasses as he scrolled intently through all the matches that the CIA Expressway software had just produced. He had fed over four thousand names into the software in dumps of raw data, and now he had over two hundred back. All the people on the list were probably there for a reason.

Palantile Expressway was a US software, so there were some weird anomalies. For instance, anybody with even the most tenuous links to Russia or Cuba would also be listed. He mentally sifted the names and quickly discounted the obvious, but then reconsidered, and sometimes put some of them back into the mix.

Nothing in the world he inhabited was that easy to solve. A self-evident truth was sometimes expertly hidden within a believable lie.

But soon a discernible pattern emerged. The commercial imperative guaranteed that a proportion of the ship's crew was recruited from some of the poorest countries on earth, several of which had problems with radical Islam. Jimmy cross-referenced again, using countries that did have such problems, and the list of possible suspects dropped to about fifty. He then extracted these names and put them through the next level of scrutiny. The names that the system would spit out would be people that might have links with any terrorist organisation. Arabic names were sometimes generational in the same tribe, while some Afghans, especially Tajiks, only used one name. He also knew that the security checks used by commercial recruitment agencies for the maritime industry could be somewhat perfunctory.

It was more about 'bums on seats' than security concerns.

He would now sift the final list until he only had the potential suspects in the right combination of demographics and threat profile, with possible motivation and access. Thousands of names of ISIS members had been found during the closing stages of resistance in Iraq, and all that data was on the CIA system.

The system also sifted and isolated any unrecorded mobile phones or burner phones used by terrorist groups during attacks, as well as the software to track those individual phones, once activated. The other software supplied on the USB stick also gave all of the team's phones fully interactive holographic maps of the interior of the Queen Mary 2, allowing the tracking of any other phone traced by link analysis to any other suspect phone.

***

Tuesday 7 September. The bridge of HMS Queen Elizabeth, Mid-Atlantic

It was the forenoon watch. The sea moved in an oily, grey, undulating motion that scarcely affected the grey bulk of the carrier. On the fore bridge Lieutenant Ted Pemberton gazed at the plot table, which seemed strangely archaic compared to the vast array of computer screens and flashing lights along the inside of the main tower. The Royal Navy still insisted that all functions could still be replicated in the old ways, in case of cyber-attack, and the plotting of a course in the old manner of seamanship was part of this functional 'belt and braces' approach.

He glanced across at the club-swinger, as naval PTIs are known, at the helm of the newest and most expensive ship the Royal Navy possessed. The Navy's attitudes, as much as its equipment, had changed in recent years. CPTI 'Smudge' Smith, his usual training partner in the gym, had the helm, and calmly controlled the vessel as if he were at the console of some giant gaming machine. The massive wipers rhythmically swiped to clear the three-metre-high armoured glass that jutted inward like the front of an aircraft control tower. It was raining hard, but when the glass cleared he could see the top of the front ski ramp shudder, almost imperceptibly, as an increasingly angry Atlantic made its presence felt.

"What's the Met like for later, Chief?" Ted asked his watch partner. He was usually careful to use rank on the bridge; the informal use of forenames was left in the gym.

"Not good, sir," said the PTI, playing the same game. "We are at Force Six, sir, expecting worsening conditions up to Force Ten for the next three days."

"Force Six, but you wouldn't know it, would you, Clubs?" Ted smiled. The rank formality had gone for a minute; his last ship had been a small minesweeper, and the smaller the ship in the Royal Navy the more relaxed was the atmosphere between ranks.

"No sir, not even the Atlantic can throw Big Lizzie around," Smudge said proudly.

Three decks below, in the Captain's day cabin, his steward had awakened Captain Jeffrey Childs, at 0100 hours, with a 'Secret UK Eyes 'FLASH'' message from Northwood, the bunkered control centre in North London that controlled Britain's nuclear deterrent and its military operations.

It simply read:

070921 07 SEP ZULU

FLASH

FM C IN C FLEET TO HMS QUEEN ELIZABETH

SECRET UK EYES

A. ORDERS/CAT A/IMMEDIATE ACTION.

B. SPECIAL FORCES INTERDICTION. C. HMS QUEEN ELIZABETH.

1. 1. 1. ASSIST PRIORITY SPECIAL FORCES MISSION

2. 2. 2. M SQUADRON SPECIAL BOAT SERVICE WILL ARRIVE YOUR LOCATION AT 03.30H

3. 3. 3. 30 PAX

4. 4. 4. 2 X MK 4 MERLINS, 2 X WILDCAT.

5. 5. 5. INBOUND YOUR LOCATION

6. 6. 6. WILL PROVIDE INTERDICTION ON TARGET.

7. 7. 7. PLEASE PROVIDE THEM ALL ASSISTANCE.

8. 8. 8. MATTER OF NATIONAL SECURITY.

9. 9. 9. STAND BY FOR RED PHONE COMMS AT 0200

10. 10. 10. HMS QUEEN ELIZABETH TO APPLY AN EXCLUSION ZONE TO TARGET OF A MINIMUM OF 100 NAUTICAL MILES.

The Captain was intrigued by the last part of the message. Conventional air ops always tried to get the platform, in this case his new ride, the largest and newest ship in the Royal Navy, as close to the target as possible. The only caveat to that would be if there were a 'significant level of danger' to his ship. He would know more after he had spoken directly to C-in-C Fleet.

I wonder what they are up to at Northwood? he thought.

Chapter Twenty-Five

Queen Mary 2, Cabin 2004, Britannia Suite, port side. Same day, 12.30 hours

Abdul Haq had always understood the way the Great Game was played. He knew that a real secret could only remain so within an accountable and tight circle of knowledge. Therefore, somebody else, not he, had chosen the sleeper unit of 'clean skins' aboard the *Queen Mary 2*. It was important that no one person had a complete picture of who was involved, and that made it the ultimate closed cell operation. The dormant terror cell was still needed, even though thousands would die when the actual device exploded.

The brigadier understood how terrorism worked. To be really successful, a ship hijack had to be seen to cause fear. The unholy trinity of terror was made up of three distinct elements: first, the act; second, the effect, and third, the audience. It wasn't enough just to kill three thousand humans with a bomb; after all, that had already been done before. It was more important that the ship attack dealt as much death as possible and was at the same time internationally visible. It needed to be recorded by terrified passengers and then immediately shared on social media. There must be blood. There must be visible and spectacular carnage. That is why he had instructed some of the attackers to use large knives.

The cell itself was to be activated using the 'reverse pyramid' method, from the top down. The brigadier would trigger the four principal cell leaders just four hours before the intended assault. He, Abdul Haq, only knew the names and contact method. The cell leaders, in turn, knew only the names of the next level of ASU leaders, who would be activated via a memorised codeword on a secure email channel. They would then organise their teams in the same way. All this would be finally confirmed by a simple password. This method of sequenced activation kept the circle of knowledge tight. The attack would be the Islamist equivalent of America's 'shock and awe' during the Iraq war of 2003. He smiled.

The carnage would indeed be shocking, and its shockwaves would reverberate throughout the kuffar world. It would be this one action that would finally cause the religious conflagration that his sponsors intended.

Haq opened the bedside cabinet drawer and took out the three small packages. He removed the green waterproof outer cover from the first one and carefully checked the wrapped brown paper; it had been sealed with six sequentially numbered clear plastic security seals, still all intact. He opened the package and removed an American-made Vipertek VTS-880 stun gun. It was a small black rubber and plastic box with two metal prongs that was capable of stunning an assailant for between three and six minutes. The ageing soldier was now too old and far too sick for fighting but, if he needed to, modern technology could give him the edge.

He unwrapped the second package, secured in the same way. It was his other piece of personal protection equipment, but this one was smaller and much deadlier. He opened the sealed cover, removed a bubble-wrapped envelope and tipped out the contents. What seemed like a jumble of spare parts of various sizes tumbled onto the Cunard Logo on the bed like bits of a dangerous jigsaw puzzle. The 'puzzle' was the standard ISI assassination gun. It had been commissioned and custom-made in a small workshop in the Pashtun Pakistani village of Darra Adam Khel.

The old man's hands moved quickly as he reassembled the weapon; he had trained himself to do it blindfold. He started with the lightweight plastic frame, with the skeleton pistol grip and trigger mechanism, and finished with the finely-machined tubular steel barrel. He finally screwed the reinforced plastic and rubber suppressor onto the end of the barrel, inserted a clear plastic magazine with nine rounds of adapted ammunition and pushed it home with a satisfying click. The bullets had been hollowed at the end to cause maximum damage and tipped with mercury: the classic dumdum round.

He picked up the last and most important package, opening the outer cover to reveal another bubble-wrapped envelope, and again emptied the contents onto the bed. A rather tatty-looking iPhone fell onto it, along with a wall charger with a SIM card stuck to it and sealed under clear Sellotape. He needed to programme it. He picked up the handset, opened the holder, inserted the SIM and plugged the iPhone into the wall.

He went to the screen and selected the Callbot automated dialling app, which allowed him to programme the time of 'ground zero'. He set it to 08.30 on the eleventh of September 2021, EST (Eastern Standard Time). The phone would send out an encrypted signal to detonate the device, along with the coded numbered sequence for the dual-time multi-frequency circuit board on the bomb. The little receiver inside the device would set the firing chain for the warhead and simultaneously send an electric charge to the military-grade detonator, which would send the 'tac' supercritical, and into fusion.

It would also allow him to use the phone as a remote detonating device if his plans changed and he needed to explode it early.

In the Great Game you have to think of every possibility.

Whether things go to plan or not.
This alarm call will wake the world.

At that exact time, another player in the Great Game detected an audible bleep in his laptop's headset. Jimmy Cohen picked up the Motorola handset lying beside him.

"Hello Sam, this is Jimmy."

"This is Sam; send."

"We've just pinged an unregistered iPhone."

"Roger that. Can we get a fix?"

"I'm working on it," Jimmy said, as he started to download the updates on the ship's computer system to allow the trace. Every phone currently on board was traced and recorded on the Panantile Expressway system. Any unregistered phone could automatically be monitored, along with any other phone that was linked to it. The iPhone showed up as a red dot on the 3D computer graphic that was now on Jimmy's laptop.

"Did you get that?" said Sam.

Taff noticed that Samantha's face suddenly seemed almost waxen, and she appeared to struggle with the next sentence as her conversation trailed off, almost to incoherence. She suddenly stopped and sat down heavily on the bed. She was worn out, having hardly slept since they had boarded the ship. Taff stopped what he was doing. She seemed to be a bit lost, ashen-faced and gently rocking, as if she were struggling to stay upright.

"You don't look well, darling. Seasickness? You OK?"

The room spun around her and she felt nauseous. The ship was encountering a slightly heavier sea than usual, but the stabilisers made the movement almost imperceptible. The *Queen Mary* wasn't just a cruise ship; she was an ocean-going liner designed specifically for Atlantic conditions.

"Nope," said Sam. Her answer trailed off and she sprinted towards the cabin's bathroom. Taff followed towards the retching sound. Sam was doubled over the sink, straining.

"Hey, darling." Taff's concern mirrored itself in his voice. He moved into the en suite and behind Sam. She felt his strong hand gently massage her tummy as it continued to spasm. "I'll get you some seasick pills. They should settle your stomach."

"I don't think seasick pills are going to cure this one, Nigel," said Sam, as she started to run the taps to clear away the debris. "This has happened a few times now, and well before we boarded."

Taff looked puzzled. "Before?"

"Yes, husband of mine," Sam smiled. "And it's been happening mainly in the morning."

Taff suddenly realised what she meant.

Chapter Twenty-Six

Wednesday 8 September

Sam's head was spinning, and the morning sickness didn't help. Although she was pleased that she had another chance of a baby, it couldn't have come at a worse time. The team had hit this task at only one speed and that was flat out. The ship itself provided the biggest learning curve, with a never-ending series of challenges. The liner had over twenty decks enclosed in its 345 metres crammed full of passengers and crew. It was a major task just to navigate from one part of it to another, and the team had spent the first few days simply finding their way around.

Even with Cunard sticking to its two-metre Covid spacing rules, the company had still managed to sell over 1,500 tickets for the trip to New York. The present clientele on board had further complicated things: the fashionistas had a habit of bunching together at the most inconvenient times, and Sam had sometimes found herself in the middle of some bizarre situations and even more deranged conversations.

Certain things had to be right if they were to keep the ship safe. The absence of the normal can sometimes indicate the abnormal, but at the moment, it was hard to gauge what normal was. Sam had delegated tasks throughout the team. Scottie and Pat were assessing the ship as SBS liaison officers, while Jimmy was handling all the technical stuff and linking with Ricky in his role as the DCA. Taff was liaising with Gav and trying to work out how everything meshed together. The ship normally had a two thousand plus crew from twenty-seven different countries and some had been security vetted, but others hadn't; it was a complicated situation that technical means alone couldn't unravel.

Ricky had found the situation just as confusing from his first day onboard. The perspective that had worked so well for him in prison, where he could just take a step back and get an overview, had proved impossible. The situation below decks was totally different, a self-levelling ecosystem. A cruise ship provided a microcosm of the consumer society in the twenty-first century. The mostly rich Westerners waited in comfort on the upper decks while the rabbit warren of corridors below constantly teemed with waiters, maids and cleaning staff suppling their every need. It reminded him of the colonies of worker ants on those wildlife shows, just non-stop organised action, fed by need. The need was for Cunard to make a few quid, while supplying jobs for the mostly third-world staff below to enhance the already privileged lives of the wealthy above. He had had no time to plan how he was going to achieve his mission. Everybody on the staff had specific tasks; he was literally learning on the job and the days had flashed by in a blur.

In his carefully crafted and rehearsed legend he was a junior stores assistant with only two years' experience at sea. His previous work record had placed him on a ship called *Stena Britannica* that had ploughed the choppy seas from Harwich to the Hook of Holland, and before that as a computer assistant at the Amazon depot in Balham. A good cover story or 'legend' stays as close as possible to the truth, to ensure both plausibility and continuity.

He was well rehearsed in its intricacies and thought that it would hold water. He also knew that he had the other option of telling over-enthusiastic enquirers into his past to *'just fuck off'*, as would ninety-nine per cent of people, if asked probing questions.

On his first few days his task was to do just what he had done in prison: keep his mouth shut and his eyes open and wait until he could work out the internal dynamics of the crew. He was confident in his abilities and those of his operational controller, Jimmy, who was his vital link back to the others. Contact between the two was made via electronic means, with a nondescript burner phone and the Telegram app that worked on a one-to-one basis, even out of reach of land-based networks. Jimmy had trained him in all the TECHINT he needed.

His new job was complicated and based below decks in the high-tech stores complex, with an official title of Trainee Inventory Controller. His workplace was where all the items necessary for a successful Atlantic crossing were stored. There was an eye-straining labyrinth of shelves that glowed with recessed LED lighting; it included everything from a can of beans to a bottle of champagne, and everything technical from a light bulb to a spare computer modem for the ship's propulsion units. Everything was numbered, recorded and accounted for. The initial training period had helped the process and being part of an Islamist organisation inside one of Her Majesty's prisons had honed his instincts. Gaining access to Islamist fellow-travellers was all about non-verbal communication and tiny visual clues.

Ricky still wore the close-cropped beard worn by the majority of the younger Muslim guys inside, and a shirt with the top collar button secured at the neck, a non-verbal signal to all that *"I'm a God-fearing, modest man"*. The button was also where he had secured the tiny pin-sized lens linked to his phone's camera. He was tasked to photograph as many of the below-decks crew as possible, and the golden opportunity to use the kit on a possible POI (Person of Interest) came quickly.

It had been on his first day at work. As his supervisor counted items, he used the Cunard issue iPad to check the inventory with another staff member. The conversation suddenly stopped as a stocky-looking figure dressed in white entered the stores space, and the two others working with him eyed each other nervously.

They're worried. Ricky picked up the vibes immediately.

There is something strange about human instinct, probably inherited from primeval times, that sensation where the hairs on the back of your neck prickle, and Ricky's previous lifestyle had subconsciously encouraged him to develop it. As soon as he spotted him, he knew that the big guy was trouble. There was something strangely familiar about him: he way he walked, the slight swagger of a former boxer, an air of menace. *It takes one to know one.*

It was only a glance between the two as the guy moved through Ricky's workstation, an almost imperceptible piece of non-verbal communication that was mutually recognised. The big man, a Filipino, gave him a long, hard stare and brushed past as he stock-checked the food inventory in the close confines of the Deck One stores complex. The Cunard issue iPad was forgotten as Ricky considered his response. The sensible thing would be to just try to find out who the guy was and then look at the options. *But that was what sensible people do! The chance of an ID pic may never come up again. I need a photo!*

It was a gutsy decision, what surveillance operators call 'going in hard'.

Ricky pressed the amulet under his shirt, put the camera on 'record' and walked after the guy that had brushed past him.

"Hey!" He sounded confident. "What's with the big hard stare, buddy? Do you know me?"

The older and larger man was temporarily put out; in his country, younger men kept their distance and had some respect for their elders. He was quiet for a moment as he gathered his thoughts; his English was good, though not fluent, but 'cheeky' was the same word in both languages.

"You talk, cheeky boy?"

"Yes, I fucking talk, buddy, I just thought you might know me. Do you?"

"No, and it's best for you that I don't," the big guy growled threateningly.

"OK, no offence meant." Ricky knew he had pushed his luck too far as he turned quickly and went back to his workstation. As soon as the large Filipino had cleared the workspace, he asked the question. "Who was that?"

The supervisor was a middle-aged Indian guy who wore a dark blue Cunard-issue turban and spoke with a London accent.

"He's trouble," he simply said. "You should have left him alone. We do."

"Who is he, though?" Ricky pressed another button inside his right-hand trouser pocket that sent an alert signal to Jimmy and recorded the conversation.

"He's a nasty bastard. He runs the Muslim prayer groups, and he hates Sikhs." He gestured towards himself and the other, younger, Indian guy.

"Why don't you complain to HR?" Ricky felt a tremor from the iPhone in his pocket that meant that Jimmy was on the case.

"Listen very carefully, young man," said the supervisor. "If you don't want trouble on this ship, remember that the Western world is confined to the upper decks. Down here we don't make trouble. The Atlantic is a big ocean and it's a long swim back to London."

"OK, thanks for the advice." Ricky was thoughtful.

Probably not a good move!

***

Same time, mid-Atlantic. HMS Queen Elizabeth

"Who are they?" a pretty, dark-haired sailor and Aircraft Handler said to her immediate superior.

"Ask me one on sport, Tania; we're chock-heads and therefore the mushroom element on this ship: always fed on shit and kept in the dark. But they do look like scary fuckers."

The killick (corporal) was amazed at the four semi-inflatable housing modules that had sprung up overnight in the previously empty hangar. The modules themselves were large structures, maybe twenty feet high, used for humanitarian missions, but they were dwarfed by the sheer size of the space they inhabited. The cavernous aircraft hangar, lined with shiny steel gantries, was now providing accommodation and briefing rooms for M Squadron of the Special Boat Service. Moving around outside the housing modules were SBS guys checking their equipment. He had been in the Royal Navy long enough to know the difference between a standard SA80 A2 assault rifle, as used by regular troops, and the kit that these guys had. He turned to Tania, stepped closer in a conspiratorial gesture and said quietly, "Special Forces of some sort, SAS or SBS is my guess, and they've arrived in two new Merlin Mark 4s with a couple of 'brand spankers' Wildcat Mark 2s during the middle watch, at about zero three hundred. I'm thinking, my lovely," he continued in an exaggerated West Country pirate accent, "we are going to be working with the SBS for a while."

Two SBS men were working together checking kit. Davey Slater was Billy Ford's sergeant and had also been best man at his wedding. The rank structure in the SBS was always fluid and sometimes non-existent: as long as you knew your job and knew who was in charge when it all 'went noisy', that was always the main thing. They worked sat opposite each other on a wooden table in the buddy-buddy way, checking the equipment that they would be using. In the SBS you checked each other's kit; it was a military thing. Davey was inspecting Billy's FRIS (Fire Retardant Immersion Suit), made of a black waterproof and fireproof Nomex material. Davey examined Billy's, and *vice versa*. Both had the suits turned inside out, checking the integrity of the glued seams. In the SBS you always tended to care more about your oppo than you did about yourself, so swapping equipment when conducting pre-operational checks made perfect sense.

These suits were what an MCT operator fought in. They were an expensive bit of kit but, even at about two grand a pop, they were still prone to the odd imperfection around the seams and the large nylon zips. A leak was not good news if you were overboard, treading water, wearing your body armour and carrying weapons, while trying to survive in the cold oily grey of the Atlantic. The FRIS went over your warmers kit, and your lightweight body armour and ammo vest went over that. Each operator then carried his primary weapon, depending on the task, a Glock 19 pistol as a secondary weapon, ammo for both, and any MOE (Method of Entry) kit that he needed, including some small explosive charges for opening doors in a hurry. Two other methods of achieving the same thing lay on the ground next to them: a 14lb sledgehammer, bought in

B&Q at Poole, and a sawn-off Remington pump-action shotgun firing a wax and lead solid shot called a 'Hatton Round' to open stubborn doors. The guys nicknamed it 'the Barclaycard', after an old TV advert claiming that 'Barclaycard can get you anywhere'.

Everything was checked meticulously. Another four-man team were at the very end of 'Big Lizzie's 260-metre flight deck, zeroing weapons. They sheltered in the windbreak caused by the flight ramp that the *Queen Elizabeth*'s twelve F35B Lightning II STOVL (Short Take Off and Vertical Landing) fighter aircraft needed to be able to use the carrier. They were in the prone position, firing off the end of the ship and zeroing their ACOGs (Advanced Combat Optical Gunsight) attached to their Diemaco Colt C4 assault rifles. There wasn't a lot of noise, just the occasional low sharp sound like that of an air rifle, as the red dots steadied, and well-aimed double taps struck the cardboard targets.

Some interested naval ratings looked on from the main hangar, trying to work out what was happening aboard their beloved new warship. They were looking at the SBS men who were working with the pilots and crewmen around the two smaller Wildcat helicopters. They were from a part of the SBS known as the Counter-Terrorist Wing or CTW. They made up a kind of Close Quarter Battle training cadre for the men at Poole and also tested new kit and trialled other specialised equipment. A sergeant called Bill Duff and one of his men had been nominated as helicopter snipers. They would be the first guys on target, hovering either side of the ship and protecting the other fire teams as they roped down.

Each would use the new H&K L129A1 Sharpshooter rifle with an ACOG sight that utilised a red-dot sight system. The weapon would use frangible ammunition, designed to kill an enemy but not to penetrate the steel superstructure of a target vessel. Their sniping platforms would be the two new Westland Wildcat helicopters that they stood beside. One of his men held what looked like an outsized 'gangster-like' Tommy gun. It was the ARWEN riot control gun, which gave the teams the ability to fire a 37mm gas grenade onto or into any part of a ship.

Inside one of the inflatable housing modules, two young SBS operators were sitting down in front of a computer console and appeared to be playing video games. They both wore Lenovo holographic VR headsets and held Logitech Freedom joysticks. They were rehearsing their mission using a 3D holographic computer simulation of the inside of the QM2, supplied by the IT specialists of the Int Corps and 30 Commando Royal Marines. Major Tom Steel entered the inflatable room and tapped one of the lads on the shoulder. He was, at that time, deeply engrossed in moving his suitably armed avatar up the right-hand staircase of the rather stately central atrium of the virtual QM2.

"Whoa, what the fuck?" was his instinctive response to the hand that had suddenly snatched him from his digital world. He raised his goggles and smiled.

"Fuck me, Boss, give me a break, I nearly crapped myself there," he said, as he recognised his squadron commander.

"Sorry, Billy," said Tom, with a chuckle, "I'm in a rush, mate, and need to know if this new-fangled shit 30 Commando Int cell supplied is working for you."

"Yeah, it's good stuff," said Ronnie, the other guy inside the same holographic image of the QM2, as he removed his headset.

"OK, Billy," said Major Steel, as he placed the other headset on his head and sat down, "take me from the RDP (Rope Down Point) on Aft Deck C to your primary objective." He paused. "And then you, Ron, you take me to the secondary objective and the Emergency RV." Another pause. "And where *is* the emergency RV, guys?"

"Yeah, Boss, the main Britannia Grill Restaurant," said both SBS men in unison.

CHAPTER TWENTY-SEVEN

Thursday 9 September. Queen Mary 2, Security Room

The last couple of days at sea had been a frenzy of activity for everybody on the team. Sam had been both concerned and confused by the ever-changing instructions coming from London. That was the odd thing about being involved in a quickly developing intelligence operation: only the people at the very top knew what was really going on. They were now almost a week into the operation and they still couldn't confirm whether or not there really was a substantial threat to the ship. The footage from the photo-recognition cameras that were supposed to identify any traced terrorists had failed, much like Jimmy had predicted. The not-so-organised mayhem of normal passengers, crew, and what looked like a cast of extras in a film about Vogue magazine, had been hard to decipher. Most of the passengers were still fearful of last year's super-virus and wore masks. The normal on-boarding system had ensured that passengers were correctly photographed to receive their on-board ID, and those had been run through the photo-recognition data but had produced nothing of interest. The ship now was in mid-Atlantic and a big decision needed to be made, and agreed upon, in open discussion.

"So, what've we got?" Sam looked around the team. Jimmy was the first to speak.

"Well, Panantile Expressway is fully operational and hoovering up much of what's going on within the confines of the ship." He pointed towards his laptop. "We have also got a direct feed from our DCA." Jimmy was referring to Ricky. The actual name of a Deep Cover Agent was never, ever, used in conversation; Ricky was always either the DCA or CORKSCREW. "But no big breakthrough as yet. When do we have to make the call?"

"Pretty soon," Sam said. "We have another three hours before M Squadron either deploy or stand down."

Pat looked across at Scottie and spoke up for their joint responsibility.

"Everything is ready to go if they have to come in noisy. We've prepped the RDPs and supplied adjusted digital data sets to Poole."

"Hang on." Jimmy looked up and adjusted his glasses as his fingers ran rapidly over his laptop. "I've just got incoming from the DCA." He was again silent for a while as he worked at his keyboard.

"We have a possible player here!" He used Intelligence 'oldspeak' to describe what is now termed a POI, or Person of Interest. His laptop chimed again, and an unfamiliar face filled the screen. He could see that the man wasn't happy, but, apart from that, the extreme convex aperture of Ricky's camera made the face look like an Asian guy with mumps.

"Who is it?" said Sam.

"It's a possible from below decks." Jimmy looked at the still photo. It wasn't a good image; the extreme glare of LED lighting had refracted the picture from the tiny convex lens of the DCA's camera. He would have to run the photograph though a converter before he got a decent image. One thing was for sure, though: the young man who was working below decks thought that it was a significant picture.

"The image needs some work." Jimmy tapped away again at the laptop. "Once I've processed it, I'll run it through Panantile Expressway and direct to VX."

"Any thoughts?" Sam said, with a hint of concern in her voice.

"No, but he wouldn't have sent it if he didn't think it was worth checking out."

"He has the same brief?" Sam said.

"Yeah, just strictly eyes and ears. The covert camera is just to gather anything that might not be featured in the standard data sets, but he would only use it if he thought this guy was interesting."

"How long to get a decent image?"

"Not long." Jimmy looked up; his eyes were magnified under his glasses and showed a hint of annoyance. "It should be instantaneous, but the programme's playing up. I've sent it direct to Tim; maybe he will know before us."

"What's up with the system?" Sam asked.

"Don't know, Sam. Every bit of experimental software has its off days." He thoughtfully pushed his glasses back on to his face with his forefinger.

"There's one other thing that could cause this, though it's highly unlikely."

"And what's that?" Sam asked.

"Someone stressing the bandwidth by using similar software."

"We hope not!" Sam looked worried.

Cabin 2004, Queen Mary 2. The same time.

Abdul Haq was smiling as he closed his laptop. He had just used some of the latest software stolen from the ISI, who had themselves stolen it from the CIA. The fading evening light was still streaming through the double doors of the balcony. He had left the door slightly ajar to let some air circulate within the cabin; like most Pakistani men of his age, he hated air conditioning. It was a waste and, as far as he was concerned, created by the Devil, although the hot flush he felt was probably more to do with his recent diagnosis of cancer than the ship's cooling system. He clicked the MacBook, and an image filled the screen. It was a picture of Samantha Holloway on her wedding day. He smiled.

CLICK.

And now it was a picture of the same girl in uniform, with a lurid tabloid headline saying, 'The Angel of Death'. As he read the story, he vividly remembered the incident – after all, he had arranged it! The ambush in Afghanistan's Helmand Province had been organised by one of his DCAs inside the country's National Directorate of Security (NDS). The brigadier's organisation, the ISI, had placed a one-million-dollar bounty on the successful capture of a British source handler, and he had planned that perhaps one or two could be snatched to order, but the girl had shot her way out.

He actually felt some empathy with the female British soldier. She was a brave fighter, and she had also been betrayed by the British Army in the same sort of way that his political masters had betrayed him. It was a strange part of the game of shadows; you could actually plan to kill an opposing operator and still have a grudging respect for him or her. The man that Samantha Holloway had killed in Afghanistan had seriously underestimated the risks and now was dead.

What do the British say? The Great Game has Big Boys' Rules, and he had paid the price.

CLICK.

Another photograph appeared, of a beautiful young girl's face at her graduation, or what was known as the Sovereign's Parade, at Sandhurst.

CLICK, CLICK, CLICK.

A series of surveillance photographs featuring Samantha Holloway with, presumably, her husband, leaving a house in the country. These were the pictures supplied by the Saudi Embassy. He smiled; even he thought it ironic that, in common with people from his viewpoint, nationality, and age group, he hated most things Western, weak-willed and liberally democratic, but nevertheless loved the tech things from the USA like his new Apple MacBook Pro. It had helped uncover the operation against him in minutes. All he had needed to do was compare the pictures of the passengers from the CCTV cameras as they boarded the ship against his facial recognition system. Now that he knew that he had a British team on board, and that they were actively looking for him, he in turn would get his people to look for them.

He had also accessed the crew records and would use the same system to see if there were any suspicious-looking members who had just joined. He knew that the next logical step, as far as the British were concerned, would be to try and infiltrate the crew as well as cover the passenger spaces. His ISI-issued Panantile Expressway system had immediately hacked into Cunard's private cyberspace and revealed the sixteen new crew members who joined at Southampton. He started to examine each name in turn.

The British now knew that there was a plot in motion, and he had adapted his plan with that in mind. He knew that they must have found out about it in one of only two ways. Either the London end of the ISIS operation had leaked, or some of his equipment was compromised.

Knowledge is power.

At this stage, he assessed that the British team still thought their secret was secure. The Brigadier smiled again, a smile of realisation, a light-bulb moment of stunning clarity. He picked up the iPhone and sent a coded message to all the other iPhones that had been smuggled aboard. He did so both to activate his sleeper cells and to send a copy of the Callbot data to all the individual handsets. Now, even if his phone were seized, the signal to initiate the ship's mini-nuclear holocaust would still be sent.

Now, if his iPhone was bugged, all he needed to do was to turn it on and wait for the British to arrive. He opened his computer case and took out the pistol. He checked that the silencer was fitted correctly by twisting it in an anti-clockwise direction, pushed the clear plastic magazine home with a click, cocked the weapon, and then checked for the glint of brass that showed him that the mercury-tipped dum-dum round had fed into the chamber correctly. He then carefully placed the pistol into the lightweight nylon holster under his sports coat.

He returned to the computer case, picked up the stun gun and popped it into his left-hand jacket pocket. In one hour, all the phones would start to transmit – the signal for the suicide teams onboard to go about their religious duty. He hoped that somebody would come and try to seize his iPhone handset.

He would be waiting. He would have one last chance of revenge before he died. A chance to kill a member of the British Special Forces, the same people who had killed his only son.

Chapter Twenty-Eight

Thames House, London

Danny always felt slightly perturbed when visiting Thames House, the not-so-secret home of MI5. The eight imposing storeys of pale grey Portland stone were only a few hundred yards from the Palace of Westminster, and it was a very easy building to spot.

Hardly like one of those nondescript US intelligence 'black' sites where they had Objective Cyclone – far too practical for the British!

He entered the building and went through the usual security checks. He smiled politely but found it frustrating. When he had worked there himself it had only been a matter of a quick wave to the guy on duty, and straight to the tubes. Now he was treated as a visitor and had to go through the whole ritual search routine. The handing over of his phone, which was placed in a steel locker, the scanning machine, the intrusive personal search and then, finally, the tubes. It seemed that Thames House made up for its lack of external secrecy by proportionally increasing it internally. He finally introduced his smart pass and stepped into the security capsule; the tube whirred, shut briefly and then re-opened. As he walked towards the lifts, he started to wonder why he had been summoned to see Tim.

Had something moved forward in other areas?

Sam's team was now on the QM2 and trying to 'find and fix' the threat. The SBS element had been activated and was already aboard its FMB (Forward Mounting Base) on HMS *Queen Elizabeth*. Mac was also still feeding in information from his source, who was obviously in some sort of relationship with the Qatari or Saudi intelligence agencies. Only Tim knew the full details of how his DCA was doing, and he was probably the only person that could see the whole picture. Danny stepped into the lift and selected the fifth floor. The conference room he was going to was 5Z, next door to JTAC. The Joint Terrorism Analysis Centre was a large computer-filled room occupied by a variety of government agencies, where the whole intelligence picture of an operation was pieced together.

Talk of the Devil!

Tim was halfway along the corridor, being handed another red folder as he used the other hand to wave towards Danny.

"Sorry, pal, I was on my way to escort you; I know you hate the rigmarole downstairs."

"Yeah, that's a big roger, but it wasn't that painful today," Danny admitted.

"Follow me, Danny, this is our conference room." He scanned his card and the electronically sealed door of conference room 5Z opened. The small chamber was of the same bland magnolia colour as thousands of other government rooms, with a light wood table for six people as its focal point. The meeting rooms at Box always seemed to smell the same, a sort of cross between pine-scented disinfectant and the acetone smell of whiteboards and markers. Danny glanced at the whiteboard that the other three people in the room were standing around. It bore the results of a brainstorming session after the latest input of data from next door, looking like some type of bizarre surrealist sketch, with all types of charts, time zones, clocks and codenames.

The usual suspects, Alex, Collette and Mac, were still standing around the whiteboard with various red folders and open laptops. A large TV monitor was fixed to the far wall, and as Tim clicked his laptop the picture changed. The new image was a photo of a pug-nosed guy who looked Filipino.

The team have been busy, Danny thought.

"Sorry to call you in at short notice, Danny," said Tim, "but we need your input on this." He glanced to either side at the others, as a way of including them in the conversation.

Danny studied the photo on the monitor. It featured an Asian man, probably a Filipino of indeterminate age, perhaps thirties, with a pitted complexion. *Maybe childhood smallpox?* He had a roundish face and large brown eyes. The one notable feature was the pugnacious-looking broken nose.

Tim impatiently tapped his fingers on the desk. Danny knew that this was his default message to others for action, or "hurry up and tell me". "Yeah, this guy looks like he's had a hard life. A boxer, maybe?" said Alex.

"Yes, it looks like he's lost quite a few as well," quipped Collette.

"How did we get this?" Danny continued to look at the picture. He had spent half his life looking at mugshots and photomontages. He examined the eyes particularly; it was something that he had learned to do by experience, when you looked at a face and immediately knew that it displayed an element of evil.

The eyes are the window of the soul! And Danny thought that these eyes reflected a dark element within.

"Have we identified him?" he added.

"No, not yet" said Tim. "And we really don't know why the DCA on the ship has sent it. It's a Filipino guy but so are seventy-five percent of the crew. We are running his image through all our assets, and so far, we've had a couple of positive hits."

"Who with?"

"The CIA and the Filipino NCTU (The National Counter Terrorism Unit), and they've ticked a box for Abu Sayyaf, but only as a partial ID."

"I hope not, but that would make sense," Danny said. "Abu Sayyaf are some of the hardcore over there. They have links with Islamic State, and tendrils and funding reaching back into Saudi Arabia and the days of the Soviet invasion of Afghanistan."

"When will we have a positive?" asked Mac.

Tim stood up and used the remote to switch off the screen.

"Soon," he replied. "But then we have a choice to make."

"Explain." Collette brushed her hair back with her fingers. "You're not going to let him run, are you?"

"What do you guys think?" Tim was considering the obvious. "If this guy is a terrorist sleeper in the crew, he may be the only link we have to lead us to any possible device. What do you think we should do?" He waited for input.

Danny looked around the room. Nobody wanted to make the call. There was only silence.

Friday, 10 September. QM2, Deck Five, Level Three. 1500 hrs

Ricky had felt the atmosphere starting to sour just after his run-in with the big Filipino. His highly developed street sense worked below decks as well as it had in Wandsworth. Nothing entirely positive at first, just strange glances from unfamiliar faces and fiercely curious eyes. He noted the faces and times, and pretty soon realised that he was under a crude form of surveillance. The catering staff had a logical reason for visiting the area in which he worked, as they often needed to collect extra provisions for the galley, but a pattern soon formed, with the same people and much too often. Ricky picked up the vibrations and knew that he was under threat. His old iPhone buzzed in his pocket. He excused himself from his work colleague and visited the toilet. It was a message on Telegram. He quickly scanned it:

> *Get close to the big guy they call Manny. He is a traced terrorist, Abu Sayaf. Get close and get him under control.*

How the fuck am I going to do that?
 Ricky made a quick assessment.
 Get tooled up!
He looked through the inventory on his company iPad under 'kitchen cutlery', made his way to storage space G, Row 15, and opened the storage bin. He quickly unwrapped one of the objects. Cold, sharp and shiny, it had a small label with a Cunard sticker and bar code that simply said, 'small kitchen knife, double bladed'. He looked at the shiny tungsten-edged blade, placed the knife in the rear waistband of his trousers and smiled.
 That's better!
In a similar storage area just fifty metres away from Ricky, Faisal Uddin was excited; he had just got the text on the iPhone that he had collected from his team leader. The text meant that he could now be a Jihadi again and attain 'Jannah'; it was the final confirmation of all his training and his past, his present, and his heavenly future. It was a coded reference that only he would understand, the code that he had memorised before he left the training camp in Pakistan. He had spent ten months on the QM2 just waiting for

the day when he could become a martyr, and that day was nearly here.

He was looking down a seemingly endless row of provisions in the main cool room of the QM2. The small LED motion sensor lights flicked on as he walked down the ship's larder, illuminating and reflecting the intense concentration he devoted to the task. He gazed unblinkingly at the multitude of items that lined the tightly packed shelves, ranging from the mundane to the luxurious. He was looking for a large consignment of what purported to be canned Beluga caviar that had been loaded at Southampton. That box contained five Skorpion machine pistols that were needed for the blessed task. He knew that, all over the ship, his brothers were doing the same. They were gathering the tools they needed to carry the war to the kuffar in the very place where they felt the most safe and comfortable. The day of reckoning was nearly here; he felt the elation of action at last and was thrilled at the prospect of eternal bliss.

Britannia Grill Restaurant, 1900 hrs

Manny Maygana looked like a professional boxer but behaved like a perfect gentleman. He was immaculately turned out, and his Cunard uniform was never less than a sparkling white. Efficient and courteous, he was a great favourite with the upmarket crowd that dined at the Britannia Grill Restaurant. He'd remembered the head chef's explanation during Cunard's training course when he first joined the ship:

"*Fine dining is all about great food, polished presentation, and excellent service,*" he had said.

But Manny had drawn his own analogy. *People are also like food: the same essential ingredients are put together in different proportions, in different ways, from different countries. But you have to look under that superficial veneer to really know the people. If only these people really knew me!*

The smiling face, good manners and white uniform were a different camouflage from the one he had worn in the jungles of the Philippines, but the godless enemy was the same. Two years before, Manny had led a group of fighters from Abu Sayyaf, the ISIS-affiliated group in his homeland. The struggle had been fierce on the island of Mindanao.

He had killed many unbelievers on his Jihad, but he had also lost friends and family to the army and the police Special Action Force. Now, though, revenge was coming. He had been in contact with the other fighters on board, and everything was ready.

Cunard Security Office, The Bridge

"What do you think?" Sam said, as she felt the collective gaze of her very experienced team. They were gathered together in the security room with Gavin, the Cunard security officer in attendance. The Cunard security suite was one deck down, on the upper bridge wing. It was a large space crammed full of TV monitors and computer screens, dotted with fixed swivel chairs spaced along a white plastic desk that ran the width of the room. The team looked worn out; in the last two days they had all been involved flat-out in a hectic learning experience that continued to curve ever upwards. They knew that the pressure to come up with a solution was increasing incrementally as the clock ticked and time was running out.

In six hours, the ship would be only eighty nautical miles from where the *Titanic* had met her watery end, well over halfway to

New York. They had one day at most, not only to find out who the opposition were, and their location on board, but also to devise a plan to deal with them. The team had had to start unpacking the clues almost as soon as they had unpacked their kit, operating on separate tasks for equally important reasons. The *Queen Mary 2* was a complicated environment in which to execute a covert mission and expect to keep it secret.

The ship represented a tiny cross-section of humanity of just about every nationality on earth, all on eighteen different decks of one the most iconic ocean liners ever built. In the first few days it had even been a problem simply finding one's way around the ship. The task was draining for all the team, but Sam, as the leader, felt the full weight of responsibility and she needed to rely on their advice to help share the load. She turned to Jimmy for the latest intelligence. He looked pensive.

"What's the latest from London?"

Jimmy had spent countless hours crouched over his computer, trying to weave together the five or six strands of incoming information.

"Mostly good," he said, "but could be better. The Panatile Expressway software has managed to give us a list of POIs and some have tenuous links to terrorist groups, although they are in no way confirmed. We have identified fifteen members of the crew that could have had the opportunity to undergo terrorist training. They are now comparing those names to seized ISIS material collected by British and US Special Forces after the fall of Raqqa." (the last ISIS stronghold in Syria, on October 17, 2017).

"And what's happening with Poole?" Sam turned her head towards Pat and Scottie, who had charge of the physical side – the bombs and bullets – of the operation. They had been in constant contact with both London and Poole and had been feeding back information to both places.

Pat spoke first. "M Squadron have deployed and are within forty-five minutes of an Immediate Action. Their only option is an air assault, as the speed of this ship precludes any other. We have recced and timed the routes from the RDPs to the PTLs (Primary Target Locations) and STLs (Secondary Target Locations), and that data has been fed into the planning process." He turned towards Scottie, who continued in a gentle Highland burr.

"Yeah, it's not that easy knowing what to plan for, Sam, though a ship takeover by Jihadists seems the mostly likely scenario." He paused and looked around the group. "Conventional maritime counter-terrorism planning has always considered the bridge area as the primary objective. Not sure that's the case with a Jihadi terrorist, though. I don't think controlling the ship is a big priority for them, like it was for the PLO guys who hijacked the *Achille Lauro* in '85, or even present-day Somali pirates. You only take the ship's bridge if you want to negotiate, and we don't think that's what these guys are about. So, we have spot-coded the vessel in six different locations including the bridge; that way, we can have some control as to where the SBS lads are directed. The teams will get both a primary and a secondary target.

"After all, if it does go noisy, these fuckers will just want to kill as many people as possible. I know it's too late now, but this ship should never have left Southampton."

"Yeah, but it has," Sam said with a shrug.

"Hold on," said Jimmy, "I've just got that suspect's photo back from London. There was a flurry of fingers across his keyboard as the technical guru decrypted the picture and turned the screen towards the team.

The photo of the POI was clear in every detail. It was the face of a big-built Filipino with a hard-man's face, the brows scarred by boxing, the eyes deep and glaring with menace. Another photo of the same man, but of when he was considerably younger, was displayed alongside it. It was an old mugshot from a montage supplied by the Filipino Security Services that had a number underneath and stated simply, '10080 Abu Sayyaf'.

"So, it's confirmed that we have at least one traced terrorist on board," Jimmy said. "I'll get a name."

"Fuck!", said Gav, "I know him. Hard not to – he's the head waiter at the Britannia Grill restaurant. His name is Manny, and he was last year's Employee of the Year." Gav turned and moved towards the ship's weapon store. He tapped out some numbers on a Simplex lock and opened the steel cupboard to reveal a row of Glock 19 pistols. Choosing one, he slapped on a full magazine, racked the slide and chambered a round.

"We need to take him out soonest. Never liked the fucker anyway!"

"No," Sam said. "He's the only link we have to where the bomber and bomb might be."

"What's the suggestion, then?" Gav placed the pistol in the waistband of his uniform trousers.

Sam looked around the team. "Options?"

Taff spoke first. "A quick surveillance operation, once we have a rudimentary start point, with the DCA trying to get close to the target below decks and the rest of the team covering the public areas. Jimmy, what do you think?"

"It's risky, but no riskier than doing sweet fuck all!"

"But how can we do it?" Samantha sounded doubtful.

Jimmy adjusted his glasses. "We can utilise the ship's CCTV cameras to follow a target. But we will need a definite start point, and we can monitor where the target works with some close-in cover."

Gav adjusted his clothing to hide the pistol and joined the conversation.

"I don't think we can keep this to ourselves any more; we need to let the Captain know what's going on. He needs to know everything, including the current threat. He's the one who has to make the final decision on whether he needs to evacuate. You roger that, Sam?"

"Yeah, I agree. More than anything else, we need his help on this one."

Sam led the team to the bridge. The journey was only one deck up from the Cunard Security office, but it gave Sam a chance to organise her thoughts and mentally rehearse how to actually break the extremely bad news to the captain. She knew a bit about him. An older guy, ex-Royal Navy and a Master Mariner, he would have read the annual security reviews that all cruise ship captains have to factor into their busy schedules. Sam also knew that John Rainer had been the ship's master when the SBS assessment team had carried out their last onboard visit a year ago.

That might help.

He was waiting for them as Sam and Gavin opened the reinforced and bulletproof glass door of the bridge. Gavin had gained access by scanning a pass card and by tapping in an entry code. The Captain was a large man in his mid-fifties, with a nautical white beard of generous proportions. He was immaculately turned out in the white Cunard uniform with lots of gold braid, and greeted Gavin with a curt nod of acknowledgement.

"So, I suppose I'm eventually going to find out what's happening on my ship?"

He had a slight West Country twang and looked a bit like a nautical version of Father Christmas, but he wasn't smiling.

"Yes, sir," said Gavin, equally seriously. "Can I introduce Samantha Holloway? Samantha is the team leader of the additional security staff that the Security Service has provided for this crossing. She has a Special Forces background and comes highly recommended."

The Captain looked across at Sam and smiled. "Quite an introduction, madam!" Sam noticed a definite twinkle in the old sea dog's eye.

"I had noticed you people on board before, but I thought that you – and especially you, Samantha – were something to do with New York Fashion Week," the captain smiled. "I spent my time in the Andrew (Royal Navy) confined inside one of Her Majesty's Upholder-class submarines, sometimes dropping off the SBS, and they didn't look anything like you." He beamed another smile. "They looked more like the gentleman behind you."

"He's my husband, Nigel, and he's an ex-Royal Marine," said Sam.

"So, I got that right, then?"

"Indeed, sir. Can I introduce the rest of my team?" Sam sensed it was time to change the subject. "Each of my men will then brief you on his area of responsibility, tell you what we think is happening and how we propose to deal with it."

"OK," said Captain Rainer tersely. "But I want it clear, concise, and up front, is that understood? I have the responsibility for over three thousand people on this ship and I know that you wouldn't be here if it weren't serious." He paused for emphasis. "So, what *is* happening on my ship?"

"We have two main problems," Sam said calmly. "We have members of the ship's crew, numbers presently unknown, that we suspect will try to mount a terrorist attack as the ship enters US territorial waters." There was a shocked silence as the old seafarer processed this information.

Sam continued. "There's also the possibility that any attack will be combined with the detonation of a stolen tactical nuclear device."

The Captain seemed to rock on his feet as he registered the scale of the threat, his ruddy complexion appearing to blanch slightly.

"All right," he said calmly. "thank you for your clarity on that." He had now partly recovered his composure. "So, what's the plan to deal with it?"

"Firstly, we intend to call our Quick Reaction Force in now. We have elements of M Squadron SBS within an hour of the ship. Once they have arrived, we can identify the terrorists by technical means and neutralise the threat. Until then, we intend to mount a surveillance operation on the only member of the crew that we have so far identified as hostile and hope that he will lead us to the rest of the terrorists."

"Who is it?" said the Captain, "Or am I not allowed to know?" Sam looked towards Gav to supply the answer.

"It's the head waiter from the Britannia," Gav answered.

The Captain's face reflected both concern and uncertainty. "Are you sure?"

"Yes, it's been confirmed," Gav quietly acknowledged.

Then we have another problem," the *Queen Mary*'s Captain said in an urgent voice. "There's a Fashion Week dinner scheduled at the restaurant tonight. Do we need to cancel it?"

"And then we'd lose our chance," Sam said.

"And how do you cover that risk?"

"We will make sure that we are there personally to deal with any threat."

"I think we should still cancel," the captain shot back.

"It's your final decision, **sir**, but if the ship's routine were to change, we'd probably lose any chance of locating the device."

Captain Rainer frowned, his face a mask of worry.

"That, to me, still seems rather dangerous. What are our chances of success?"

"They're good," said Sam. "But we won't be truly safe until the SBS arrive. They will have all the expertise necessary to deal with the situation." Sam really didn't know whether they had a chance or not, but it wouldn't improve matters by worrying the Captain any more than she needed to.

"Then get them here as soon as you can!" The Captain had made his decision.

"Sir, with your permission," Gav said, as he picked up the ship's phone and dialled the secure number to Northwood. M Squadron of the Special Boat Service would be on the way in minutes.

Chapter Twenty-Nine

Friday 10 September, QM2 First Class, Cabin 2004. 1300 hrs.

The brigadier had always been able to think one step ahead of his adversaries. It had been the same in Afghanistan: he knew the way the British thought and he had planned his mission with that in mind. He looked in the mirror of his stateroom and smiled at his reflection. He could almost predict what would happen now. The British team that he had identified were probably frantically trying to work out what was going on. They would have good technical people who would soon identify the threat and then call in people to neutralise it, but it would be too late. The planning for this operation had been years in the making, and it was a completely closed-cell one. Even he didn't know the twelve battle-hardened ISIS operatives that had hidden themselves amongst the crew; they had been recruited separately, in different places and at different times, by a man known only as the 'Controller". Each cell operated independently; until now its members had only known the three other people in their own group and could only be activated by Abdul Haq alone.

He smiled. *A terrorist incident is like a theatre performance, and he had chosen the stage.*

The Live Letterbox

Ricky looked out over the North Atlantic as the tops of the waves just started to show flecks of white. Both the weather and his personal situation had started to worsen. He had made his way to the life raft that was both his emergency muster station and the Dead Letter Box that his controller, Jimmy, had nominated. The ship's regulation stipulating that all new joiners must know how to reach their emergency station from all areas of the ship gave him natural cover, a reason to be there. He pushed his back against the orange life raft pod and waited for the call. The wind had started to blow a bit and he felt a slight chill slowly permeate his body. *Or was that fear?* The phone buzzed; he took it from his pocket, placed it to his ear and recognised Jimmy's voice.

"OK, Ricky. Don't talk, just listen, understand and try to answer just yes or no!"

"Yeah." Ricky detected the urgency in his voice.

"OK, things have changed, mate. We need to try and get close to the big guy you identified. Roger so far?"

"Yeah."

"We need a start point for a surveillance operation. Roger so far?"

"Yeah."

"You will need to go in hard. A 9mm Glock will be at the LLB in fifteen minutes. Got that?"

"Yeah," said a confident-sounding Ricky.

"Get close and keep close and trigger him to us." Jimmy looked at his watch; the time available for finding the device was ticking away.

"Yeah," Ricky said.

"Any problems?" Jimmy sounded concerned.

"No."

"Remember to use the emergency button if you need to, and don't try to be a hero," Jimmy said as he rang off.

After Repton, Ricky now understood the difference between an LLB (Live Letter Box) or Live Drop and a DLB (Dead Letter Box), sometimes called a Dead Drop, but in this case the location of both was the same. The Live Drop was just somewhere where the drop could be made while being covered by another team member, and Ricky knew that he was expected to supply that cover. The drop was on the inside of the bright orange life raft pod. He left the lifeboat station and looked around for an instant OP (Observation Point). He needed to have good all-round arcs of observation on both sides of the drop. Ricky glanced upwards, took the small metal crew-ladder to the deck above and looked down. He pulled out a packet of cigarettes and lit one.

He coughed violently; he didn't smoke, but the ostensible habit was another handy reason for a crew member to be off his station. He recognised Jimmy, walking along the deck below, observed the drop and then waited until his controller had started to leave the LLB. Jimmy had looked around casually and then leant on the guardrail, as if he were just looking at the increasingly choppy Atlantic. He waited the required minute to mark the drop, then turned and ambled towards the ship's stern. Ricky got ready to clear the drop and was just about to descend the same ship's ladder when he stopped; he had spotted a man following Jimmy. He recognised him: it was one of the faces that had been shadowing Ricky himself!

As soon as the man had moved on, Ricky quickly and quietly climbed back down. The sea spray had now made the ladder slippery, and he had to squeeze the rails hard to control his descent. He looked to his right and caught sight of the shadow, in a Cunard-issue windbreaker, just as he turned aft in the same direction as Jimmy. Ricky felt for the knife in his waistband, held it in his right hand and followed him. A close-up foot follow is not really covert surveillance at all; the layout of the ship's deck made any covert drills very difficult.

Because he had to stick close to his target he could be 'blown' at any second, but the man following Jimmy seemed preoccupied with his own task, intent on just staying glued to his target's back. A hundred different 'what ifs' flooded Ricky's mind.

Is Jimmy under threat?
What if the guy pulls out a gun?
What if he pulls out a knife?
What if he follows Jimmy all the way back to the security room, houses the whole team and organises an attack?

Ricky still held the knife, blade down and out of sight, against his right thigh.

If I see a knife, or if he reaches for a pistol, I'll stab him in the back just below his ribcage, try to get the knife into his heart and then get rid of the body overboard. But what about the blood?

Ricky adjusted quickly and faded into the darkened walkway. He decided to close the distance, and then something that any operator secretly dreads, on a too-close follow in an exposed area, actually happened. The man just stopped dead, furtively glanced around him and then took a mobile phone from his pocket. Ricky managed to stop just in time and stayed in the shadows. The ex-gangster's finely-honed street sense clicked in as the man turned and started hurriedly walking in the opposite direction. As he passed, he was speaking in hushed but seemingly frantic tones into his iPhone. Ricky could hear what he was saying but didn't understand much, as the language was strange. *Maybe Filipino?* But he understood its nature well enough. It had been a rushed call, blurted out with a sense of urgency, and therefore apparently important. Jimmy's watcher was obviously passing or receiving urgent information.

Something is happening!
I'll stick with him.
Ricky had to make a quick assessment: more 'what if**s**'.
Do I follow? Would it be safer to pick up the Glock before I do?
No time, I gotta just get close to him!

He pulled back slightly, giving the man just enough space to maintain visual contact. He watched from about fifteen metres as the target undid the latch on a watertight crew door and stepped into the ship's service corridors. The DCA waited by the door. He was holding the knife in his right hand while he slowly pushed down the latch with his left. Once inside, he just had time to hear another door shut in front of him in the next corridor, and he speeded up in pursuit.

Ricky was almost frantic now. *I've lost him!*

He was breaking all the rules now, running along the long service corridor in the half-light as consecutive motion-triggered lights flashed on. All the need for a covert follow, all the lessons from Repton, were forgotten. He now was just the same old postcode gangster closing in on his prey.

I'll just fucking stab him! The idea leapt out from his subconscious, but was it prompted by crude bloodlust or reasoned thought? His street sense told him that all he could do was close with the enemy! As he drew nearer to his target, he had a weird thought:

This is the first time I've thought about stabbing someone to actually try to kill him. How could I justify that?

He heard another door close just as he opened the door in front of him. He sprinted up the next corridor, this one in the ship's electrical store. Individual storage bays lit up in a bright fluorescent glow as he passed them, like a weird internal light show. He controlled himself as he stopped before the last door; he was breathing heavily now. *Poor fitness or fear? No, definitely fear!*

More deep breaths. *Control yourself!* And, suddenly, he did. In that instant he became something that all his training had been designed to achieve – he became an intelligence operator.

He pulled the fire door open, slowly, carefully, so that the spring in the mechanism clicked almost soundlessly. He peered through the chink in the door, focusing his left eye onto a brightly lit corridor. He was very close, and he identified the target just as he was welcomed at the door of storeroom X8. He also recognised the man who welcomed him, the same man he had argued with, the big Filipino bruiser.

Chapter Thirty

HMS Queen Elizabeth. Same time

Captain Childs had asked to see Major 'George' Hunt, although George wasn't his Christian name. The Marines of his troop in 41 Commando RM had rechristened him when he had joined them forty years earlier. They had said that Darren wasn't a proper name for a commando, and he had been called George ever since. The sandy blond hair that had once upgraded his nickname to 'Gorgeous George' had long since lifted off during an action-packed career that had taken him from a rifleman in 6 Troop, F Company, 41 Commando to a commissioned Royal Marines major flying the Special Forces. During that time, he had been shot down over South Armagh, been mentioned in dispatches, won a Military Medal with 45 Commando in the Falklands and flown hundreds of missions in Iraq and Afghanistan. George was now the oldest serving, most decorated and most experienced helicopter pilot in the Royal Marines, which was why he was flying the SBS and why the Captain of 'Big Lizzy' wanted to talk to him.

"Major Hunt, the skipper wants to see you," said the door gunner.

"Roger that," said George, who was sitting in the cab of his Merlin Mark 4 doing some pre-flight checks.

George tapped on the door of the bridge five minutes later and the watchkeeper let him in.

The ship's Captain was in a murmured conversation with the Aviation Officer and flight deck senior. He looked over his shoulder from an array of computers and screens under the bridge windows.

"I need some advice here, George." The *Queen Elizabeth*'s skipper had known the Royal Marine for a long time on Air Ops, and George was one of the few people on the ship that rated first-name terms.

"We're looking at Red-Red for Air Ops, according to the Met officer. What's the maximum sea and wind state we can mount the SBS in?"

George looked thoughtful. "Depends on the combination of both sea state and wind, and the mission priority," he answered.

"Top priority, mission essential," the skipper answered.

"This new airframe can survive most things. It's at Force 4 to 6 now, with a 15-knot side wind; we can fly off a stable platform and into wind. Once we are up, it's all good."

"Great. Any problems with that?" said Captain Childs.

"Yeah, but that's a risk mitigation problem, sir. With the weather worsening, we won't be able to cover the SAR (Search and Rescue) side. We will be on our own. If an asset ditches, it will stay ditched!"

"Oh, I see," said the Captain. It was decision time; careers in the Royal Navy had been scuppered by much less.

"You know the mission. What do you think?"

"We have no choice. It's an SF QRF mission, and if people are dying, we have to go."

"Thanks, Royal," said the most senior ship's captain in the Royal Navy. "We go." He had made his decision.

He turned to the ship's 'Jimmy' (Executive Officer).

"OK, Number One, record this decision in the ship's log and then the buck will stop with me. This ship will start the way it will go on, and the Big Lizzy will never let anybody down."

Storeroom X8, Queen Mary 2

He received all his guests in the same formal way: they were his brothers, and they would be bound together for ever in sacrifice. They were all the blessed 'Shahid' (martyrs). He embraced them, kissed them on each cheek and just said to each one in Arabic, "Ahlaan akhi," (welcome, brother), "Nadhhab illau aljanet maeaan" (we go to heaven together).

Ricky watched from about ten metres away; there was just a chink of light seeping through the door, but he could see and hear. He had heard enough Arabic in Wandsworth to know a few key words, especially 'Jannah', which the Beardie fuckers never stopped taking about: it was almost like a fucking death cult! The door had closed as the last man entered.

Manny had gathered the brothers together at this prearranged place as soon as he received the call on the mission's iPhone. The other information he needed was on the encrypted Telegram App downloaded on the handset. The brothers had already completed 'wudhu' (ritual ablutions for prayer) and they had spent the last hour in contemplation.

They were all smiling now as they prepared their equipment. The only person in a Cunard uniform was the team leader, resplendent in his spotless white jacket with brass buttons. The uniforms of the other three had gone; their servitude to the kuffar had finished, and they were dressed in black overalls and training shoes.

Ricky continued to observe from the doorway, but he could no longer hear what was happening. He needed to get nearer.

The room was readied for action. All the equipment they needed was still on the floor, laid next to the rolled prayer mats. The primary weapon lay in the middle, in its ominous deadly outline. It was a shrapnel-packed suicide vest that had just been recovered from its hiding place, along with four shiny kitchen knives, an AK47, and two gleaming black Skorpion machine pistols. Manny Maygana whispered his pre-op pep talk.

"OK brothers, the time has come for Jannah, Allah be praised."

He produced a small plastic container from his trouser pocket, unscrewed the lid and placed four lozenge-shaped 100-mill tablets of Captagon into each of his group's outstretched right hands - their clean hands - in an almost sacred way.

"These will make our work easier," he said.

Each of the team then unrolled a prayer mat, knelt, prayed and prepared himself until the chemicals stiffened his inner resolve.

Outside storeroom X8. 1700 hours

I'm exposed here! Ricky knew that he was breaking all the rules as he approached the source of the low drone of voices seeping through into the corridor. He had to wait for what seemed like hours before the motion-activated lights in the main corridor clicked off. He was just outside the door now and waiting in the darkness, with only the eerie glow of the corridor's blue safety lights for company. His heart was beating as he held the knife in his right hand and his iPhone in his left. As he listened, he heard the prayers from inside the room and thought he understood what was about to happen. He tapped his mobile. He had to carefully limit his movement, or the action-activated corridor lights would flicker on and possibly warn the men in the storeroom. His screen glowed as he tried to tap out a message on the Telegram App. He remembered his training: keep messages short but concise.

SITREP, XRAYS IN X8, MINIMUM 4 PAX, READY TO GO! STAND BY! The prayers were finished now; they were talking in low friendly tones, and again he heard the word *Jannah* several times. It wouldn't be long. He had to get a signal, but he had no coverage.

I'll have to take a chance.

Ricky took a deep breath as he moved towards the nearest access door. The lights flashed on as he moved but mercifully didn't disturb the low drone of conversation that leaked from the room. He slowly closed the door, and heard the gentle click of the lock, as he frantically tried to get a signal. The screen of the old iPhone glimmered. He changed direction and tried again. Now he had three bars and he sent the message.

The Cunard security office

Jimmy was looking at the ship's CCTV system. He had worked out how to reprogramme the screens to operate in sequence because of the target's assumed finishing point in the kitchen of the Britannia Restaurant. That was where he was due on shift, and where he should then be 'housed' by Taff and Sam when they were 'eyes on' in the restaurant, but he could only surmise his intended direction of travel. His iPhone buzzed in his pocket. He quickly glanced at the DCA's message and smiled.

Good man!

He now had a start point and began to look at the CCTV camera covering the darkened corridor outside the storage area near X8. There were seven different cameras spaced along the corridor, but the door numbers were hard to see in the low glow of the blue-tinted safety lights. He needed to know which door sheltered the terrorist group.

He quickly tapped out a message to the DCA: *CONFIRM AND MARK THE DOOR,* and he hit Send.

Ricky looked down at the message and immediately understood. He re-entered the corridor and the nearest set of lights clicked on in a harsh glare of neon. He approached the door of storeroom X8 as soundlessly as possible. There was still just a low buzz of whispered conversation, with the leader sometimes raising his voice to maybe emphasise a point, and the occasional grunt of acknowledgement. He couldn't understand the language, but he thought he understood the intent.

Orders for the Op.

He looked left and right and pointed towards the door with an outstretched hand. The phone again vibrated in his pocket. The message said, '*GOT IT!*'

Ricky was already moving back along the corridor to retrieve the Glock from the drop.

I'll feel safer when I have it!

Jimmy worked quickly to sequence the cameras along two different probable routes. He knew, though, that this was very unlikely to work without actual physical surveillance. The team would also have to crash out quickly.

He moved rapidly from the CCTV room along a short corridor and back into the Cunard security office. The team were prepping weapons and equipment as he arrived. Pat was attaching the suppressor to a Glock pistol; Scottie was unpacking ammunition, Samantha and Taff were already dressed for a surveillance serial at the restaurant and Taff was helping her fit her comms kit. Despite his sense of urgency, Jimmy couldn't help thinking, *she looks stunning*.

"We've got a start point for an ISIS ASU." He was talking quickly. "The DCA will give us the trigger."

"How much time have we got?" Sam racked the slide of her Glock, checked the chamber for the glint of brass indicating that a round was good-to-go, and put it into a handbag.

"None. They could leave any time."

"OK, Jimmy, what's the camera layout?"

"All the cameras are sequenced from the place where they are housed, with a possible finish point at the restaurant."

"OK, guys, listen in!" The team moved closer to Sam. "QBOs (Quick Battle Orders)."

And then Captain Samantha Holloway MC, ex-operator of the Special Reconnaissance Regiment, gave the quickest set of orders that she had ever delivered.

Below decks, stores area

Ricky was running now; he dashed past two of his co-workers on his way back to his DLB and the Glock.

"Where's the fire?" said one, as Ricky sidestepped around him.

Another held up his hand to try and stop him, but Ricky dropped his shoulder and sent him flying. The man cannoned into the corridor wall with a grunt, then he was past him and climbing the crew deck to the emergency station.

As he opened the door to the deck a blast of icy air hit his face and he tasted the tang of salt spray. The weather was getting worse. His 'interior' issue Cunard work shoes slid on the deck as he made his way along the last twenty metres towards the drop, using the guard rail to steady himself. He could feel the big ship actually swaying now; he looked out into the North Atlantic. The large black waves had developed angry white-flecked tops, and they were getter bigger.

He reached his nominated Dead Drop, but the sway of the ship meant that he struggled to keep his balance as he reached inside the life-raft. He pushed his whole arm in up to the shoulder and felt around for the package where it was supposed to be. His hand skimmed over, and then grabbed, what felt like a plastic bag. He pulled it clear, tore it open, and there it was: a Glock 19 pistol. His hands were slippery, and he found that they were also shaking as he felt the first tendrils of fear creeping through his body. He checked the rest of the bag. There was also a full magazine, a small package and a dark green baseball cap with just the word 'ARMY' on it in large, bright fluorescent orange letters. He understood immediately what it was – it was meant to identify him as one of the good guys when what Jimmy called the 'other assets' arrived. He thought he knew what the small package contained and was proved right when he ripped off the waterproof plastic, removed a QuikClot dressing and placed it in his pocket. His mind was racing now with a thousand more 'what ifs'. He needed to do something.

He had a job to do. He cocked the pistol and tucked the weapon into the front waistband of his trousers and moved to return to where the ISIS fighters were preparing their assault. He pulled out his iPhone and hit the Send button. Jimmy answered immediately.

"SITREP. I'm going back in."

"No, stop, stop, stop and listen." Jimmy was calm, but with an urgent edge to his voice. "Have you got the drop?"

"Yeah!"

"OK, you are probably blown, mate, just stay where you are and protect yourself when it goes noisy. Other assets are on their way, and I can handle the trigger to the team. If you meet the other guys coming in, SBS men in black, ditch the weapon, put on the hat, just shout 'SPARTAN' as loud as you can and do exactly what you are told. Do you understand?"

"Yeah!"

"Good luck, Ricky." And Jimmy rang off.

The ship was rolling now, and the odd fleck of sea spray was spitting onto the young Londoner's face. He looked around for somewhere dry and found it: an upper-deck paint store. He undid the door clip and got a blast of turpentine and gloss paint as he opened up his refuge. There was a selection of industrial-sized paint pots and white sheets, paint brushes and rollers. It was a good place to hide.

He was now in the inky black darkness, with his thumping heart for company.

How the fuck did I get myself into this? Ricky took the pistol, cradled it in both hands, placed his back against the wall of his refuge and slid down until he was sitting on his haunches. He was cold, so he pulled one of the white dustsheets around him for warmth. He was now cocooned in a safe place, but he didn't feel safe.

This was the first time in his life that he'd ever felt really scared.

Chapter Thirty-One

Friday, 10 September. The Britannia Grill Restaurant, 1930 hrs

Samantha and Taff thought they had chosen their table far enough away from the target so as not to arouse suspicion. The surveillance plan was basic, but they knew that simple plans are sometimes the best. Gavin Loach had come up trumps with the props they had needed to blend with such a fashion-conscious crowd. He had opened one of the storage rooms, 'liberated' a range of Julien Macdonald evening dresses from the 2020 season and let Samantha help herself. Taff was somewhat more conspicuous in an ill-fitting dinner jacket and black tie and looked more like her minder than her consort. Sam glittered with borrowed Swarovski costume jewellery that hid her earpiece, and she carried a Furla evening bag that contained her Glock, radio and loop. She blended into the fashionistas crowd as much as Taff didn't. His evening jacket was loose enough, though, to conceal his pistol and radio fit.

The Britannia was full. Every table in the very stylish Art Deco restaurant was buzzing with conversation and, whenever another cork from a bottle of Veuve Clicquot champagne popped, the laughter got louder. The dinner was to both celebrate New York Fashion Week and welcome all involved in it. Sam and Taff's jobs were, first, to protect the diners against attack and, second, to trigger the target if he left the restaurant. Jimmy could then follow him, on a pre-sequenced relay of CCTV cameras, to wherever he was heading on the ship. He also had the overview on the Panatile Expressway system.

In the Cunard control room, Jimmy was 'eyes on' Storeroom X8. The ship's CCTV cameras were sequenced along the likely route to the Britannia Restaurant, where Sam and Taff had already started the surveillance serial. Pat, Gav and Scottie were sitting alongside him, acting as a QRF. They couldn't yet put on their full body armour as they needed to move around the ship without spooking the passengers: panic could sometimes do as much damage as a bomb.

"How long till M Squadron arrive?" Jimmy asked Pat.

"Not sure they're even going to make it, with the current sea state." Pat was placing a mag onto his MP5 Kurz machine pistol.

TING! The Panatile Expressway system alarmed.

"Fuck!" Jimmy was now looking at the screen.

"A phone has just come onto the system. They've been activated."

"Where?" Scottie was adjusting the bungee cord that hung from his shoulder. Hanging on the business end was his MP5K.

Jimmy looked at the screen. The phone was highlighted as a bright red dot on the 3D overlay map of the ship. He looked up at the CCTV monitor covering storeroom X8, and saw its door opening. The first terrorist to leave was the big Filipino dressed in white. He went left down the corridor and then, thirty seconds later, three other men dressed in black and carrying bags went right.

"It's started," he shouted.

Pat confirmed that his phone had loaded the ship's mapping correctly. He could see the red dot moving inside the holographic representation of the QM2.

"Can you see it?"

Scottie checked as well. "Yep, buddy. I've got it!"

"OK, we are moving to the ERV, mate," Pat said, as both operators covered their weapons with their jackets and left.

Jimmy picked up the handheld.

"Hello, Sam, X-ray One towards you, three other X-rays moving in the stores area."

A calm voice whispered, "This is Sam, roger that."

Sam and Taff had just got the call when they first spotted Manny Maygana moving behind them from the kitchen area. He was holding a silver platter aloft in the way that only a properly trained waiter could. It seemed to hover effortlessly over his raised right hand, as if gravity had ceased to exist. He was carrying a bottle of champagne. He looked relaxed and was beaming a smile.

"Do you think we've got the right guy here?" said Taff.

"Yeah, that's him," Sam replied.

"He's coming towards us," Taff whispered. A loud bray of laughter erupted from the adjoining table. The subject of their surveillance was suddenly next to them. The people at the table, buyers for a London fashion house, were tipsy and getting louder by the minute. The broken-nosed waiter placed the bottle on the table with a flourish.

"And keep it coming," said a guy with a London accent. Taff thought he could see the waiter's smile fade very slightly as he replied.

"Of course, sir. The table has another four bottles ordered."

"Well, why not bring them all?" said the Londoner. "We can't get pissed in instalments." The comment was accompanied by laughter.

"Of course, sir," Manny replied in an apparently deferential tone, though his eyes glittered with hate and were large as saucers.

"Sam," whispered Taff as the waiter turned towards the kitchen, "this is happening tonight. He's as high as a kite; they've already broken out the happy pills, and it's going to happen soon."

Sam and Taff watched the target return to the kitchen, then walk out without a tray and make straight for the restaurant's door.

"That's X-ray One towards the exit" said Sam.

"Roger that," Jimmy confirmed. He was monitoring the target's progress: he was clearly sighted leaving the Britannia Grill, was seen again by the cameras mounted in the central lobby's main corridor, and then was gone.

"Hello all stations, target unsighted. I repeat, target unsighted." Jimmy looked at the screen of his MacBook Pro and confirmed that the one target on the Panatile Expressway program had suddenly become five, as that number of individual red dots had appeared at different locations throughout the ship. Jimmy spoke in clear over the Spartan net.

"Sam, Taff, get to the ERV ASAP. Something big is happening. We now have five targets."

"Roger that," said Taff, and immediately stood up and led Sam out of the restaurant.

"We've got trouble," Sam said as the couple hurried past the glittering bronze reliefs along the corridor that led into the ship's central atrium and lobby. "Five targets, six operators."

The packed atrium by the left side of the central staircase was their ERV (Emergency Rendezvous), and the other guys were there already. Jimmy briefed in low tones as passengers strolled by. A small boy wearing a pair of trainers with flashing lights darted in between the operators, playing hide-and-seek with his baby sister, as the ex-Shin Bet guy explained the situation.

"We have five different locations where the device might be, and the SBS won't be on target for at least ten minutes." He looked at the team leader. "What do you think, Sam?" he asked.

"OK guys, go with our QBOs. We can't take the option of just doing nothing. Any one of those contacts could be heading for a nuclear device." They nodded in agreement.

A pianist seated at a large white grand piano started to play a souped-up version of Vivaldi.

"We split up, and each of us takes a location to see if we can find the trigger or the actual device," said Sam.

"No, you stay here," Taff said in a worried voice.

Sam pulled him to one side and whispered, "Hey, Nigel, I'm your wife but still your team leader. No favouritism, we all take our chances." Her eyes reflected a steely determination to take the lead.

"OK, who takes what?"

"I'll go to Deck 5," said Sam, "Gav will work from the Bridge and coordinate with M Squadron." Sam and the rest of the team looked at the mapping on their iPhones.

"I'll go Deck 8 in the lift," said Taff.

"I'll take Deck 6 and then move to 7," said Pat.

"I'll chase the contact on 9 and then join Pat on 6 or 7," said Scottie.

"I'll take down the primary X-ray, once I locate him, and then join Pat," said Jimmy.

The QBOs ended when all the respective locations were assigned, and the team members rushed to their designated targets. Sam felt utterly alone in the main lobby surrounded by passengers that she could not ask for help. She glanced down at her iPhone and could see the green dots that represented each member of her team diverging, all over the QM2, towards the red dots of the unknown activated mobile phones.

All were heading in entirely different directions over the ship's eighteen decks, chasing the positive hits they had on the system. It was a near-impossible task with a minimal chance of success, but Sam knew that they had to go, as the stakes were too high not to. 'No action' was never an option: an IA (Immediate Action) was just that, and only happened when lives were at stake. Sam took a deep breath.

Game on. I need to get a move on!

She was hurrying now but having problems with her slightly higher borrowed heels and the somewhat increased sea state. She thought about just running barefoot, but she needed to remain covert to get to her particular target, now on Deck 2.

You just need to act on the information available and trust your training and instincts.

In conventional military thinking, you always relied on a three-to-one advantage for a military assault, but this didn't apply to counterterrorism. Special Forces teams were normally outnumbered and usually surrounded.

Situation, no change!

Her small team's chances were at best fifty-fifty. In rushing to minimise the risk to the passengers and crew they had maximised the risk to themselves. No time for preparation, no body armour or detailed orders. Sam was wearing a long evening dress and heels and had her evening bag covered by a long pashmina wrap.

Not an ideal outfit for an 'advance to contact'.

She checked the mapping on her phone; the quickest way to Deck 2 was via the grand lobby. Sam looked up at the Grand Staircase, designed in homage to the Art Deco elegance of all former

Cunard liners. It was the ship's focal point, sweeping upwards from the richly carpeted atrium in two graceful arcs to left and right. The sounds of a tinkling grand piano, laughter and the hum of conversation provided the background to Samantha's advance to contact.

She now felt responsible for all the people she passed. The young couples tenderly holding hands, the older lady in an evening dress, leaning on a black ebony walking stick, and the group of giggling children that played in between them. The New York fashionistas blended into the mix. Beautifully dressed women and elegantly attired men wandered round, talking about this show or that. It was hard to believe that all this opulence could soon be the scene of an atrocity. Sam realised that during her entire military career she had never actually been without back-up and unsupported.

There's a first time for everything. It's just grab a gun and go!

She had had to make that decision because the stakes were just too high. Any of the red dots on the system could be the site of a nuclear device. Each dot almost certainly represented a terrorist, and thousands of lives were at risk. Sam's team had 'bombburst' in five different directions inside the vastness of the ship She flicked the holographic mapping data on her handset. Her own red dot was now stationary, in a port-side cabin on Deck 2. Her earpiece buzzed.

"Zero, this is Spartan Two. I have a fix, one hundred and tracking."

"That's OK." Jimmy sounded breathless as if he was running.

"Zero, Spartan Three, I'm foxtrot towards Deck 4 and tracking a contact at four hundred metres."

"Zero, this is Spartan Four, I'm tracking on Deck 6."

"Zero, Spartan Three, tracking contact towards Deck 8," Scottie said. The buzzing of the urgent, intense messages on the Spartan net, and the realisation that her guys were preparing to engage, froze her very core. All those 'what ifs' now haunted her. Her team was vulnerable because she had failed! Sam tried a service door at the side of the central atrium, and it opened. She hesitated for a moment at the entrance to this warm, dark space, then entered it. She felt the panic start to build, closed her eyes and tried to focus. Her head was spinning; it seemed like her brain had detached itself and was rotating like the blades from one of the Merlin helicopters that were even now speeding towards the ship. The small service area seemed a dark and comforting space to shelter in, a safe place.

A place to hide?

All the inner turmoil that she had hidden, all the fear, and all her symptoms of post-traumatic stress syndrome just seemed to implode. As her sense of dread grew stronger, her legs became heavier and her chest tightened. She panted, her breath now coming in small gasps as she fought to control her emotions. Sam's past and her perilous present, combined with her uncertain future, piled in on top of her to crush her spirit. The tough SF soldier's face was suddenly wet with a flood of tears. So this was fear?

I'll have to wait until M Squadron arrives. I can't do this on my own.

Sam had never felt this way. Her only fear in the past had been that of failure. Now, for the first time since her dad had died, she felt truly alone.

But she wasn't. She held her left hand over her tummy and envisioned the small bean-size person, of indeterminate sex, that was keeping her company. She tried to regain control after that thought. She took a long, deep breath and she was over it. *His grandson or granddaughter, his legacy?* she rationalised.

So that's a panic attack? My hormones are all over the shop. Get a grip, you're a British soldier, and you're fighting for two now.

And then, in a heartbeat, she was back and focused. She flicked the pashmina away, raised the Glock, pulled back the slide with the index finger and thumb of her left hand and checked for the glint of brass that showed that a round was in the breech. She covered the weapon again and listened at the door. A whispered conversation filtered through from the atrium. Sam eased it open slightly and glanced out. The young couple opposite was engaged in a seriously intimate clinch. Sam smiled, opened the service door and slipped past the pair, who failed even to notice her. She was now on the other side of the service corridor and walking on the thick, blue pile carpets that led to the single Premium suites. A quick glance at the iPhone confirmed that the potential target was now within one hundred metres. She needed to make a decision, and quickly. She checked the GPS overview for the team: no one was close, and the nearest green dot signifying a team member was on Deck 6.

I'll have to go it alone.

Every SF mission tiptoes that fine line separating action from consequence. And this was the contractor equivalent of the Charge of the Light Brigade!

The Upper Deck

Ricky was running through the options in his mind. The fear had subsided as he had rationalised his thoughts. He knew that the bad guys were 'good to go' and he guessed that the team that he now felt part of was seriously outnumbered. He looked at the Glock.

It's wasted, hiding in a paint store!

He was still dressed for his job below decks. He could still blend with the rest of the crew. He checked his old iPhone; he was sure that it could still transmit video from the covert camera behind his shirt button.

That could be a valuable asset for the team! Yeah, I've got to try and do something. I'll go back down to X8.

The team's DCA had made his decision; just doing nothing had become too heavy a burden to bear. He stood up, shook the white sheet from his shoulders, took a few deep breaths and then checked his equipment. He quickly ran through the inventory in his mind.

I've a Glock and two mags, should be 30 rounds. I have my knife and my comms kit. And my CQB skills.

He checked his phone; the battery was only at 50 per cent. He made sure that the camera was linked, then tapped out a message on Telegram to Jimmy, and pressed Send.

SORRY MATE, I'M MOVING TO X8 TO USE CAMERA.

He checked the Glock and slid it into the front of his trousers. He pulled his polo shirt over it and then reversed the procedure, to make sure he could draw it quickly. He adjusted his belt, let it out a notch and repeated the draw.

That's better!

The knife was placed at the rear of his belt, to his right, but he felt better having the Glock.

Never good, just having a knife in a gunfight!

The wind was picking up now, and he had to push against the door before he once again hit the salt spray of the North Atlantic. He thought he knew the route back; he tried to envisage the internal mapping of the ship. He would have to make his way along the staff corridors on Deck 8 and then drop down to the stores complex. He walked quickly along the exposed outer deck, ducking down as he passed some small portholes that leaked light. He clambered quickly up a crew ladder, found his bearings and was then ready to make his way back to storeroom X8 - and danger. Just as he pressed down on the latch his phone buzzed. He quickly looked at the Telegram message from Jimmy:

STOP! DANGER! ASSETS ON WAY IN, 10 MINUTES! GO BACK

This, now, was his individual decision point.

What his handler, Lou, had said back at Repton Manor flashed into his mind:

Always remember that what some people call the Great Game isn't a game at all, it's life or death, and you can never just cheer from the sidelines.

He opened the door, stepped through and turned towards the interior of the ship. Towards danger.

CHAPTER THIRTY-TWO

Cabin 2004.

At the end of the corridor, Abdul Haq had prepared his trap. It was now twenty minutes since he had activated his group, and they would be gathering in their four-man teams, ready for action and its consequences. They all knew that they would die today, and they all embraced the idea of death.

The British team would now have to react quickly to find him. If they were tracking the iPhone, they would be coming straight for him, drawn away from where the real carnage would begin, in the Britannia Restaurant. There would be at least twenty SF troops on board. He knew a team would come his way.

The brigadier placed the iPhone on the bathroom cabinet, over his ticking gift for the ship and the Western world. Opening the double sliding doors that led outside onto the cabin's private balcony, he stepped out, partly closing the doors behind him. He also pulled the curtains to, checking that he could still observe the bathroom through the softly swaying dark blue drapes. He took the silenced pistol from its shoulder holster, brought it up on aim and scanned the room over its open sight. *Maybe the Brit SF will use a flash/crash grenade first, but perhaps not, especially if they expect an IED. I will plan for either option. They will have body armour, so head shots only!*

It was cold on the balcony; he could hear an angry sea behind him as the odd speck of spume splashed across his face. He could taste the salt spray. All his senses were sharp now, and time had slowed. *All I have to do is wait.*

Samantha crept now, as she approached the target cabin. The red dot and the green dot on the mapping had converged. She felt that old familiar feeling deep in the pit of her stomach: pre-combat nerves knowing that death could come with the red dot. Her pulse started to race as the adrenaline kicked in. She liked the feeling and was now in the zone, truly alive in that unsafe space between life and death. She looked at the surroundings, a very upmarket suite, thick carpets and luxury. Her mind was racing now, trying to rationalise what she was thinking as her heart was beating out of her chest.

If this is where the red dot says a terrorist is, maybe he's the team leader – and maybe he has control of the device.

She took a deep breath to calm herself, plucked the universal key card from her shoulder bag and inserted it into the lock with her left hand, with her Glock 9 mill in her right at waist level. The lock clicked, and she eased the door slightly open. The balcony curtains were drawn, and the cabin was in semi-darkness. One of the small bedside lights was on. An opened book lay on the bedside table with a half-filled glass alongside it. The room's key card that kept the power on was missing. Some discarded clothing lay on the bed.

It looks like someone left in a hurry.

Sam pushed the door open with her very expensive left shoe and entered the cabin in a controlled rush, looking over the sights of her modified Glock 19, first pressure on the trigger. She scanned the room as she had been trained, with the Glock in the Weaver position, the right arm holding the pistol fully extended, the left shoulder forward and the left hand pressing back against the right, applying gentle pressure.

LEFT- RIGHT- CENTRE

She quickly searched the room, a quick visual scan and then under the bed, the wardrobe and drawers. It was a frantic search; she was trying to remember all those pointers from her previous training. *When searching a series of drawers open the bottom one first, just like a thief, so you can then open them moving upwards. It saves time.*

She looked to the right again. The bathroom door was open, and in the dim light she spotted an iPhone handset on top of the cabinet by the washbasin. She moved to the door, banged it hard with her shoulder, checked behind it, and then she was in the bathroom.

She looked for somewhere large enough to hide a device. She checked for anything out of place in the bathroom. The plastic panel below the wash basin looked like it had been disturbed. She pressed with the palm of her hand and it gave way. She removed the faux marble panel and then she saw it. She pressed the Send button on her comms.

Deck 8, Corridor C

Taff's eyes were drawn to a blur of movement just where the mapping had indicated a hostile presence. A black-garbed figure had rushed into a cabin with a bag. Somebody was in a real hurry, and that's unusual on a cruise ship. He quickly snatched the Glock from the shoulder holster under his dinner jacket, took the suppressor from his right pocket and pressed it home. He half smiled at the absurdity of it.

It's like a clichéd scene from a James Bond movie. The hero, dressed in black tie, pulls out the pistol, fits the silencer and prepares to kill the bad guys.

But that's just what he was going to try to do. He always could sense danger; it had kept him alive in Iraq and Afghanistan. He brought the pistol up on aim and moved up to the door.

The terrorists on board had to meet somewhere. Maybe this room was it.

He moved soundlessly, placing his feet carefully on the thick carpet until he had reached the cabin. He stood with his back to the wall, weapon in the Weaver stance and pointing towards the threat and listened to the conversation from within. At least three men were speaking in low tones in a language he didn't understand. He heard the odd metallic clink and the sound of a large zip being undone, then there was silence and some murmured prayers in classical Arabic. Taff understood the prayer: they were ready for death.

He had to go. He mentally prepped himself. STAND BY! STAND BY!

Cabin 2004

Abdul Haq's hands were steady. He had seen the blonde girl clear the room very professionally. *But she didn't check the balcony.* He smiled because he knew who she was.

So, this is the Angel of Death!

He sighted his silenced pistol on the back of a head with long blonde hair and applied the first pressure to the trigger. The dum-dum bullet, with its mercury tip, would enter the back of that pretty blonde head and exit through her face, splashing it against the wall.

She's dead.

But no! That was too easy!

She was bending over the washbasin with the bottom half of a very shapely evening dress facing his way.

I want to make her suffer. I want to humiliate her.

In that split second, the professional soldier wrestled with his sadistic sexual tendencies. But the ISI man had always been a risk-taker, and the sadism won. The brigadier quickly returned his pistol to its nylon holster on his right hip, removed the stun gun from his pocket and got ready to move through the balcony doors.

He heard her send her location: "All Spartan call signs, this is Zero sending blind, I have the device, it's located in cabin 2004, Deck 2."

She needed both hands now. He saw her put the Glock into her bag and pull out a small Maglite torch. She shone the torch at the area under the hand basin, where the white panel had been removed. Underneath the sink was the expensive piece of Louis Vuitton luggage.

The girl was occupied and easy prey. Abdul Haq moved soundlessly across the thick carpet. She still had her slender backside pointing towards him. He admired her long blonde hair and caught the first faint scent of her perfume. But she had changed almost instantly, when he had decided not to shoot her, from a worthy adversary to a piece of meat. He wanted to abuse her, to humiliate her, to rape her and then kill her.

He was now within arm's length, and he extended the stun gun. He hit the sweet spot on her neck with the two small metal electrodes and 7,000 volts sparked into her body. The spasm was dramatic – she looked like a marionette whose strings had been slashed. Just a little scream of pain and she was out, and entirely senseless on the bathroom floor.

He was going to enjoy this.

He picked her up like a discarded rag doll and pulled her roughly by the ankles of her shapely legs over to the bed. She was light. He lifted her easily and dumped her onto the mattress, her bag still over her shoulder. He opened his briefcase and removed the handcuffs, smiling as he felt his power growing.

Deck 8, Corridor C

Ricky was moving quickly now. The staff corridor was strangely quiet, although he could hear the buzz of people and entertainment coming from the adjacent passenger area. He was trying to get as close as possible to where he had first listened to Manny give his orders. Once again, he suddenly felt that danger was nearby. It was the same eerie sensation that had kept him safe throughout his young life, a sort of warning signal, an itchy tingling at the back of his neck.

Where are all the staff? This corridor should be busy.

The abnormal is the absence of the normal.

Ricky slowed now; he just *knew* that danger was nearby. He pulled out the Glock and held it by his side as he approached another door that led into corridor C. He slowly opened the door and pulled it inwards to look along the corridor, and then he saw the burly figure of Taff waiting outside another door further down, with his pistol in the ready position.

Taff could still hear the odd murmur and clink of metal from inside the room as he stepped back to ensure the full force of his left shoulder against the door. He launched himself, it splintered easily, and he was in the room. He just had time to register the surprise on the first man's face as he killed him with two well-aimed shots to the head, a double tap. Taff pivoted to his right and engaged the second man as he was scrambling for a Skorpion pistol inside the black bag in the centre of the room. The two rounds hit him in quick succession: one burrowed deep into the shoulder of his outstretched arm, and the young Filipino was still looking in Taff's direction as the other 9mm round hammered into his face.

And that was when the ex-Marine ran out of luck as quickly as the two Jihadist terrorists had. He felt a sudden searing pain in his upper back as if someone had pushed in a red-hot poker.

Didn't check behind the door. Poor skills!

Taff felt his assailant's presence hard up against his back, heard him screaming, "ALLAHU AKBAR".

As Ricky saw the door being forced and heard the first muffled gunshots, he was already running to close the gap between him and Taff. His weapon was in full view now, but as soon as he heard the terrorist's shout, he stopped dead in his tracks and dived onto the floor. His immediate thought was *suicide vest! a*s he tried to make himself as small a target as possible.

At the same time the big Marine felt the indescribable pain of every part of the twelve-inch butcher's knife as it sliced through his body and grated on bone. The shock almost paralyzed his brain as his attacker tried to free the blade, stuck between the upper rib cage and shoulder blade, by vigorously rotating the knife's black plastic hilt. Taff heard himself scream; it was an almost primeval wail as he felt the knife come free.

The Jihadist held up the knife and prepared to slash it downwards in a deadly arc to finish the job. Relying more on instinct than thought, Taff moved the Glock under his left arm and pushed the silenced muzzle hard up against his assailant's chest.

PHUT- PHUT

The dead ISIS man hit the floor only a split second before Taff did himself. They landed almost together, their bodies intertwined and momentarily wedged in the instant before he brought the Glock on aim again.

PHUT

Another round smashed into the temple of the ISIS fighter's head.

He was definitely dead now!

Taff knew enough about trauma management to see that he also was probably dying. He then underwent the weirdest sensation, almost like an out-of-body experience. He was looking down at the scene from the ceiling, observing himself in an almost dispassionate way. There were three dead bodies and the one he had inhabited, with its life slowly leaving it.

So, this is death. At least I've had a good run.

There was very little pain now, just a dizzy, lightheaded feeling and an intense bodily heaviness, an overwhelming sense of tiredness. The adrenaline had gone, and death was slowly and painlessly creeping in. The warrior had turned his eyes towards home. He thought of his wife, and of a baby that would grow up without him. He could feel the blood bubble from under his white evening shirt. Even now, though, his highly trained mind automatically diagnosed the problem. The knife had sliced and punctured his lung. But … the storeroom's shelves were packed with ancillary items for the cabin stewards and the ship's offices. He used every last ounce of strength to pull himself towards the racks and selected the two things that might just help: a plastic-wrapped pack of toilet rolls and a large, thick, roll of Sellotape.

He tried hard to inhale but he was beginning to gasp now.

I have a sucking chest wound, and I've got to stop the bleeding. Taff somehow pulled his rapidly fading body upwards as he reached for the toilet rolls and the tape. He tried to tear the plastic sheeting from the outside of the toilet rolls but then his strength failed. He just couldn't do it!

Ricky was still lying on the floor waiting for the explosion that he knew he might not survive … but there was only silence. He stood up quickly, moved his pistol into the ready position and edged towards the opened door. As he got closer, he could hear a panting sound from inside the room. He edged up to the door with the Glock on aim. Inside, the former Marine had only the fighters he had killed for company. The waxen face of his knife attacker looked accusingly towards him, with stone-dead eyes. He didn't really know how much time he had left.

The guy with the staring dead eyes thought he had inflicted a killer blow. And maybe he had.

In that instant Taff rationalised that it was only a matter of incremental blood loss and time. His immediate intimacy with death clarified his thoughts. He didn*'t really believe in God as such, even at this late juncture in life, but he thought there was something beyond that final curtain. There were definitely greater powers at work in the universe than a simple bootneck could comprehend. He was not a philosopher, he was very much a soldier, but you do tend to think about 'what comes next?' when you have been around war, death, and killing as much as he had. He had resigned himself to it and felt calm. He thought about Sam: if only she was safe, he could cross the bar painlessly.* Then he heard the bang on the door and a shout.

"TAFF, SPARTAN, SPARTAN." He recognised the voice. "It's Ricky, I'm coming in, mate."

Taff managed to grunt a reply "OK, it's clear."

Ricky looked down at Taff while he tried to assess the situation. "OK Taff, everything's going to be OK, bruv."

Ricky was thinking ABC. *Airway:* he's talking, so unobstructed. *Breathing:* he's breathing – but only just, it's laboured. *Circulation: it looks like he's losing a lot of blood; his white shirt is covered in it.*

He pushed the Glock into his waist band and drew the knife he had on his right hip. At that very moment Taff opened his eyes, and what he saw seemed to confirm all his suspicions about Ricky. He tried to reach for his silenced pistol but had no strength.

So, this is where it ends!

"Right, Taff. Listen, mate. I'm going to cut away some of your outer clothing to look at the damage." Ricky took out his Quik-Clot package and cut the end of it. "Sounds like you have a sucking chest wound, buddy, so I need to seal up your chest."

There was no response. Ricky quickly cut away Taff's clothing from both the back and front of the wound, moving him as gently as possible, and prepared to apply the QuikClot to the large entry wound on his old instructor's back. He also used the plastic wrapping from the outside of the toilet rolls to seal the small bubbling wound in his chest.

"Don't worry, Taff, you're going to be all right." Taff heard the voice, but nothing after that.

Chapter Thirty-Three

Cabin 2004

Sam felt her leg being lifted as she woke with a heart-stopping rush of adrenaline, and immediately worked out what had happened. Fighting hard not to scream, she assessed the situation. She felt the handcuff bite as her assailant roughly attempted to manacle her right wrist to her right ankle. The man was smiling as he pulled her leg upward.

"BITCH", she heard, as the tightly fitted evening dress impeded his progress. He solved the problem by dropping Sam's leg and arm and ripping the French lace dress along its seam. It tore easily, and the man lifted her leg again. Sam was now wide awake but pretended not to be. He grunted as he once again grabbed her leg by the stainless-steel cuff around her ankle and pulled it roughly towards her right wrist. Sam resisted the almost involuntary need to wince in pain as her eyes momentarily flicked open. A manacled ankle, and her right foot wearing a very expensive evening shoe, loomed into view.

"I'm going to FUCK that before I kill you." He was leering at Sam's now-exposed bottom half.

The shoe was nearly up by her right ear when Samantha acted, as her rapist was distracted and looking between her legs. She rotated her trapped right wrist against her attacker's thumb, freed it and snatched the stiletto-heeled shoe from her foot. Sam now had her weapon. With a supreme effort she half-twisted her body so that she was now facing Haq, whipped the heel of the shoe into the left side of his face and kept it there, pressing the other side of his head with her left hand as she rapidly found the ear, inserted the spiked end of the tapering heel and rammed it through the soft membrane of his eardrum. The brigadier screamed in agony and fought to withdraw his pistol from its shoulder holster. Their eyes were locked together now, and they writhed together like lovers, but in the polar opposite of love.

Both pairs of eyes reflected fear and hate in equal proportions, as the panicking and frantic Abdul Haq tried to push her away with his left arm, while trying to free his pistol with his right. But he had lost his last battle, and felt the strength leaving him. Sam saw the last vestiges of arrogance drain from his face as he suddenly realised that she was stronger than him. She studied his face intently as she pushed the spike deeper into his brain. One convulsive shudder of pain, one final scream, and he had gone. She smashed the stiletto deeper still into his head with a sharp blow of the heel of her hand. The weight of his body slumped onto hers. She reached for her bag, snatched the Glock from it, pushed him upwards and fired the pistol at him.

BANG-BANG-BANG-BANG

Four shots struck the brigadier's body at point-blank range. She rolled the corpse off her with all her strength and it hit the carpet with a thump. Sam stood up on shaky legs and straddled him.

BANG, a final shot to the head.

"You're the one that's just been fucked," she snarled, with an expression of pure hate on her beautiful face. She had killed before, but always in combat. Undue emotion in a firefight usually confuses the senses and clouds good judgment; a professional soldier tries to operate entirely without rage. This time it was different.

This is the first time I've enjoyed it. It excited me.

The realisation of what she had just become now hit her. The strength drained from her body as she sat down, almost in a trance, on the bed.

I'm a stone-cold killer!

9/11/2021. Over the Atlantic

The Merlin was flying at 2,000 feet and 120 knots over an increasingly angry North Atlantic. The three powerful RTM322 Rolls Royce engines throbbed, straining, as the rotor blades pitted themselves against the force of the storm. The interior of the darkened cabin vibrated with each surge, and the gearbox strained as the aircraft made headway, only to be buffeted by high winds that almost seemed to halt its progress. The red glow of the cabin's nightlight silhouetted the swimmer canoeists of Purple Troop as Tom listened intently on the spare crew headset for any updates on the target.

"How are you doing back there?" the pilot asked.

"Good, George," Tom answered.

"Green light in ten, Tom."

"Yeah, roger that; we're all set here, mate."

The crewman in the seat next to him stood up and turned on his filtered head-torch.

An icy blast of air hit the cabin as he opened the starboard cargo door of the aircraft. He leaned out and checked the winch arm that protruded from the side. A shackle secured the ninety feet of neatly coiled, thick, black rope inside the door of the aircraft. A Cyalume stick was secured to the top of the rope with black masking tape; he cracked it, the chemicals mixed, and the plastic tube started to glow a bright orange. The SBS troopers began their final preparations by checking their weapons and kit. They tested their radios, confirming the net with a quick burst of squelch into their earpieces. They adjusted their lightweight black Pro-Tec helmets and pulled their respirators into position. Hands moved in unison over equipment, making sure that nothing would snag while roping down. They also made sure that their assault life vests were clear of their ammunition, flash-bangs and weapons.

Tom checked the chamber on his C8 and then put on his fast-rope gloves.

"Hello, all stations Purple." His voice was calm but with a steely edge. "A quick battle update, lads: we are going in hot." All the members of Purple Troop M Squadron knew what that meant. "Spartan is in contact."

They were about to land on the ship during a firefight.

"Roger that," all the Purple call signs answered sequentially, in an equally calm manner. Purple was just back from Syria, so it wouldn't be the first time.

Tom looked at his guys and raised his thumb, they all responded, and everybody was ready as the Merlin turned. His stomach churned as the aircraft dropped and increased speed as it spiralled downwards to its attack height. He moved his right hand to the release lever on his seat belt. It was always a good thing to do when over a rough sea at a low level – if a helicopter creams in when at attack height you only have seconds to try and exit the aircraft and swim clear. Tom checked that all the SBS men done the same thing.

Here we go!

And it *was* rough as the aircraft vectored onto its attack line. The airframe was now pierced by a cold Atlantic side wind that found its way through the opened starboard cargo door and into the very bones of the cabin's occupants. The Merlin was now skimming over force 6 seas at only 200 feet.

"Two minutes." Tom heard the ultra-professional and dispassionate voice of Gorgeous George on the Purple Troop net. "The Whisky call signs are on station now." He turned the aircraft into its final vector and into the wind.

The Whisky call signs were the two Wildcats with the heli-snipers on board. They would now be scanning the deck of the QM2 from both the port and starboard sides, looking for any armed terrorists.

"It's all clear from Whisky 1 and 2." George's voice remained emotionless.

"Hello, Queen Mary Two, this is Mike Tango One, deck lights in one minute."

"Yeah, roger that," said an equally terse Gav Loach from the bridge of the *Queen Mary 2*. A darkened deck would give the attacking troops an edge if opposed.

The green light went on, and the troops struggled to stand up. The crewman moved to the cargo door. They all knew what would happen now. They were the lead Merlin and they would be the first into contact. The helicopter would go even lower and approach under the level of the stern of the massive liner, effectively out of sight of anybody on the deck of the ship. The pilot would skim the waves at sea level and, at the last second, flare the Merlin into the wind above the nominated RDP at between sixty and ninety feet above the deck. The crewman would throw the rope out over the Landing Zone. The SBS men would then slide down, using the rope like a fireman's pole, into the pitch darkness below, with at least three of them on the rope at the same time. They would only use their NVGs when they hit the deck.

The Bridge, Queen Mary 2

The *Queen Mary*'s captain peered out into the night from the darkened bridge. The lights had been out since they had heard the massive explosion that had shaken the ship. Now, the vessel's internal communication systems were alive with the sound of gunfire and frenzied screams for help. As the fire alarm sounded, the First Officer gasped as he looked at the CCTV monitor and surveyed what had once been the Britannia Restaurant. The once joyous space, crowded with voyagers from the New York Fashion Week, was now a scarlet butcher's shop, littered with body parts and splintered furniture. The occupants of the bridge were silent and in shock. The swishing of the wipers to clear the rain on the bridge windows was the only sound until the ship's radio squawked into life and broke the spell.

"Hello *Queen Mary*, this is Mike One, one thousand metres and closing,"

"Roger that," said Gav. The occupants of the bridge all studied the TV monitor covering the ship's stern.

"Here they come!" said Gav.

"Mike One, on target now." And then the first Merlin loomed over the rear of the ship, and the rope was out.

The sound of gunfire rattled over the ship's internal communications system and then reverberated with a slight delay from inside the structure of the vessel. Jimmy, Pat and Scottie were working together to stop about eight Jihadists gaining access to the upper deck and bridge. The terrorists were trying to move along the carpeted accommodation corridor on Deck 3 towards the bridge and the Spartan guys were stopping their progress. An incoming torrent of gunfire rattled down the long narrow space, a deadly mixture of long bursts of either AK47 or Czech VZ Skorpion machine pistols. Jimmy and Pat had only their MP5Ks to return the fire and therefore kept low, popping up when they could. In between, they tried to melt into the thick pile of the carpet as either the AK's 7.62 bullets or the stubby 7.65 round from the VZ sprayed random patterns around where they had taken cover.

They had cover from view but not from fire. The heavier rounds from the AK were literally ripping down parts of the walls above their heads. Jimmy was lying flat at the end of the corridor, on the right-hand side. Pat was sheltering from the next stairwell up; it gave him an excellent field of fire right along what had become a shooting gallery. The gunfight had settled into a pattern; it was obvious that the terrorists hadn't quite worked out how to use fire and movement on a ship. They would spray the area with bullets and then try to rush the ground. Scottie, on the opposite side of the corridor to Jimmy, was the only Spartan call sign properly armed with a 'long': he had his 5.56 SIG Sauer MCX in his shoulder, with his back hard up against a steel safety door so he could engage along a target-rich environment when the Jihadists charged. The four dead terrorists in the corridor paid testament to Spartan's superior tactics.

The Merlin MK 4

Tom was first. The rain had spattered against the darkened lenses on his respirator, and he couldn't make out the black rope against the ink-black sky. He took a deep breath, reached for the Cyalume, found the rope with both hands and he was away. As he was halfway towards the deck another SBS man was already sliding down the rope above him. Tom hit the solid teak deck hard and rolled away; he had to fight hard to stop the downdraught from the Merlin pushing him into the ship's swimming pool. The entire troop was on deck now, and the helicopter was away and standing off. Tom placed his weapon into the shoulder and scanned the LZ. The rain was still falling hard as he tipped down the NVGs mounted against his helmet. He spoke calmly into his throat mike.

"Hello Mike One, all down safe. Thanks, George."

"You're welcome," said Gorgeous George in a fake American accent.

There was another call in an urgent voice.

"Purple Zero, Whisky One, X-ray on deck, SHOT."

The heli-sniper, with his ACOG sight in night mode, had spotted movement in the area of the LZ and scanned a suspicious figure. He held the H&K Sharpshooter sniper rifle as steady as possible as he considered who, apart from a terrorist, would be on the upper deck in a storm.

Maybe a crew member or a Spartan operator, or even a drunk passenger?

The red dot flickered over the figure, searching for a weapon. And then he spotted the distinctive outline of the AK 47, with its banana-shaped magazine, just as the figure brought the rifle into his shoulder. The heli-sniper aimed for the head, kept the dot steady and put first pressure on the trigger.

On the deck, the Jihadi fighter had watched the whole scene with amazement. He hadn't heard or seen the helicopter until it was almost on top of him. He had hidden, but now he must fight. The men dressed in black had arrived, sliding down a Devil's rope, a falling of black-garbed demons from Hell. He aimed the iron sights of the old AK 47 towards the new arrivals.

That looks like their leader.

The blade of the foresight steadied onto the black figure. He took up first pressure on the trigger and then the ship rolled; he had to steady himself against the outside bulkhead with his left hand. He again brought the assault rifle up on aim, steadying the foresight onto the central mass of the leader. He controlled his aim. Then he died. A 7.62mm frangible bullet, made of lead and wax and designed to shatter on impact, entered his left cheek and threw him violently sideways, smashing his head backward against the bulkhead.

"Whisky One – SHOT, OUT. Tom, you owe me a pint, mate."

Tom recognised the voice. "That's a big roger, Bill."

"OK Purple, let's get this done," Tom said into his radio fit.

"Roger. Purple one to the primary," said one team leader.

"Roger. Purple two to the secondary," said the other. And the SBS went to war.

Chapter Thirty-Four

Queen Mary 2, Deck 2

Tom's team had killed three X-rays so far and they could hear sporadic bursts of gunfire as they gained access to Deck Two. They arrived in the corridor via a small set of service stairs. The black-clad SBS men moved as a team in one fluid motion, with a confidence that comes only from constant practice. A Sabre Squadron in its 'Black Role' spends hundreds of hours shooting and practising room combat. The team flowed along the corridor in a controlled rush, weapons extended and looking over their sights.

Tom had nominated himself as lead scout. After they entered the ornately decorated corridor the sounds of screams, bangs and the rattle of small arms had faded. There was just a low, vaporous fog of smoke that swirled around the floor. He was leading from the front, looking through the darkened eyepieces of his respirator. As a former counter-IED operator, the role of lead scout was one with which he was more than familiar. But trying to maintain your awareness was a problem in a black-tinted Scott M94 respirator. Within its confines, his senses were dominated by the smell of rubber and the magnified roar of his breathing as he made his assessment. Small rivulets of sweat made the inside of the mask uncomfortable and misted his eyepieces.

He had slung his short-barrelled Colt C8 carbine over his shoulder. In his left hand he held a Thermo Fisher RadEye radiation detector that was starting to register as he moved down the corridor. In his right hand was a bit of kit from the other end of the technical spectrum: a spray can of Silly String, a children's party accessory. Tom sprayed the can in front of him. The ultra-light strands of plastic string drifting to the ground allowed him to detect tripwires. It was an old school trick that had kept Tom alive before, when he had had the unenviable job of searching caves in Afghanistan.

The ship's corridor seemed to rise and fall away slightly as the *Queen Mary* made a turn in the heavy seas. There was sometimes the heavy thump of a wave hitting the side of the ship that sent a shudder through the frame of the mighty vessel. The only sounds now were the tinkling of some of the cabin sprinkler systems and a kind of collective low moan of terror emanating from the passenger cabins.

Tom's peripheral vision could pick up the barrel of one of his men's C8, hovering over his right shoulder. They were shuffling forward in perfect unison and mutual support, trying to address the two separate threats: Tom was looking for something that might blow them up and his companion was looking for someone who might want to shoot them. As the corridor lurched again, a cabin door suddenly sprang open.

"TARGET RIGHT," the man behind him shouted, as he moved the red dot on his ACOG swiftly onto the centre of mass of the rather pretty brunette head that had suddenly popped into sight. A red spot from the sight shimmered on her forehead as Gary prepared to double-tap the threat. The girl screamed, in a howl of bright red lipstick, as she saw the black-garbed and masked SBS guys. He relaxed his trigger finger as he identified the girl.

"NO THREAT. BRITISH SPECIAL FORCES. CLOSE THE DOOR, LIE ON THE FLOOR" he shouted, as he pointed to the

Union Jack stitched onto Tom's right shoulder. The door slammed immediately.

A tap on Tom's shoulder signalled when it was OK; they hadn't far to go. Nature had marked the exact spot. A dark stain of not-yet-congealed blood had seeped into the thick blue carpet under the door of cabin 2004 and indicated the way. He put the RadEye into his chest webbing, raised his arm and made the clenched-hand sign, indicating to the rest of the team that he intended to breach the door. He grabbed the shortened pump shotgun from the rear of his body armour.

Tom shouted "British Special Forces" as the shotgun pointed towards the door lock.

"Sam Holloway, Spartan," she said in a loud but calm voice. "Please come in, it's clear."

He lowered the shotgun and replaced it on his back. The door appeared to be partially open and didn't need the firepower. He flipped up his respirator, pressed against the door and tried to fully open it, but something from inside seemed to push back. He pushed harder, the door yielded, and he detected the source of the resistance and also of the blood seeping from a middle-aged man's very dead body. His dead eyes were still gazing up at a very elegant Art Deco light fitting. Tom noticed two things straight away: the man's gleaming dental work and the shiny high-heeled shoe sticking out of his left ear. But he didn't need to be a trained pathologist to deduce that the unusual ear accessory was not the only cause of death. The torso was smothered in blood from perhaps four different gunshots, and there was also a neat entry hole placed very precisely between two amazed-looking eyes. A curious pistol fitted with a suppressor was clutched in the lifeless right hand.

Tom's face registered his surprise.

"Hi, Tom," said the girl sitting on the bed. She was breathing heavily and seemed in a state of mild shock, so the gently smiling face surprised him. "Yeah, an unusual sight, I suppose. Not a good way to die, is it? And the room's in a bit of a mess, I'm afraid."

She paused and looked down at the body. "I haven't had time to call Housekeeping yet."

She was sitting bolt upright, in a white, ripped but still elegant evening dress smeared with blood. She held a Glock 19 in her right hand that was similarly bloodied. One half of a pair of stainless-steel handcuffs was attached to her right ankle. On her left foot, Tom spotted the matching stiletto for the one protruding from the dead man's ear.

"Jimmy Choo, Romy 65, 2020 season, they were," Sam said, "and I've only just borrowed them."

"I suppose that's the bad guy?" Tom looked towards the corpse.

"Yeah, that's a big roger," Sam said, as she wiped the blood-smeared Glock pistol on the Cunard-logo bed cover.

"I don't think you've had the pleasure of meeting the man who brought the bomb on board." She nudged the body with her bloodstained right foot. "Unfortunately, he's not seeing visitors at the moment."

"Doesn't look like he sees fuck all, Sam," said the SBS man.

The bleeping of his radiation monitor changed the subject and put a stop to the black humour.

"You need to get out of here now – the radiation level is off the scale."

Sam glanced down at the bracelet that she was wearing, which was her dosimeter. It had changed colour from a mint opal to an opaque pink, registering high.

"Where's the device?"

"It's over there, under the sink." Sam pointed limply with the Glock towards the bathroom. "I got ambushed by our dead friend before I could confirm it."

"OK, Sam, you have to leave NOW," Tom said with some urgency. "Let me deal with this."

"Can you defuse it?"

"I haven't got a fucking clue," Tom answered, as he removed his backpack while stepping over the body.

"Gary, look after Captain Sam, mate. Get her back to the top deck." The other SBS Marine, who was propping the door open with his shoulder and looking back down the passage, suddenly had a thought.

The Spartan team had been isolated, outnumbered, and scrapping for at least five minutes before we hit the LZ during a full-on firefight.

What if they are all dead? What if she's the only survivor?

"Roger that, Boss. Do we need to organise the evacuation of the ship?"

"No mate, hardly worth it," Tom said, placing his black bag on the floor of the bathroom. "We just haven't got time."

He opened the heavy-duty zip that ran around his Ops bag to reveal the glitter of various tools, gauges and monitors.

"Everything will be atomised for two clicks around if this fucker goes bang, so why bother to panic them any more than they already are?"

He opened another layer of his Ops bag and pulled out a mirror on a cantilever-type device that looked like a thin black robotic arm. It extended almost magically to its full height and its function was immediately apparent: it was a magnifying glass with a powerful LED light. A small video camera was mounted on the end to record Tom's efforts if he were successful. As he set up, M Squadron's battle static that had reverberated in his earpiece since they had roped down was suddenly quiet. The frantic mixture of calls, shouts, explosions, screams and intermittent gunfire had stopped. The firefight was over.

It was an all-stations call.

"Hello, all stations Mike, this is Purple Zero Alpha." He recognised the calm voice of Sergeant Davey Slater, his second in command on this operation.

"Ship secure. I say again, ship secure." The transmission paused and then supplied the information that Tom was keen to hear, known in the military as a contact report.

Were any of his guys dead or injured? Tom steeled himself for bad news as reports from M Squadron's sub-units were fed into the control station. Then finally:

"Hello, all stations, this is Purple Zero Alpha. Twelve X-rays (enemy) neutralised, 20 pax (passengers) down (dead or injured). No Purple call signs down. Ammunition at fifty percent. CASEVAC is due from the FOB in 30 minutes."

"Purple Zero Alpha, this is Purple Zero," Tom transmitted. "Hello, all stations, well done, lads. Comms will now go dark as I look at a device found in Cabin 2004, Deck 2, that appears to be the obvious."

Chapter Thirty-Five

The SBS teams on the other end of this radio transmission all knew why their radios would temporarily cease to function. Tom was going to turn on his mini-Antler, his radio-jamming device, while he examined the bomb. The jammer would interfere with all incoming radio and phone traffic, just in case another firing mechanism was on the ship. Sergeant Slater would talk to Gav on the bridge, to make sure that the ship's phone and Wi-Fi system also went dark.

Tom removed the cover from underneath the washbasin to get a good look at the device. Everything from now on was just a matter of pitting his ten years of experience in defusing IEDs against the level of skill of the bomb-maker. He knew that lots of IEDs were modular systems; the spider might have been put together at an entirely different place from the engineering work.

There were certain places in Pakistan where IED workshops employing skilled technicians competed with each other to produce the best radio-control set up. 'The spider' was the name given by British Army bomb disposal personnel to the DTMF, the Dual-Time Multi-Frequency unit. A DTMF was simply a circuit board attached to a small antenna that decoded phone or radio signals and was, therefore, the key component in the IED's firing chain. It would be on a fail-safe as well; you wouldn't put a thing like this together without a timing device incorporated into it. Tom glanced at his SBS 'Omega Seamaster Pro'. It was set on the operations Zulu time and read 07.50 am.

Tom had defused scores of different IEDs, ranging from the simple to the complex. In the early days in Helmand, the Taliban had used the crush-initiated device, like a simple plastic water bottle, to trigger anti-vehicle mines. Pakistan's ISI-had issued the more sophisticated IEDs to kill the Coalition's counter-IED specialists, but any bomb could be built with a variety of anti-tamper functions to detonate it. If it were picked up it could be triggered by a pressure release switch; if moved, an anti-tilt switch; if exposed to light, a photosensitive micro-switch. Tom looked at the device and discounted all anti-tamper options with this piece of kit.

Anti-tamper would make it pretty hard to install and use on a ship.

He turned on the small video camera at the end of the skeletal black arm. He would now talk through his observations for the next poor bastard who had to defuse something similar.

"Guys, getting ready to take a look at this now."

"Yeah, roger that, Boss," said an SBS Marine, as he started to search the dead body on the floor.

Tom looked at the device now illuminated by the sharp LED light. He cleared his throat nervously.

It seemed a bit fucked up, chatting on your Jack Jones. But here goes, he thought.

"The suspect device is inside an oblong trunk. It doesn't appear to have any anti-handling systems, or at least it would be highly unusual if it did in this scenario."

As if to test his theory the ship lurched violently to starboard and the bomb moved with it.

"That sort of checks out my thinking," he said casually into the mike, as his heart pounded in his chest.

"So, the first thing I'm going to do is move this thing so I can work on it."

Tom moved towards the device and carefully picked it up by the carrying handle. He carried it into the centre of the cabin, very near to where the ex-brigadier continued to stare blankly at the ceiling. The rest of the team now sealed the corridor, with one operator listening in at the door in case help was needed. Tom removed a long, thin, articulated cable from his open bag and threaded it under the lid. The cable was an endoscope camera, and the video screen now showed the inside of the trunk.

"It looks like there are no anti-tamper switches on the inside. I'm going to take the lid off now." He switched the camera to exterior view and opened the trunk.

"I'm looking inside now. It looks like a titanium plate with four screws." Tom took a small battery screwdriver, removed the screws and then released the plate.

"Gotcha!"

Tom recognised the type of spider that was at the heart of the firing mechanism. A small, thin, plastic-covered wire antenna extended from a transparent plastic circuit board. It was the Dual-Time Multi-Frequency unit, and Tom smiled as he realised that he had seen this type of spider before.

"This device was manufactured at an ISI-sponsored workshop in a border town called Chaman, in Pakistan. The Chinese writing on the main section of the DTMF indicates that the parts originate from a mobile company called Zong, that used to trade as China Mobile Pakistan. It therefore has a bandwidth of 1800 MHz: it can cover from GSM up to 5G and is capable of using advanced encryption."

"Now this is the difficult bit," he said into the mike.

Tom took a deep breath as he quietly thought of his next step.

He thought back to the last time he had seen such a colour and wiring configuration. It had been on a complicated Pakistani-made device when he was attached to 40 Commando in Sangin. He thought he recognised the configuration of the wires. It was a nightmare device. Every spider in the same batch was identical, but that's where the similarities finished, and the difficulties started. The ISI issued devices were designed to defeat the Coalition's best bomb disposal officers. One of the wires was designed to trigger the device if it was disabled in the wrong order, and the whole thing triggered anyway if the wires were not all cut within a 300 second time frame.

"I don't know the wiring sequence; I will need to check my disposal log," he said calmly and clearly. But Tom was far from calm on the inside – although he had felt this pressure before, the stakes had never been so high. He took several deep breaths and tried to calm his nerves. He looked down at his right hand; there was a slight tremor. He concentrated until the tremors stopped and he was ready to crack on.

Get a fucking grip. Tom mentally visualised his next step.

I've got butterflies in my stomach the size of those fucking seagulls that stole my ice cream in Newquay last year.

The funny memory calmed him as he rummaged into his bag once again and removed a small green plastic notebook. The book was both sequenced numerically and dated chronologically. The spider he remembered was the twenty-third bomb he had defused on that tour. He turned to the tattered page and looked at the wiring diagram he had scrawled on the page at the time.

I wish I'd taken more time over that.

"OK." Tom resumed his commentary, glancing at his Omega Seamaster; it was set on the operation's Zulu time and it was 08.25. Once he snipped the first wire, he knew he would have just 300 seconds to defuse it. The IED men in Afghanistan called it the 'five minutes of fear'.

The SBS major returned to his shiny tool kit. "I'm taking out small-size snippers. There are seven wires and, according to the last time I dealt with this spider, two of them are dummies." He steadied his hand; it was beginning to tremble again. Tom stopped as he consulted the wiring diagram. A small area of it had been partially obscured by a drop of Helmand-generated sweat that must have dripped from his brow when hastily copying the wiring. He wasn't sure whether the last wire was black or white.

Then: BEEP-BEEP-BEEP.

"That's the firing mechanism," he said calmly. "Here goes," he muttered, as he clipped the yellow, blue, and red wire in quick succession. His heart was booming now; his eardrums were banging like bass drums as he held his breath slightly after each snip.

"Now the guesswork,'" he said into the mike as he checked his watch. The brow wire on the diagram had a D next to it, meaning danger. He left it alone.

BEEP-BEEP-BEEP.

It said 0827: Tom steadied his hand again. "I have a white wire and a black wire, but they can only be snipped in sequence … Here's the green." He snipped. *No bang!*

"I was sure of that one. Now the guesswork: black or white?"

Tom felt as if a palpable sense of fear was leaving the pit of his stomach and rising into his throat. He fought his natural urge to shout, if only to release some of the tension. He tried to concentrate as his hand hovered between the two wires.

BEEP.

Now he had to make a choice, and time had almost run out. White or black, light or shade, joy or mourning? The thought of his wife on their wedding day suddenly flashed into his mind. *I'm going for the white.*

BEEP.

SNIP. He cut the white wire and then:

BEEEEEP, then sudden silence.

"Thank fuck for that!" he said. He checked his Omega: it was 08:29.30.

Thirty seconds to spare.

Tom reached across, turned off the Antler jammer and transmitted.

"Hi, all stations Purple, this is Purple Zero." He thought of how well his men had done, smiled and said just four words.

"The bomb is safe."

Tom could hear the joyous whoop from his lads in the corridor, just as he leaned over the cabin's washbasin and was violently sick. An SBS man shouted into the cabin with a concerned edge to his voice. He glanced down at the left sleeve of his FRIS and checked his dosimeter. It was high.

"You OK, Boss? You been sick? Probably radiation sickness."

"No, Simmo, abject fucking fear!"

Chapter Thirty-Six

Queen Mary 2, Ground Zero plus ten

Samantha's face registered her shock at the carnage as she and the SBS man carefully picked their way past the epicentre of the suicide attack and into the main concourse. The luxury liner looked and smelled like an abattoir; the metallic scent of the blood that had drenched the carpets still hung in the air. They stepped over two bodies interlocked at the very moment of death. A black-masked terrorist still had a foot-long carving knife embedded in the half-severed neck of what had once been a beautiful young woman excited about New York Fashion Week. The terrorist had two neat holes in the back of his head, courtesy of M Squadron.

Sam stopped and looked back at the young girl whom they had just stepped over.

Her only mistake had been being in the wrong place at the right time.

"Give me a hand here." Her dazed demeanour suddenly evaporated, and she was back. She started to untangle the two bodies.

"Boss Tom said to leave that for the SOCO (Scenes of Crime) guys, Sam."

"I'm not going to leave this young girl to get photographed like that, with this wanker," Sam replied decisively. "You got your body fit (camera) rolling?"

"No, wait one," he said, as he pressed the button to record the scene. "Yeah, roger that." Gary understood; his footage would have to do.

He watched as Samantha knelt by her side and tried to recover some of the young girl's lost dignity. She first pulled her murderer free, without thought or emotion. She then gently started to rearrange the girl's clothing. The two opposing halves of an act of savage violence: the victim and the perpetrator, the innocent and the damned. With the arrival of violent death, the young woman's arms looked porcelain white and painfully thin. The deep wounds from her assailant's carving knife had incised her left forearm in scarlet streaks like a wild animal's claw marks, and the blade that had almost severed her right arm was still lodged halfway through her neck. Sam ripped off the hem of her own tattered evening dress. Once she had laid the young girl alongside the passageway, she briefly bowed her head in thought and then covered the girl's face in the most delicate Chantilly lace Paris had to offer.

"We've got to move, Sam. Must get you back to Taff soonest," the SBS man said, though privately thinking that the big lad was probably dead.

Gary's earpiece buzzed with the post-contact radio traffic, mostly medical requests, as M Squadron and the onboard Cunard medical staff prioritised evacuation for the most severely injured. The Britannia Grill restaurant was the worst hit: dead bodies and human debris of all types littered the ground. A bloody shoe here, a severed hand there. A shrapnel-filled suicide vest had killed ten and maimed scores more.

As she climbed the stairs, Sam reached down and picked up a child's training shoe covered in blood. It had once been covered in twinkling lights as the little boy played below; now it was singed with explosive residue. Sam had never seen anything sadder. She slowly and reverently put the tiny shoe back onto the carpet as she continued up the stairwell towards the upper deck.

"The main casualty triage point is on the aft sun deck; they have made that the ERV, Sam," Gary said. "We can find out what's happening with the Spartan guys there."

"OK, I'm on it," said Sam. She was slightly ashamed that during the whole contact she had not actually thought about the safety of her husband. The fast-changing situation and her own perilous position had just compartmentalised the compassionate side of her nature. But she now felt a sense of dread. *Was he OK?*

Gary opened the door as Sam stepped through onto Deck 8. The acrid smell of smoke, burning plastic and blood faded as they walked upwards, to be replaced by a cold blast of wind from the North Atlantic. The teak-floored deck of the terrace pool was covered in blood and the injured. Some were still lying on stretchers, with others occupying the sun loungers. The medically trained Cunard staff and the SBS first responders busied themselves trying to help. The ship's doctor, who had once served as a military medical officer in Iraq, triaged the casualties as soon as they appeared on deck.

As in any disaster the victims were graded by survivability, with the saddest part of the deck reserved for the shattered corpses of the dead. They were lying side by side around the ship's main swimming pool, cocooned within thermal blankets that had been taped tight around them to prevent the downwash from the helicopters exposing their hideous injuries. The swimming pool was tinged pink with their blood.

A seemingly never-ending relay of improvised stretchers moved the severely injured and wounded casualties onto the upper deck, where the helicopters that had delivered M Squadron were now ferrying the wounded back to HMS *Queen Elizabeth*.

Sam spotted Taff straight away, as two SBS men with a stretcher exited the stairwell door. Ricky was walking beside them, holding a saline drip. Taff was secured to the stretcher on his injured side, to help him breathe. The SBS medic who had hooked him up to the saline drip was now holding an oxygen mask over his patient and talking to him. Taff's face was a waxen white, and his eyes were closed. "Come on, buddy, don't give up, hang in there, mate," Sam heard him say. She ran towards her husband, who lay ashen-faced and still.

Sam was sobbing now. She reached out, touched his face and stroked his cheek. His face felt cold. Sam had seen death before, and her soldier side resurfaced.

"Is he dead?" She mouthed the words, hardly wanting the sound to come out.

The medic understood immediately. "He's strong and he's going to make it," he said loudly.

In that instant, she realised that the ostensibly upbeat assessment was because he thought the seemingly unconscious Taff might be listening. He looked at Sam and smiled reassuringly, but his eyes were sending a different message. The stretcher was laid in the triage line, and the two SBS men immediately turned and rushed back to help others. The medic secured the drip to a wooden sun chair, checked the flow and shot the drip with a needle. "Look after him," he said to Ricky, and quickly followed the others.

"Hang in there, Taff." Ricky's voice was tight with emotion.

Sam looked at her husband. He looked at peace, and that worried her. She placed her hand on his face and gently kissed him. His face still felt icy cold. She whispered urgently in his ear.

"Don't leave me, Nigel, I love you, and I need you, and this baby needs a father." She thought she saw his eyelids flicker in response. Two Cunard crewmen then gently picked up the stretcher to carry it to the landing site on the next deck, as the sound and downdraught of an approaching Merlin made any further conversation impossible. Taff was leaving, and Sam wept.

Ricky, in all his young life, could never have imagined himself in this position. He held out his arms, still stained with Taff's blood, towards the sobbing Sam, and she stepped towards them.

***

MI6 Operations Room, Vauxhall

The live Operations Room at Vauxhall was high-tech, with lofty ceilings and the inevitable government-issue magnolia walls, most of which were covered with television monitors and computer screens. Danny's stress levels had risen steadily since the first "Contact, Wait Out" from Sam's team, and had skyrocketed as the first SBS guys had roped onto the deck. Now the live feed from M Squadron's communications crackled over the wall-mounted speakers, interspersed with the constant boom of explosions and bursts of gunfire. Tim was beside him, cradling his head in his hands as the contact reports continued to reflect the tenacity of the opposition. He above all others felt personally responsible for the teams now in contact on the ship. He had understood the threat, and he had directed them to apply his solution to the problem.

Mac sat next to them and stared ahead impassively with an expression that he had perfected in many high-stress situations over the years. The outer façade of stoic resolve actually masked an agile mind racing hard to keep one step ahead of events on the ground. He fully realised that they, collectively, had no influence on whatever might happen aboard the QM2, and Mac was now thinking about other operations that still might unfold.

The sense of relief was palpable when they had finally heard the codeword "Citadel Secure", meaning that M Squadron had full operational control of the ship and that the device had been neutralised and made secure. There was a brief moment of jubilation, but then the mood darkened as the data feed from the helicopter overview changed to pictures instantaneously transmitted from the SBS men's body cams. The true horror of the attack immediately hit home as the carnage in and around the Britannia Restaurant flickered jerkily onto the largest monitor, accompanied by involuntary gasps of shock from the webcams. Danny had seen a trail of such carnage from Belfast to Baghdad, from Karachi to Kabul. Such sights are always indelibly seared into the memory and truly unforgettable, but this raw footage still shocked even his hardened soul.

The random nature of the application of high explosive liberally laced with fragments of steel was all too visible. All that was left at the seat of the explosion was some of the charred wreckage of the furniture and the scattered remains of ten human beings that had been haphazardly and horrifyingly disassembled by the blast and were now only just recognisable as such. It was as if some ravenous carnivore had simply ripped them apart, limb from limb, sparing no one. Danny had to avert his gaze from the mangled body of a young child; it was just too sad for the old warrior as he contemplated the fragility of existence. A child's life ripped away for an evil ideology in an ugly twist of fate. Danny had debriefed failed suicide bombers before, and he knew how Islamists justified the death of the innocent. In their twisted version of Islam, the child, if a Muslim, would just be going to a better place, along with the wanker that sent him there. *Absolutely fucking mindless.*

They had at least twenty dead on the ship, probably thirty; only time would tell. That was the difference between success and failure – just the body count and timing. The team had done exactly what had been required of them, and he was proud but sad. He felt a single tear roll down his face before he checked himself and thought of what might happen in the future if this and other evils were allowed to continue to flourish.

Epilogue

Humberside, Toronto

Little Tommy clung to his mummy's leg as she was attempting to put on his winter coat. He was crying.

"Come on Tommy, you'll need your coat," Samantha said. "Else you'll miss seeing your friends at Tiny Bears."

Tommy just cried some more; it was the same battle every time he had to leave his mother. It had been nearly three years since her last job, and those hideous sights and sounds on the QM2 had faded into memory, to be replaced by the quiet and stillness of Humberside, a safe and prosperous suburb of Toronto in a place aptly named Baby Point Crescent. They lived within a gated community with everything they could possibly want. The house was detached within beautifully kept communal gardens and came with sport facilities and a pool. Sam's life had changed beyond recognition, and everything had just seemed to click into place. Taff had fought his way back to health after three weeks in intensive care and six months of recuperation and had managed to achieve full fitness in time to welcome his new son into the world. Tommy bound them together like they were wrapped in army black masking tape.

They could afford the place; they had moved to the new house when Danny had offered them both the job of running the North American arm of his company. They had worked hard to promote

Hedges and Fisher Canada, and it was now beginning to blossom as a profitable arm of the London end. They worked almost full time while sharing the responsibility for the two-year-old bundle of non-stop energy they had both created. They shared the job, and they shared the bundle. It was Taff's turn to take Tommy to his pre-school, but only Samantha had the mothering skill necessary to cajole him into putting his winter coat on.

"There you are, Tommy!" Sam kissed him after the struggle, and he was smiling now.

"OK, we are good to go!" Taff said, holding out his arms towards his son.

"Let's get going, Tommy, the Tiny Bears wait for no man. Go for Lift Off!"

Tommy ran to him and was immediately held aloft in his Daddy's arms. The stress of the anti-coat wearing ritual was over.

Taff checked his watch. It was 08.30.

"We're going to be late!" He smiled.

"Yeah, just like yesterday." Sam was smiling as well.

It was the domestic normality of everyday life that she was enjoying now. No more gunfights, no more government contracts, she and Taff had given enough. *It was now somebody else's turn.*

Brecon Beacons, South Wales

Ricky was tired. Very tired. In fact, he was, in military terms, *'fucked'*, but he still seemed to be doing better than most of the others on his selection. He had prepared himself well and he was fitter than most. This was what they called the 'Fan Dance', the final test on the SRR selection before they moved to Camp One for the rest of the course. His face was wet with the almost constant rain, and his back was soaked in sweat as he powered up the hill. He could feel the combined weight of both his decision to take up Tim's offer, which would, as the MI6 man had said, 'broaden his horizons' with a 'slightly different career path', and also the wet 40lb rucksack that was now cutting into his back as he hauled it up the slippery sandstone gradient.

The last three years had changed his life in many different ways. He now had a new identity and a fresh start in life. He had used the money he had earned from his Wandsworth days to move his mum out of London, and she was happy. His gangster days and Frobisher House had been officially eradicated from the record. Coco the teenage gangster was gone. He now had a different alias and was just student number 88, on SRR selection course 1/25, and he had as good a chance as any of passing and receiving the brown/grey beret of the Special Reconnaissance Regiment, before completing his attachment and returning to the security services.

Maybe!

As Tim had said, it was definitely broadening his horizons, *although this fucking one on Pen Y Fan seems to go on for ever and ever!*

The Author

W.T, Delaney is the pen name of the author. He was born in London and joined the Royal Marines in 1973. He spent twenty-four years in the Royal Marines employed in a variety of roles. He served with 45, 40 and 41 Royal Marine Commandos and was attached to the Special Boat Service and also engaged in special duties with the British Army in Northern Ireland. After his retirement from the Corps, Bernie joined the London Security 'Circuit' as a contractor. His tasks ranged from body-guarding an Arab Royal family to providing media security protection for news teams in both Iraq and Afghanistan. He retired in 2016 from his employment as a US DOD contractor teaching intelligence methods to the Iraqi and Afghan Army. He uses this experience to enhance the realism of his books. This book *'An Evil Shadow Falls'* is the final part of the Sam Holloway trilogy. The previous two were.

A Shadowing of Angels

A Falling of Angels

He can be reached on his web site wtdelaney.com

Printed in Great Britain
by Amazon